Henry Abbey

The Poems of Henry Abbey

Vol. 2

Henry Abbey

The Poems of Henry Abbey
Vol. 2

ISBN/EAN: 9783337407216

Printed in Europe, USA, Canada, Australia, Japan

Cover: Foto ©Andreas Hilbeck / pixelio.de

More available books at **www.hansebooks.com**

THE

Poems of Henry Abbey.

THIRD EDITION, ENLARGED.

KINGSTON, NEW YORK:
Author's Edition.
1895.

The Riverside Press, Cambridge:
Electrotyped and Printed by H. O. Houghton & Co.

AUTHOR'S NOTE.

THIS third edition contains, to date, all the poems of mine that I wish to have live. Some of these, doubtless, should not be here; but they have been widely copied and recited and are beyond my power to recall. They here stand emended by me, or as I first wrote them. The thirteen following the "Invocation to the Sun" are added to what comprised the first and second editions and are chiefly occasional, but I trust that these too take hold on life.   H. A.

KINGSTON, NEW YORK,
      September, 1894.

CONTENTS.

 CONTENTS.

THE POEMS OF HENRY ABBEY.

FACIEBAT.

As thoughts possess the fashion of the mood
That gave them birth, so every deed we do
Partakes of our inborn disquietude
That spurns the old and reaches toward the new.
The noblest works of human art and pride
Show that their makers were not satisfied.

For, looking down the ladder of our deeds,
The rounds seem slender : all past work appears
Unto the doer faulty : the heart bleeds,
And pale Regret comes weltering in tears,
To think how poor our best has been, how vain,
Beside the excellence we would attain.

ALONG THE NILE.

WE journey up the storied Nile ;
The timeless water seems to smile ;
The slow and swarthy boatman sings ;
The dahabeyeh spreads her wings ;
We catch the breeze and sail away,
Along the dawning of the day,
Along the East, wherein the morn
Of life and truth was gladly born.

We sail along the past, and see
Great Thebes with Karnak at her knee.

To Isis and Osiris rise
The prayers and smoke of sacrifice.
'Mid rites of priests and pomp of kings
Again the seated Memnon sings.
We watch the palms along the shore,
And dream of what is here no more.

The gliding Cleopatran Nile,
With glossy windings, mile on mile,
Suggests the asp: in coils compact
It hisses — at the cataract.
Thence on again we sail, and strand
Upon the yellow Nubian sand,
Near Aboo Simbel's rock-hewn fane,
Which smiles at time with calm disdain.

Who cut the stone joy none can tell;
He did his work, like Nature, well.
At one with Nature, godlike, these
Sphinx figures of great Rameses.
'T is seemly that the noble mind
Somewhat of permanence may find,
Whereon, with patience, may be wrought
A clear expression of its thought.

The artist labors while he may,
But finds at best too brief the day;
And, tho' his works outlast the time
And nation that they make sublime,
He feels and sees that Nature knows
Nothing of time in what she does,
But has a leisure infinite
Wherein to do her work aright.

The Nile of virtue overflows
The fruitful lands through which it goes.
It little cares for smile or slight,
But in its deeds takes sole delight,

And in them puts its highest sense,
Unmindful of the recompense;
Contented calmly to pursue
Whatever work it finds to do.

Howadji, with sweet dreams full fraught,
We trace this Nile through human thought.
Remains of ancient grandeur stand
Along the shores on either hand.
Like pyramids, against the skies
Loom up the old philosophies,
And the Greek king, who wandered long,
Smiles from uncrumbling rock of song.

THE STATUE.

In Athens, when all learning center'd there,
Men reared a column of surpassing height
In honor of Minerva, wise and fair;
And on the top, which dwindled to the sight,
A statue of the goddess was to stand,
That wisdom might obtain in all the land.

And he who, with the beauty in his heart,
Seeking in faultless work immortal youth,
Would mold this statue with the finest art,
Making the wintry marble glow with truth,
Should gain the prize: two sculptors sought the fame —
The prize they craved was an enduring name.

Alcamenes soon carved his little best;
But Phidias, beneath a dazzling thought
That like a bright sun in a cloudless west
Lit up his wide, great soul, with pure love wrought

A statue, and its changeless face of stone
With calm, far-sighted wisdom towered and shone.

Then to be judged the labors were unveiled;
But, at the marble thought, that by degrees
Of hardship Phidias cut, the people railed.
"The lines are coarse, the form too large," said these;
"And he who sends this rough result of haste
Sends scorn, and offers insult to our taste."

Alcamenes' praised work was lifted high
Upon the capital where it might stand;
But it appeared too small against the sky,
And lacked proportion from uplooking land;
So it was lowered and quickly put aside,
And the scorned thought was mounted to be tried.

Surprise swept o'er the faces of the crowd,
And changed them as a sudden breeze may change
A field of fickle grass, and long and loud
Their mingled shouts to see a sight so ·strange.
The statue stood completed in its place,
Each coarse line melted to a line of grace.

All bold, great actions that are seen too near,
Look rash and foolish to unthinking eyes;
But at a distance they at once appear
In their true grandeur: so let us be wise,
And not too soon our neighbor's deed malign,
For what seems coarse may yet be good and fine.

TRAILING ARBUTUS.

In spring when branches of woodbine
  Hung leafless over the rocks,
And fleecy snow in the hollows
  Lay in unshepherded flocks,

By the road where dead leaves rustled,
  Or damply matted the ground,
While over me gurgled the robin
  His honey'd passion of sound,

I came upon trailing arbutus
  Blooming in modesty sweet,
And gathered store of its riches
  Offered and spread at my feet.

It grew under leaves, as if seeking
  No hint of itself to disclose,
And out of its pink-white petals
  A delicate perfume rose.

As faint as the fond remembrance
  Of joy that was only dreamed,
And like a divine suggestion
  The scent of the flower seemed.

I sought for love on the highway,
  For love unselfish and pure,
And found it in good deeds blooming,
  Tho' often in haunts obscure.

Often in leaves by the wayside,
  But touched with a heavenly glow,
And with self-sacrifice fragrant
  The flowers of great love grow.

O lovely and lowly arbutus!
As year unto year succeeds,
Be thou the laurel and emblem
Of noble, unselfish deeds!

THE TROUBADOUR.

So many poets die ere they are known,
I pray you, hear me kindly for their sake.
Not of the harp, but of the soul alone,
Is the deep music all true minstrels make:
Hear my soul's music, and I will beguile,
With string and song, your festival awhile.

The stranger, looking on a merry scene
Where unknown faces shine with love and joy,
Feels that he is a stranger: on this green
That fronts the castle, seeing your employ,
My heart sank desolate; yet came I near,
For welcome should be found at all good cheer.

Provence my home, and fancy not, I pray,
That in Provence no lords save Love abide;
For there, Neglect, that, coming down the way,
Or priest, or Levite, takes the other side,
Neglect, false neighbor, flung at me the scoff:
"Honor is cold, and is the most, far off!"

Love is the key-note of the universe —
The theme, the melody; though poorly decked,
Masters, I ask but little of your purse,
For love, not gold, is best to heal neglect.
Love yields true fame when love is widely sown;
Bloom, flower of love! — lest I, too, die unknown.

WHILE THE DAYS GO BY.

I SHALL not say, our life is all in vain,
For peace may cheer the desolated hearth;
But well I know that, on this weary earth,
Round each joy-island is a sea of pain —
          And the days go by.

We watch our hopes, far flickering in the night,
Once radiant torches, lighted in our youth,
To guide, through years, to some broad morn of truth;
But these go out and leave us with no light —
          And the days go by.

We see the clouds of summer go and come,
And thirsty verdure praying them to give:
We cry, "O Nature, tell us why we live!"
She smiles with beauty, but her lips are dumb —
          And the days go by.

Yet what are we? We breathe, we love, we cease:
Too soon our little orbits change and fall:
We are Fate's children, very tired; and all
Are homeless strangers, craving rest and peace —
          And the days go by.

I only ask to drink experience deep;
And, in the sad, sweet goblet of my years,
To find love poured with all its smiles and tears,
And quaffing this, I too shall sweetly sleep —
          While the days go by.

MAY IN KINGSTON.

Our old colonial town is new with May:
The loving trees that clasp across the streets,
Grow greener sleeved with bursting buds each day.
Still this year's May the last year's May repeats;
Even the old stone houses half renew
Their youth and beauty, as the old trees do.

High over all, like some divine desire
Above our lower thoughts of daily care,
The gray, religious, heaven-touching spire
Adds to the quiet of the spring-time air;
And over roofs the birds create a sea,
That has no shore, of their May melody.

Down through the lowlands now of lightest green,
The undecided creek winds on its way.
There the lithe willow bends with graceful mien,
And sees its likeness in the depths all day;
While in the orchards, flushed with May's warm light,
The bride-like fruit-trees dwell, attired in white.

But yonder loom the mountains old and grand,
That off, along dim distance, reach afar,
And high and vast, against the sunset stand,
A dreamy range, long and irregular —
A caravan that never passes by,
Whose camel-backs are laden with the sky.

So, like a caravan, our outlived years
Loom on the introspective landscape seen
Within the heart: and now, when May appears,
And earth renews its vernal bloom and green,
We but renew our longing, and we say:
"Oh, would that life might ever be all May!

"Would that the bloom of youth that is so brief,
The bloom, the May, the fullness ripe and fair
Of cheek and limb, might fade not as the leaf;
Would that the heart might not grow old with care,
Nor love turn bitter, nor fond hope decay ;
But soul and body lead a life of May ! "

THE SPIRIT OF THE MOUNTAIN.

THE POET.

Who art thou, mighty spirit,
　That, in the twilight deep,
Makest a deeper twilight,
　Invading tired sleep?
The new moon, like a jewel,
　Shines on thy forehead high,
And shows thy wavy outline
　Along the mellow sky.

Thy ample sides are shaggy
　With maple, oak, and pine ;
Thy foot is shod with verdure ;
　Thy breath is more than wine.
The brooklet is thy laughter ;
　The light cloud likes thy brow.
Speak from thy breezy summit,
　Say, spirit, who art thou ?

THE SPIRIT OF THE MOUNTAIN.

I am the far-seen mountain
　Before thee towering high,
Where, peak beyond peak reaching,
　Rise others such as I.
Our dark-blue robes at twilight
　We draw about our forms ;

Ours is the boundless quiet
  That dwells above the storms.

I am a patient spirit
  That worked beneath the sea,
And, from hills pre-existing,
  Built up the hills to be.
To shifting sands I added
  Pebble and limy shell,
And laid, in briny chasms,
  My deep foundations well.

THE POET.

O Spirit of the Mountain!
  O toiler deep of yore!
Vast is thy past behind thee,
  Thy future vast before.
We call thee everlasting;
  Our life is like a day;
Are time and tide against thee?
  Must thou too pass away?

THE SPIRIT OF THE MOUNTAIN.

I see thy generation,
  Who wither as the rose,
And feel the isolation
  That wraps unmoved repose.
What through uncounted ages
  I wrought in sunless deeps,
Now, with the suns of heaven,
  Its lofty vigils keeps!

Yet slowly, ever slowly,
  I melt again, to be

> Lost in my grand, gray lover,
>   The wild, unresting sea.
> I cannot hear his moaning;
>   But know that, on the shore,
> He flings his spray-arms toward me,
>   And calls me ever more.

RECOMPENSE.

In spring, two robins from the southern lands
Built a brown nest upon an unsafe limb
Of the large tree that by my window stands,
And every morn they praised God with a hymn;
And, when a certain season passed away,
Five light-green eggs within the building lay.

Above the rush and clatter of the street,
Devotedly was guarded each green trust,
And the round house was an abode most sweet,
Roofed with expectant wings: better to rust
With iron patience, than forego a hope,
And pent life in the shells was felt to grope.

But one dread day, before the sun went down,
A cloud arose, a black and monstrous hand,
That robbed the sunset of its golden crown,
Filled the wild sky, and shook the frightened land.
The portals of the storm were opened wide,
And pealing thunder rolled on every side.

Then was it some unchained, malicious gust
Broke off the limb on which the nest was stayed,
And to the ground the tender dwelling thrust,
And wrecked its hapless store. The birds, dismayed,
Were shrill with grief, and beat the moving air
With wings whose frantic whir was like despair.

At dawn, my friends who live across the way,
Sent me the whisper that their child was dead;
And, when they led to where the body lay —
The free, winged spirit's shell, untimely shed —
And the wild cries of their distress I heard,
My sympathy again was deeply stirred.

Yet grief is but a cloud that soon is past;
Hither the mated robins came once more,
And built, with cunning architecture, fast
In the same tree beside my friendly door;
And in the soft-floored building could be seen
Five sources of sweet music, new and clean.

Time passed, and to the good home opposite
Another babe was born, and all the love
That was bereft that fierce and stormy night,
Fell to the latter child as from above:
And in the nest five yellow mouths one day
Of their impatient hunger made display.

DONALD.

O WHITE, white, light moon, that sailest in the sky,
Look down upon the whirling world, for thou art up
     so high,
And tell me where my Donald is who sailed across
     the sea,
And make a path of silver light to lead him back to me.

O white, white, bright moon, thy cheek is coldly fair,
A little cloud beside thee seems thy wildly floating
     hair;
And if thou would'st not have me grow as white and
     cold as thee,
Go, make a mighty tide to draw my Donald back to me.

O light, white, bright moon, that dost so fondly shine,
There is not a lily in the world but hides its face
    from thine ;
I too shall go and hide my face close in the dust from
    thee,
Unless with light and tide thou bring my Donald back
    to me.

IN THE VALLEY.

THIS is the place — a grove of sighing pines ;
Their fallen tassels thatch the roofs with brown,
The narrow roofs, beneath whose small confines
No dweller wakens: tho' the rains weep down,
Tho' winds, the mighty mourners, by the spot
Go unconsoled, the inmates waken not.

Along the unbusy street my way I keep,
Between the houses tenanted by death,
And seek the place where lies my friend asleep,
Alien to this the life of light and breath.
And here his grave, where wild vines bloom and grope,
Makes recollection seem as sweet as hope.

For he, my friend, was gentle, wise and true ;
Pleasant to him a beggar's thankful word ;
He spoke no ill of others, and he knew
And loved clear brooks, green dells, and flower, and
    bird ;
And now the flowers strive to return his love
By growing here his humble grave above.

But tears are more than flowers, and make for peace,
Tho' God by grief is oft misunderstood.
In tears I made complaint of his decease
Whom I had loved, for he was young and good ;

I made complaint that He who rules on high
Should suffer here the young and good to die.

O Death! sole warder at the gates of time,
For ever more to those thy hinge swing wide
Whose hope is flown, whose souls are stained with
        crime —
Give way to all who are dissatisfied
With their recurrent days, and long to cease;
Swing wide for such, and to the old give peace.

But close and bar thy black and mournful gates
Against the good, the beautiful, the young,
Whose lives the lamp of hope illuminates,
Whose harp-like souls for highest strains are strung.
O warder Death! give way, swing wide for sin;
But close, and bar, and keep the good within.

LOW TIDE.

UNDER the cliff I walk in silence,
    Where the wide waters ebb and flow;
And white birds, changed by the sun into silver,
    Glitter against the blue below;
            And the tide is low.

Here years ago, in golden weather,
    Under the cliff, and close to the sea,
A pledge was given that made me master
    Of all that ever was dear to me;
            And the tide was low.

Only a little year fled by after,
    Then my bride and I came once more,
And saw the sea, like a bird imprisoned

Beating its wings at its bars, the shore ;
And the tide was low.

Now I walk alone by the filmy breakers —
A voice is hushed I can never forget ;
On my saddened sea dead calm has fallen,
My ships are harbored, my sun is set ;
And the tide is low.

THE PATIENCE OF LIBERTY.

As in a dream I saw her, where she stood,
Calm, self-contained, the goddess of the free,
Upon a height above the storm and flood,
Looking far off on what was like the sea.
Her gown was plain : her freedman's cap she wore,
And, by her side, the rod magistral bore.

The lofty heights whereon she dwells alone,
To many hearts seem hard indeed to scale ;
Wilder than those above the Yellowstone,
With rugged paths swept by the leaden hail
Wherewith Oppression, in his selfish rage,
Drives back her worshipers in every age.

Few are the ways that lead to where she stands,
Not filled with slain and hedged with bloody death ;
But now I saw her on the misty lands,
And sweeter than the morning's was her breath,
And radiant with glory shone her face,
Kindly, sublime, and of immortal grace.

" Thine is the land where all, at last, are free ;
But is the freedom real or a dream ? "
She asked ; " and dost thou not despair of me,

To see my rights abused, wealth made supreme,
Truth scorned by party zeal, and everywhere,
Honors dishonored?—dost thou not despair?"

I knew that these, her questions, were a test,
And from the fullness of my faith I said:
"O Liberty! there is not in my breast
Harbor to moor thy doubt; the blood we shed,
The bitter tears, the long, heart-rending pain,
Were all for thee; they have not been in vain.

"Often a public wrong a use fulfills,
And, tho' not left unpunished, leads to good;
I look to time to cure a thousand ills,
And make thee widely, better understood.
True love of thee will heal the wrongs we bear;
I trust to time, and I do not despair!"

She stood with one hand on her eagle's head,
The other pointed to an age to be.
"Neither do I despair," she proudly said,
"For I behold the future, and I see
The shadow and the darkness overpast,
My glad day come, and all men free at last!"

MARY MAGDALENE.

ALL night I cried in agony
　　Of grief and bitter loss,
And wept for Him whom they had nailed
　　Against the shameful cross.

But in the morning, in the dark,
　　Before the east was gray,
I hastened to the sepulcher
　　Wherein the body lay.

The stone was rolled away I found;
  And filled with fear and woe,
I straight to His disciples ran,
  Thereof to let them know.

I said, "The body of the Lord
  Is not within the tomb;
For they have taken him away
  Unnoticed in the gloom.

"Where have they laid him? who can tell?
  Alas! we know not where."
The words were slower than my tears
  To utter my despair.

Then two disciples, coming forth,
  With hurried footsteps sped,
Till, at the garden sepulcher,
  They found as I had said.

They saw the door-stone rolled away,
  The empty tomb and wide,
The linen face-cloth folded up
  And grave-clothes laid aside.

The morn was cold; I heeded not,
  With sorrow wrapped about;
Till both were gone to tell the rest,
  I stood and wept without.

Then stooping down and looking in,
  I saw two angels there,
Whose faces shone with love and joy,
  And were divinely fair.

In white effulgence garmented,
  That showed the hewn rock's grain,

2

One at the head, one at the feet,
  Sat where my Lord had lain.

To look on them I was afraid,
  Their splendor was so great:
They said to me, " Why weepest thou ? "
  In tones compassionate.

" I weep," I said, "for that my Lord
  Is taken hence away,
And that, alas ! I do not know
  Where he is laid to-day."

I sadly rose, and turning back,
  Beheld One standing by,
And knew the lily of the dawn
  Unfolded in the sky.

But in the pale, uncertain light,
  Too blind with tears to see,
I thought it was the gardener
  There at the tomb with me.

It soothed me much, the day before,
  To say it in my mind,
That in a garden they had laid
  The Flower of all mankind.

Until Thy fragrance fell on me,
  A thrall to sin was I;
O Flower of Peace ! O Flower of Grace !
  Thy love is liberty !

But they had taken him away,
  Who is of sin the price ;
I held the gift that I had brought,
  Of perfume, oil, and spice.

I had not staid to braid my hair,
  And, in the early breeze,
The long, black luster, damp with tears,
  Down fluttered to my knees.

I dimly saw the gardener;
  In grief I bowed my head;
"Why weepest thou? whom seekest thou?"
  He softly, gently said.

"O sir, if thou have borne him hence,"
  I eagerly replied,
"Tell me where thou hast laid my Lord,
  Whom they have crucified,

"And I will take him thence away;
  Oh, tell me where he lies!"
"Mary!" he said — I knew the voice,
  And turned in glad surprise.

For he was not the gardener
  That I advanced to greet;
I cried, "Rabboni!" joyfully,
  And knelt at Jesus' feet.

THE AGE OF GOOD.

I HAD a vision of mankind to be:
I saw no grated windows, heard no roar
From iron mouths of war on land or sea;
Ambition broke the sway of peace no more.
Out of the chaos of ill-will had come
Cosmos, the Age of Good, Millennium!

The lowly hero had of praise his meed,
And loving-kindnesses joined roof to roof.

The poor were few, and to their daily need
Abundance ministered: men bore reproof;
On crags of self-denial sought to cull
Rare flowers to deck their doors hospitable.

The very bells rang out the Golden Rule,
For hearts were loath to give their fellows pain.
The man was chosen chief who, brave and cool,
Was king in act and thought: wise power is plain
And likes not pomp and show; he seemed to be
The least in all that true democracy.

O Thou, the Christ, the Sower of the seed,
Pluck out the narrowness, the greed for pelf;
Pluck out all tares; the time let come, and speed,
When each will love his neighbor as himself!
The hopes of man, our dreams of higher good,
Are based on Thee; we are Thy brotherhood.

KARAGWE.

Because the sun hath looked upon me.
THE SONG OF SOLOMON.

I.

AN African, thick-lipped and heavy-heeled,
With woolly hair, large eyes, and even teeth,
A forehead high, and beetling at the brows
Enough to show a strong perceptive thought
Ran out infallibly beyond his sight —
A savage with no knowledge we possess
Of science, art, or books, or government —
A captive black bereft of rights, inthralled,
Bought from a slaver off the Georgia coast,
His life a thing of price with market rate;
Yet in the face of all, a brave, true man,
Named Kara-gwe in token of his tribe.

His buyer was the planter Dalton Earl,
Of Valley Earl, an owner of broad lands,
Whose wife, in some cold daybreak of the **past**,
Had tarried with the silence and the night;
But parting, left him of their love a child.
He named it Coralline: by sad waves tossed,
She was a spray of coral fair to see,
Found on the shore where death's impatient deep
Hems in the narrow continent of life.

II.

Each day brought health and strength to Karagwe;
Each day he worked where white the cotton grew,
And every boll he picked had thought in it.
Strange fancies, faced with ignorance and doubt,
Came crowding, peering in his heathen mind,
Like men who, gathered in some rich bazaar,
Elbow to see arrive the caravan.

All things were new and wonderful to him.
What were the papers that his owner read?
What meant the black and ant-like characters?
He found a leaf of them and gazed at it,
Trying to understand their voiceless speech.
This, Dalton Earl with cloudy look beheld,
And seized the print, commanding that the slave
Have twenty lashes for this breach of law.

Long on his sentence pondered Karagwe.
Against the law? Who then would make a law
Decreeing knowledge to a few proud men,
To others ignorance? Surely not God;
The white-haired negro with a text had said
That God loved justice, and was Friend to all.

With blood replying redly to each stroke,
With dark skin clinging ghastly to the whip,

The slave bore up beneath his punishment;
His heart, indignant, shaking his broad breast,
Strong as the heart Hippodamè bewailed,
Which, with the cold, intrusive brass thrust through,
Shook the Greek spear to its extremity.

III.

Henceforth the black man's energy, enforced
By one opposing argument, the lash,
Pursued a quest for knowledge, and secured,
In paths familiar, pleasant wayside flowers.
The old slave preacher knew the alphabet,
And taught it, when he might, to Karagwe,
Whose books were crumbs of paper printed on,
Found here and there, strewed by the handless wind.
He studied in the woods and near the falls
That shoot in watery arrows from the cliff,
Feathered with spray and barbed with hues of flint.

Once, looking up, he saw, upon the verge,
Fair baby Coralline, that, laughing, leaned
Over th' abyss to grasp a butterfly.
Ere paused he panting on the dizzy height,
A shriek rose shrill above the water's roar;
The child had fallen, and a young quadroon
Lay on the slanted summit, swooned away.
The child had fallen, but was yet unharmed.
The slave slipped down where ran a narrow ledge,
And, reaching forth, caught fast the little frock,
Whose folds were tangled in a bending shrub,
And drew his frightened burden safely back.

He told not of this peril he had braved,
Nor spoke of any merit he possessed,
Or any worthy act that he had done.

IV.

By being always when he could alone,
By often wandering in the woods and fields,
He came at last to live in revery.
But little thought is found in revery,
But little thought, for most is useless dream;
And whoso dreams may never learn to act.
The dreamer and the thinker are not kin.
Sweet revery is like a little boat
That idly drifts along a listless stream —
A painted boat, afloat without an oar.

The negro preacher with the text had said
That when men died the soul lived on and on:
If so, of what material was the soul?
The eyes could not behold it: might not then
The viewless air be filled with living souls?
Not these alone, but other vague, strange forms
Around us at all times could dwell unseen.
If air was only matter rarëfied,
Why might not things still more impalpable
Exist as well?   Whence came our countless thoughts?
They were not ours: he fancied that they all,
Or good, or bad, were whispered to the soul:
The bad were sleek suggestions from a shape
With measureless black wings, that when it dared
Set on the necks of men its cloven foot;
But, winged with light, a spirit eloquent
Named Wisdom, with his son, Humanity,
Whispered good thoughts, and told this groping heart,
That sunset splendors were as naught beside
The fadeless glory of a noble deed.

He proudly dreamed that to no other mind
Had been revealed these trite imaginings.
Alas! poor heart, how many have awoke,

And found their newest thoughts not new but old,
Their brightest fancies woven in the silk
Of ancient poems, history or romance,
And learning still elusive and far off!

v.

The young quadroon who fainted on the cliff
Was Ruth; she, born a thrall to Dalton Earl,
Was now a conscious rose of womanhood.
She looked on Karagwe, and saw in him
A man above the level of the slave,
A palm-tree in a wide, neglected land.

While both, at twilight, on a rustic seat
Sat talking, laughing with that careless mirth
In which their race forgot its chains and toil,
A drunken overseer staggered up,
And seeing a woman sitting in the dusk,
Swayed toward her, caught her rudely by the arm,
And, with an insult, strove to drag her forth.
Ruth trembled, fawn-like; but the negro rose,
And, with his grasp, freed her the white man's hand
Then in the face the coward struck the slave,
Who neither struck him back nor uttered word.

But to a whipping-post they bound the black,
And many stripes his unhealed shoulders flayed.
Stung by the wrong, but lifted with just scorn,
That men, who claimed to be superior,
Would thus degrade their unoffending kind,
He wept at heart; no groan, no cry of pain,
Made audible their inhumanity.

Quickly thereafter he was forced to go
And toil beneath the summer's burning glare.

In foaming basket, on his wounded back,
Up a steep hillside to a cotton-gin,
The long day through, he bore the tyrannous,
Truth-smothering product of the slave-worked fields.

VI.

Ruth, in her household cares and restful hours,
Thought of the one dark face and noble heart.

He, when the labor of the day was done,
Moved through the dusk, between the dewy leaves,
And, softly as a shadow, climbed the wall,
And waited in the garden, crouching down,
Hidden and breathed on by abundant bloom,
Hoping that she again might come that way.
He saw her, by a window of the house,
Pass and repass within, and heard her sing
A wooing song of love and pity blent;
But would not call to her, nor give a sign
That he was near; to see her was enough.
Perhaps, if those she dwelt with knew he came
To meet her in the garden, they would place
On her some punishment, some sharp restraint,
That she, tho' innocent, might have to bear.
So he went back again to his low cot,
And on his poor, straw pallet, dreamed of her
As loyally, may be, as any prince,
Lying asleep on down and broidery,
Dreams of his queen.

VII.

      Ruth was but tinged with shade
Her black, bright eyes, so proud and passionate,
Showed that the deep and everlasting soul,
Who through their liquid portals saw the world,

Was mixed with elements of storm and gloom.
For never bird of thought flew down her sky,
But that the shadow of its flitting wing
Passed in her eyes: like leaves along the brink,
Above the depths her thick, long lashes hung.
Such excellent adornment was her grace,
That, tho' her gown was of the coarsest kind,
Hers was apparel more desirable
Than costly splendor woven by the loom.

VIII.

A vast plantation, joining Dalton Earl's,
Was held by Richard Wain, a hated man —
Hated of owned and hired and in the town.

But where the river limited his lands
Seclusion sweet was found by Karagwe.
For there a noble temple, pillared, aisled,
Toward heaven rose: aloft, the verdant roof
With sun-gilt frieze and cornice, and beneath,
A fragrant carpet and mossed seats of stone —
A grove of pines. Here, hidden in a tree,
Was treasure kept — a Bible small and worn.
From it the past arose before the slave:
The folk were vague, and their procession seemed
Like figures moving slowly in the dusk:
Yet One there was, who, center'd in great light,
Stood out, determinate, and full of life:
A pure, surpassing face, with silken beard:
Long, golden hair that waved about the neck;
Mild eyes of deepest azure, thoughtful eyes
Serene with knowledge of eternity:
A patient man, beneficent, divine,
Friend to the poor, and Messenger of love.

IX.

While walking near the house of Richard Wain,
The slave beheld a paper in the grass,
Whose sheets were closely written, signed and sealed.

Thus came the chance for which he oft had sought,
To learn the older letters of the pen.
That night the writing, wrapped about his book,
Lay nestled in the hollow, up a tree.

There once, indeed, a wedded pair had been,
That with white softness lined the balmy place,
And hatched within it callow occupants;
These being fledged, all, singing, flew away.

X.

"What token shall I give," thought Karagwe,
"That she may know from it my love for her,
And I learn whether love has answered mine?"
A straying bee, of sweet and golden wealth,
He caught and killed, and carried it to Ruth.
"I bring you, Ruth, a dead bee for a sign;
For if to-day you wear it in your hair,
When once again you come to walk this path,
I thus shall find that you are mine alone,
Content to be my wife, and share my lot,
And let me with you toil like bee with bee;
But if you do not wear it, I shall care
No more for anything; but waste my life,
A bee without a queen." Ruth said no word;
But when she went that way at one-starred dusk,
The dead bee glimmered in her dusky hair.
And meeting him for whom the sign was meant,
She laid her hand in his, and fondly smiled.

XI.

Came, trilling wildly sweet, a bird-like voice,
When Richard Wain next day went riding by,
And caught, mid foliage, a glimpse of Ruth —
A momentary picture framed in flowers.
"The prize I covet most is near," he said ;
"She shall be mine to-morrow, weep who may!"

Returning on his over-driven horse,
When shadows slowly lengthened from the west,
He near the house dismounted, fastened rein,
Strode to a threshold, asked for Dalton Earl,
And told him for what chattel he had come.
The maid was not for sale, the owner said.
"You talk at random now," said Richard Wain ;
"You know I hold the deed of all your lands.
If it be true, the wench is not for sale,
Your lands shall be for sale, at sheriff's sale!"
Pale turned the haughty planter, Dalton Earl,
And knowing, for his trouble came of it,
Whose blood made blue the fiery veins of Ruth,
Fixed blindly on a price immoderate.
"To-morrow I shall come," said Richard Wain,
"And take the girl, and pay the price I choose."

When Dalton Earl had told the thrall her fate,
She swooned, and to the floor fell heavily.
Recovering, she rose upon her knees,
And begged of him that she might still remain.
At this he told her how the lands were held,
And, if she went not, these would all be sold.
"Then let the lands be sold, and sold again;
If his, they are not yours. What good will come
If I do go to him? Then all were his ;
And I have given my hand to Karagwe.
Oh, it will break my heart to go away!"

XII.

To Karagwe's low roof Ruth went that night,
And said in loud, wild words the evil news,
She must be slave and worse to Richard Wain.
The negro sadly strove to soothe her woe
With consolation from the book he read;
For, to the souls of black and Afric slaves,
The gospel came unhindered by a doubt;
And there accepted freely, being free,
Was rapturous delight — enthusiasm!
Masking the dreary face of hopelessness
With gospel cheer, the negro talked with Ruth,
While walking toward the home of Dalton Earl.
Glory of night, the restless moon was like
A pale cloud-sheeted ghost of a dead day,
Gliding abroad to ease the ache of hell;
For heavy sorrow, disappointment deep,
Sickens the heart not only, but the eyes,
Transforming nature to ill shapes of gloom.

XIII.

A troublous morning came to Valley Earl,
And Ruth was sold away from him she loved.

The sad day died, and in its vaulted tomb
The Afric lolled upon the river's bank,
His mind a flowing tide that wandered back
Along the course and valley of the past.
It eddied round his loss as round a rock,
And roused the snake. revenge, that lay thereon.
Sprang up the slave, and wildly beat his breast,
His eyes enkindled with an evil fire.
Then came some memory of holy writ,
And in the depths the serpent disappeared.
The negro mourned that justice seldom was;

Yet knew that in God's hand the scales were set,
And, tho' His poor down-trodden waited long,
They waited surely for the balancing.

A step was heard, and Karagwe beheld,
By aid of ghostly moonlight, Richard Wain;
Behind, another followed stealthily,
With a drawn dagger in his lifted hand.
The steel, as if it feared a deed of blood,
Gleamed. to the slave its dread intelligence.
He followed swift the weaponed follower,
He grasped the hand, he wrenched the blade away,
And stood before the planter, Dalton Earl!
"Forgive," he said. "Forgiveness is a slave;
She has no pride nor hate; she does no harm;
For she is light of heart, and meekly good,
And patient when the lash of anger smites."

Rebuked, the master stood before the slave;
And Richard Wain, who sneered when he was told
That Ruth and Karagwe had plighted troth,
Went on unscathed, saved by the man he scorned.
Thus Dalton Earl: "I thank you for this act,
Thwarting a bad intent; yet I had cause
To take the sullied life of Richard Wain.
He drugged the wine he gave me at his house,
And knew the deed of my plantation there
To be my only title: while I slept
He, shameless, stole it from me: when I woke,
He feigned that I had staked the deed and lost.
For this and more I hate him: to forgive
Implies the wronger seeks to be forgiven."

XIV.

Like a great thought that full expression finds,
In happy buds mild spring found utterance.

But never bud or bloom so fresh or fair
As Coralline, daughter of Dalton Earl.

It was in spring, they say, that Stanley Thane
Came from his northern home and met this May,
This Coralline, the joy of Valley Earl.

XV.

High up, with sapphire over and below,
Blithe birds flew northward, singing as they flew,
And Love flew southward, sighing all the way.
They met him flying, heard him sighing so.
"Whither away?" they musically asked,
"Whither away? and why should Love be sad?"
The voice o' the words of Love is soft and sweet:
"Southward I go; but I shall soon return,
And help you in your art, and with you bide.
You will not flout me, scout me, make me sigh!
O wingers, kindly singers, fare you well!"

XVI.

Worthy a maiden's love was Stanley Thane.
Riches were his, and he had deeply quaffed
The tonic spring of knowledge practical.
Along his veins ran potent, old-world life,
Strong English, Huguenot, and Celtic blood
All by the climate blended and subdued
To that distinctive and peculiar kind
Which is American. Dark eyes he had,
Straight, deep-black hair, firm, fair rose-tinted flesh,
And the full bloom of evanescent youth.
High thoughts and purposes, like mountain chains
Linked and white-peaked, rose in his pleasant mind,
That was as clear and fresh as air at morn.
Hating oppression and intolerance,

Courageous, generous, but firm of will,
Of the strong North he was a character,
A stamp, a type incarnate in a man.

XVII.

Seeing her fair, he boldly kissed her hand;
He kissed the hand of southern Coralline.
He saw that she was stately, lithe and tall,
And deemed her proud, but thought her beautiful.
What if the air was fragrant, honey-sweet,
With the magnificent magnolia's breath?
What if the odorous white avenue,
From house to highway, with magnolia trees
Graceful and tall, was hedged and garlanded?
He heeded not: the dear, chief flower of all,
The one superb magnolia of a life,
Thrilled at his touch, as with enraptured lips
He kissed the snowy petal of her hand.

He galloped with her through the idle town,
He wandered with her in the orange groves,
And watched, beside the falls, the busy brook
That seemed a maid, who, sitting at a loom,
Wove misty lace to decorate the rocks.

XVIII.

Long on the writing hidden in a nest
Pondered the slave, and found it was the deed!
Then conscience, bold and prompt to tell the truth,
Upspoke, and said he had no right to it.
Yet if he gave the deed to Dalton Earl,
Unjustly Richard Wain might claim it still.

He thought of Ruth as of the loved who rest,
Mourning for her that she to him was dead,

And once he gathered wild-flowers for regret,
And placed them where they would be found by Ruth,
As if he someway laid them on her grave.

XIX.

When Richard Wain knew he had lost the deed
He feigned he won at cards from Dalton Earl,
Rage and chagrin were ready at their gate,
Like pent-up water, to surpass the race,
And turn that mill-wheel voluble, his tongue.
If he mistrusted Dalton Earl the thief,
His threat's effect, Ruth's sale, disproved the thought.
Lest he might lose the power he wished to keep,
The waters rushed not, and the wheel was dumb
To tell his secret that the deed was lost.

XX.

A skiff shot out from under-reaching shore,
And Stanley Thane, with stately Coralline,
Sailed down the river through a peaceful vale.
About them hung the shadow of the earth ;
Beneath them flowed the deep and glossy gloom
Emblazoned by the inaccessible stars.

Already there were portents of dread war,
For Slavery, a dragon fell and foul,
Opposed the youthful knight of Liberty.
But Coralline, within the dragon's spell,
Was mute to what of shame the shape had done,
And praised its hateful life with heated words.
Then Stanley, loath to weakly hold his peace
And hear a wrong defended, said, " O South,
Your chiefs, who claim the name of democrat,
Pervert the sense of that which they profess.
They democrats ! They do not understand

3

The baby letters of democracy;
For they deny that all should govern all,
And will to make men slaves and ignorant.
But God is just; He knows nor white nor black;
If war must come, the shackles, cleft amain
By the uncompromising sword, shall fall,
And the whole people of the land be free."

Seeming a dull machine that worked the boat,
The dusky oarsman, silent Karagwe,
Heard the winged words and caught them in his heart.
But Coralline, like an idolatrous
And cruel priestess of an ancient fane,
Who, proud of altars and of sacrifice,
Heard her base god dishonored, rose enraged;
She scorned the Northern thought of Stanley Thane,
She wished it had not been their fate to meet.
"If that you mean," he said, "then let us part,
And let us hope we shall not meet again.
Farewell! for I will see you never more."
The boat was near the shore; he sprang to it,
And left her standing darkly in the prow —
Her pride engaged against a host of tears;
This Paris of her high heart's Ilios roused
To drive the Greeks back to the salty sea.

Oh, far apart as east and west are they
Whom pride divides! They wander aimlessly;
They err; their hope is dead; their hearts are cold.
O pride! O foolish, shallow! that is stayed
On small and petty points, on nettles, thorns —
Oh, leave us, and go hence, that in thy room
May bloom the violet, humility!

XXI.

A mighty angel, with triumphant face,
The torch and sword of vengeance in his hands,

Swept overhead with trailing, crimson robe,
And roused a people with the cry of war!

Wake! for the night has passed, and dawn is come!
Sons of the new world, wake! turn scythes to swords.
Wake, busy town! and quiet village, wake!
The shame that is nourished stings to the death.
Voices of viol and flute are as dreams;
But bugle and drum sound a call to arms!
The pulse of the guns, in a prostrate time,
Is the heart-beat fresh of a nobler day.
Oh, strike, tho' you die, if you make men free!
Wake! there is war with the South in the south.
There is war begun, and who knows the end?

XXII.

O rash wife, South! Thy true husband, the North,
Loveth thee yet, though thou wentest astray.
In Truth's great court, where thy trial was held,
To thee was granted no bill of divorce.
Thy child, misshapen, and proud of its shame,
Was not the child of thy husband, the North.
It has led thee into the mire, and raised
To thy famished lips the cup of despair;
It were better that such a child should die.

XXIII.

When, like a soldier marching to his death,
A year of battle passed with measured step
And took its chill decease, dark Richard Wain
Prepared for his departure to the war.
To-morrow he would go, and in the night
He idly sat in his forbidding house;
Thinking, he drowsed; his chin couched on his breast;
A dim lamp wrought at shadows on the walls.

Slowly the sash was raised behind his chair.
Perhaps he slept; he did not heed the sound;
But Karagwe sprang in and faced his foe,
And held a long knife up and brandished it,
Saying, "As surely as you call or move,
Your life will not be worth a blade of grass;
But if you do not call, and sign the words
That I have written on a paper here,
No harm will come, and I shall go away."
He drew the paper forth; the planter read:

"By virtue of this writing, I disclaim
Title or right or any interest
In Dalton Earl's plantation joining mine."

"Why, this I surely will not sign," he said.
"You might have asked me to give up your Ruth,
And I should not have minded; but your game
Lies deeper than a check upon the queen."
"Sign!" cried the slave; and at the name of Ruth
A sudden madness leaped along his nerves,
Like a blown flame among dry prairie grass:
"Sign! for unless you sign this writing now,
You shall not live ; now promise me to sign!"
He fiercely caught the planter by the throat,
Starting his quailing eyes: "Now will you sign or not?
You have ten seconds more to make your choice."
"Give me the paper then, and I will sign."
The name was written, and the negro went;
But not an hour had passed before the hounds
Of Richard Wain and Dalton Earl were slipped,
And scenting on the track of his escape.

XXIV.

The slave ran swiftly to the hollow tree;
There left the paper signed by Richard Wain,

Folding it in the deed ; then took his book,
And up a tireless road fled on and on,
Until he reached the border of a marsh.

The night was dark, but darker still the clouds
That loomed along the rim where day had gone.
The wind blew cold, and, sighing, hasted by,
Escaping, like a slave, the hound-like clouds
Whose thunder-barking sounded deep and far.

Along the dark the bay came dismally,
Of savage dogs set on the negro's track —
Swift, monstrous blood-hounds trained to fight with men.
He knew a swamp-path safe for hoof or foot,
And even in the blackness followed it,
Finding a covert hummock, where a hut,
Built up of logs by some poor fugitive,
Held a rude thatch against the sun and rain.

XXV.

Men over-estimate what they desire
Through ignorance of it : credulous Pursuit
Thinks his betrothed, Possession, is divine ;
But finds she is a mortal like himself.
And in the hut, to which the slave was tracked,
That night was painted, with a facile brush,
On thin, unwoven canvas of the gloom,
Wild visions of a freedom unrestrained.
For long the slave had thought of Liberty,
And worshiped her, as in that elder time
A tyrant's subjects worshiped. praying her
That she would not delay, but hasten forth,
And bridge the gulf between the rich and poor
By making knowledge paramount to wealth,
Freeing the common from their ignorance,
And lifting up the worthy of the world.

Oh, strange, that in our age, and in a land
Where liberty was laid the corner-stone,
A slave, perforce, should be obliged to dream
And dote on freedom, like the poor oppressed
Who lived and hoped long centuries ago!

And slavery to this slave was like a fruit,
A bitter and offensive fruit to taste,
The fruit of wrong grafted on avarice,
Foul, pulp and pit, with rank and poison sin.
Yet tho' this fruit was bitter to the core,
Many there were who died for love of it.

Oh, many they who listened through long nights
To hear a footstep that will never come!
There is scarce a flower along the border blown,
From Lookout Mountain to the Chesapeake,
But has in it the blood of North and South.

XXVI.

When sleep left Karagwe, above the marsh
The flush and whisper of the morning went.
Then, when he would have ventured from the door,
A large, black blood-hound rose, and licked his hand.
The dog was Dalton Earl's, and did not know
That men were bought and sold for current coin;
He only knew with joy he saw his friend.

The thrall went back, and on a paper wrote:
"Your dog has harmed me not, tho' sent for harm.
I never wronged you; I have served you well.
I risked the life of him who wronged us both,
To do you one great service for the last.
You made me slave, you sold my plighted wife,
And now you set your blood-hounds on my track,
Because I flee to freedom that is mine.

"But tho' you wrong me, I repay with good;
For in the nested hollow of a pine,
In the high grove, on ground of Richard Wain,
Is the lost deed that holds your house and lands."
The paper fastened at the hound's strong neck,
The negro bade him go, and forth he leaped;
And Dalton Earl read what the slave had sent,
And found his deed safe hidden in the tree,
And that day made an end of all pursuit.

XXVII.

Long wandered Karagwe to find the North,
Fed from the wild abundance that the sun
Ripens on southern soil: above him leaned
Tall trees with bowers beneath their wrestling arms,
Fringed with dependent moss, and overrun
By thorn-speared and leaf-shielded Vandal vines;
Below, the water, murky with decay,
Stirred with a sluggish ripple, where had plunged
The wrinkle-throated alligator, clad
In the dark coat of his impervious mail.
Like mermaids with white faces to the sky,
An idle bevy floating on their backs,
The water-lilies lay, and over them
Birds of gay song and wing in sunshine flashed,
Or poised in thickets of lush emerald,
Where shrub and vine and frondage intertwined
Inextricably as the affairs of men.
This freedom to excess in mindless things
Appeared a happy omen to the slave,
That henceforth he should have such liberty.

XXVIII.

But now across his solitary path
A blue, wide, ebbing river sought the sea.

Two heavy logs he launched and firmly withed,
Then, with a pole for help if he should need,
Cast off, and drifted slowly down the stream.
Thus for long days he drifted, eating not,
Save of the berries growing near the shore.
Once he enlarged the uncomfortable raft,
And set a bushy sapling for a sail.
The wind and tide agreed, and hasted him
Along the sparkling way, till he, unharmed,
Passed by at night a hushed, street-lighted town,
And saw at morn the hot sun leave the sea.
A red buoy tossed upon the nearer waves,
As if it were the ocean's joyful heart,
Or his own heart upon a sea of hope ;
And ships were in the offing, sailing on
Like the vague ships that with our hopes and fears
Put from their havens to return no more.

Ere night he hailed a vessel, gained the deck,
And found he was with friends, and on his way
To Freedom, guided by her fixed North Star.
But he, without a dread, had left the land,
And sailed away, to have his wish or die.

Thus ever he who seeks his heart's desire
Sets forward on a sea unknown and large,
And leaves behind the steadfast, certain shore.
The rooted trees exclaim, " The fool will go.
There is no land beyond, for all is sea,
And it is wide and deep : he must go down,
And the wet turbulence will bury him."
He takes no heed ; the trees are left behind ;
He sails away, and in his dream beholds,
With peaceful harbor, under pleasant sky,
The city of Delight, his heart's desire.

XXIX.

Three years of war, three years of blood and tears,
And Richard Wain in front of battle fell.
There, grim with powder, he led on his men,
With cheer or oath, and gory, waving sword —
As if, through him, the spirit of his cause,
Foul Slavery, expressed itself, and fought
With desperation for its ending life.

XXX.

Forth in the garden dewy and perfumed,
Walked Coralline and Ruth, sad and alone;
For Ruth was owned again by Dalton Earl.

Tho' two leal hearts, when severed by weak pride,
Dwell far apart, there is a sting remains
That rankles, and the melancholy years
Of separation are more sad than death.
Or look or smile to Coralline recurred
Dreaming of Stanley Thane : of him she thought
Regretfully, with tender trust : for him
Her love welled up like water in a spring,
From which the more she gave the more was left,
And purer for the gift : down from the north
Came tidings of his daring; and the war
And the deep gloom of absence were as night,
And he the lovable, exalted star
Whose image was reflected in her soul
As in a shadowed lake.

     "From day to day
I grieve," said Coralline, "that Stanley Thane
So rashly left me, and that he should think
My hasty words were said with earnest thought.
Would that a bird might fly to him and sing :

'She loves you, Stanley Thane — she loves you still.'"
Ruth answered quickly, "You shall have your wish;
For I will go to him who once was here,
And say to him the words that you have said."
Then on the bosom of the wronged quadroon
The other fell with sisterly embrace,
And kissed her through her tears, and promised her
Her freedom, if she went to Stanley Thane.

That night one stole a knife, and sharpened it,
Sipping the poison sweetness of revenge.
Those that she loved were now all lost to her;
Her child was sold away, she knew not where.
She thought of Stanley Thane, and felt regret
That he should be the victim she must strike;
But wished that Coralline might look on him
After this violent knife had wrought his death.

XXXI.

Alike unmindful of all joy and woe,
Insensible to both, the day-god rose
From the black valley of unmeasured space
To the fresh summits of the waking world.
Then crazed Ruth started forth from Valley Earl.
For weary days she journeyed toward the north,
And reached the camp she sought: cheating the guard,
She in the night discovered Stanley's tent,
And, stealing in, bent over where he slept.
He dreamed of Coralline, and, sighing, said,
"Dear Coralline, forgive me. I was rash."
Then Ruth cried to the sleeper, "She forgives;
She loves you, Stanley Thane — she loves you still!"
At this he woke, and saw the woman there,
And saw the weapon held above his breast;
But horror at the mockery of her words,
Mixed with delight to find them not a dream,

Bound voice and limb as by a wizard's spell.
Then a swift hand passed in and seized the wrist,
And snatched the knife; and mild-faced Karagwe
Confronted Ruth, and turned her rage to tears.

XXXII.

But afterward, Ruth sickened in the camp.
While she lay dying, Karagwe stood near,
And holding her thin hand. he sadly said :
" Farewell, farewell ! Forgive the wrongs you had,
That you may be forgiven in the skies.
I pray that you will there find happiness,
That God will give you rest and joyful morn
After the toilsome night of these sad years."
Ruth faintly said : " 'T is sad to die, O friend ;
But it is not so hard when those we love
Are near us, and we see their grief, and feel
We shall not be forgotten while they live.
I know that Coralline with Stanley Thane
Will wed ere long ; that they will dwell in peace,
With loving children round them, and be glad
To be alive, and live their days of joy.
But you and I were slaves ; we could not wed.
Some men are born to laughter and delight,
To rule and always lightly have their will ;
But more are born to sorrow and to tears,
To serve and have for wages scorn and blame.
But blame and scorn and sorrow fell to Him
Who can forgive my dark intent of wrong."
She rose, sitting upon the couch. reposed
Her head against the breast of Karagwe,
And pointed toward the east's forerunning gray ;
Then saying, with bright eyes, " See ! morning comes."
Then, " 'T is morning ! " and " I love you. Oh, fare-
    well ! "
Breathed out her spirit gently in his arms.

And at Fort Pillow, when the iron storm
Had gone against us, and the rebels killed
Five hundred men who had laid down their arms,
Brave Karagwe was shot, and with a prayer
For his whole country, he fell back and died.

XXXIII.

O Thou, to whom is neither large nor small,
In whom we trust, and, trusting, feel that Thou
Allowest wrong that vaster good may come,
Accept the sacrifice of boisterous war,
To be the red atonement for our sin.
Henceforth let not the rocky echoes roll
The beaten summons from our vales of peace.
Bring Thou true peace, and make our Union strong,
And make us one in heart as one in name,
And let forgiveness heal the cannon's hurt.
For we have battled not against the South,
We battled for the South, to set her free;
She fought against herself in battling us.
Oh, let there be or South or North no more,
But a free people, generous to share
Their precious liberty with all mankind!
    1876.

THE TREE OF JULY.

WHEN vulture and falcon dash down on their prey,
And the burden is great and oppresses the day;
When the dragon-fly darts like a spear that is thrown,
And swiftly the reaper sets blade to his own,
Escape to the wildwood, and come and be free,
And dwell in the shade of our wide-spreading tree;
The tree like the chestnut, so strong and so high,
That bursts into blossom in fervid July. .

The blossoms are spun with that seeming delay
That is wedded to fate, and is prompt to a day.
The blossoms are golden, and cover the tree
With clustering promises tasseled and free.
The burr's round resistance may bristle, in sooth,
But crisp are the triplets and sweet to the tooth.
The tree spreads abroad, bringing love from the sky,
And is dressed in its best for the bridegroom, July.

O bride of all brides in the love of the free!
And tree of all trees as a sheltering tree,
Thy fibers are knit like the thews of wide wings;
Thy talon-like root to the ribbed earth clings;
In the journey of man thou art rest by the way;
To thy shade bring the world from the heat of the
        day!
O liberty tree! thou shalt spread as the sky,
And bloom in all lands in some happy July!

THE DRAWBRIDGE-KEEPER.

DRECKER, a drawbridge-keeper, opened wide
The dangerous gate to let the vessel through;
His little son was standing by his side,
Above Passaic River deep and blue,
While in the distance, like a moan of pain,
Was heard the whistle of the coming train.

At once brave Drecker worked to swing it back,
The gate-like bridge that seems a gate of death;
Nearer and nearer, on the slender track,
Came the swift engine, puffing its white breath.
Then, with a shriek, the loving father saw
His darling boy fall headlong from the draw!

Either at once down in the stream to spring
And save his son, and let the living freight
Rush on to death, or to his work to cling,
And leave his boy unhelped to meet his fate —
Which should he do?   Were you as he was tried,
Would not your love outweigh all else beside?

And yet the child to him was full as dear
As yours may be to you — the light of eyes,
A presence like a brighter atmosphere,
The household star that shone in love's mild skies —
Yet, side by side with duty stern and grim,
Even his child became as naught to him.

For Drecker, being great of soul and true,
Held to his work, and did not aid his boy,
Who, in the deep, dark water, sank from view.
Then from the father's life went forth all joy;
But, as he fell back pallid of his pain,
Across the bridge in safety shot the train.

And yet the man was poor, and in his breast
Flowed no ancestral blood of king or lord;
True greatness needs no title and no crest
To win from men just honor and reward;
Nobility is not of rank, but mind,
And is inborn and common in our kind.

He is most noble whose humanity
Is least corrupted : to be just and good
The birthright of the lowest born may be.
Say what we can, we are one brotherhood,
And, rich or poor, or famous or unknown,
True hearts are noble, and true hearts alone.

THE EMIR'S CHARITY.

In Samarcand, the nether Morning Star,
There lived a Vizier, treasurer of the realm,
Who did not wed until the treasurer, Time,
Had counted down to him his fortieth year.
His loving bride was younger by a score
Of such good coin, and beautiful as dawn.
Mismatched the twain, for she was generous,
And sent no beggar empty from the house:
Yet gave her own, nor touched her husband's gold.
But he, the treasurer, was miserly,
And tightened up the purse-string as he said,
"I too must beg unless you cease to give."

Disguised, the great Emír once went that way,
And, hearing of the kindness of the wife,
Had will to test it: knocking at the door,
No wife appeared; but in her stead, in wrath,
The Vizier, cursing the rag-clad, crust-fed churl
Who dared to seek for dole and break his peace;
Then stroked his beard, and swore by Tamerlane,
By the silk cerements and the sacred tomb,
That Charity herself should cease to be.

"Hold!" quoth the beggar; "say not so of her.
I pray rather that on the common street,
Yea, on the crowded corners of the street,
She yet will stand, this virgin, Charity,
And, hearing her true words, the people there
Will all espouse her cause, and make the world
Mount up and spurn the level of to-day.
Despise no man who asks alms at thy door;
A precious diamond may be meanly set.
It does not soil the angels' holy wings

To hover round the poor. I doff disguise!
Behold! I am Emir! And yet, to prove
That I am not devoid of charity,
Still keep the boon of office that I gave."

Then to the threshold came the generous spouse,
And saw her husband kneeling on the step,
And knew at once the good and great Emir.
She smiled on him, and kissed his gentle hand.
From that day forth, the alms-folk testify,
The purse-string was not tightened round the gold;
But ever more the wife, with cheering smiles,
Doled bountifully to the grateful poor,
Until, at last, when at the door of heaven
She knocked, herself a beggar, Allah smiled
And gave her alms of everlasting peace.

THE BEDOUIN'S REBUKE.

NEEBER, a Bedouin of noble heart,
That from good men received of praise the fee,
Owned a brave horse, with which he would not part,
Because from death he once had run him free.
The man and beast were friends, and it is vice
To sell our friend or friendship for a price.

The horse was black and strong, his step was proud,
His neck was arched, his ears alert for sound,
His speed the tempest's, and his mane a cloud;
His hoofs woke thunder from the desert ground;
His eyes flashed lightning from their inmost core:
Victor of Distance was the name he bore.

Daher, a Bedouin of another tribe,
Had often wished to buy this famous beast;

And as he smoked, and heard his friends describe
Its comely parts and powers, the wish increased;
But Neeber said the horse should not be sold,
Tho' offered wealth in camels and in gold.

Then Daher put on rags, and stained his face,
And went to wait for Neeber, seeming lame.
Him soon he saw approach at daring pace
Upon the envied horse, and as he came
He cried to him: " For three days on this spot
Have I lain starving — pity me my lot."

And, seeing Neeber stop, said on, "I die —
My strength is gone!"   Down Neeber sprang,
And raised him gently with a pitying sigh,
And set him on his horse: a laugh outrang,
And Daher shouted as he plunged his spurs,
"Fair price refused, one sells at last for burrs."

"Stay! stay!" cried Neeber; Daher paused to hear:
"Since God has willed that you my beast should take,
I wish you joy; but tell no man, for fear
Another who was really starved might make
Appeal in vain; for some, remembering me,
Would fail to do an act of charity."

Sharper than steel to Daher seemed remorse!
He quickly turned, and, springing to the ground,
With head bowed low brought Neeber back his horse;
Then, falling on his peaceful breast, he wound
His arms about his neck to make amends,
And ever afterward the two were friends.

THE ROMAN SENTINEL.

Death, or dishonor, which is best to taste? —
A Roman sentinel, with courage high,
When God's hot anger laid Pompeii waste,
Answered the question, and resolved to die.
His duty was upon his post to bide
Till the relief came, let what might betide.

He stood forgotten by the fleeing guard,
Choosing that part which is the bitterest still —
His face with its fixed purpose cold and hard,
Cut in the resolute granite of his will.
"Better," he said, "to die than live in shame;
Death wreathes fresh flowers round a brave man's name."

Life is the wave's deep whisper on the shore
Of a great sea beyond: the soldier saw
That day the light in broad sails hoisted o'er
The drifting boat of dawn; nor dreamed the flaw,
The puff called death, would blow him with them by,
Out to the boundless sea beyond the sky.

He watched the quaking mountain's fire-gashed cheeks,
And saw come up the sand's entombing shower;
The storm darts out its red tongue when it speaks,
And fierce Vesuvius, in that wild hour,
Put forth its tongue of flame, and spoke the word
Of hatred to the city from the Lord.

The gloom of seventeen centuries skulked away,
And standing in a marble niche was found
A skeleton in armor all decay;
The soulless skull was by a helmet crowned,
Cleaving thereto with mingled rust and sand,
And a long spear was in the crumbling hand.

Pompeii from its burial upsprings —
Paved streets with pillared temples on each side,
Baths, houses, paintings, monuments of kings.
But the arched gate whereat the sentry died,
The rusted spear, and helmet with no crest,
Are better far to see than all the rest.

O heart, whatever lot to thee God gives,
Be strong, and swerve not from a blameless way;
Dishonor hurts the soul that ever lives,
Death hurts the body that is kin with clay.
Though Duty's face is stern, her path is best:
They sweetly sleep who die upon her breast.

THE FRENCH MARSHAL.

MACMAHON up the street of Paris came,
In triumph from Magenta; every one
Had heard and praised the fearless marshal's name,
And gloried in the deeds that he had done.
Crowds packed the walks, and at each pane of glass
A face was set to see the hero pass.

Grand music lifted in the morning air
Its eloquent voice; loud-mouthed bells were rung;
Guns boomed till echoes welcomed everywhere;
On buildings and in streets the French flag hung,
And, of a breeze, like fortune, made the toy,
Thrilled every heart with patriotic joy.

But while the marshal up the street made way,
There came a little girl clothed all in white,
Bringing in happy hands a large bouquet;
Her flower-sweet face seemed fragrant with delight.
Well pleased, the soldier, dark and fierce at need,
Raised up the child before him on his steed.

The pearly necklace of her loving arms
She bound on him, and laid her spring-like head
Against the autumn of his cheek, with charms
Of smile and mien ; while to his shoulder fled
Her gold, loose hair with flowers like jewels set,
And made thereon a wondrous epaulet.

He seemed more like an angel than a man,
As, father-like, he paid back each caress ;
Better than all his deeds in war's red van
Appeared this simple act of tenderness.
The people cried " Huzza ! " and did not pause
Until the town seemed shaken with applause.

THE ARTIST'S PRAYER.

WASHINGTON ALLSTON, in a foreign land,
Went to his studio, and knelt to pray :
Starving and weak, he bowed, hand clasped to hand,
With no more strength to keep the wolf at bay.
Conscience, whose still, small voice grows loud and
        clear,
Had risen in his heart now sad and drear.

Within the vast cathedral of the night,
The stars, the altar-lamps, their thanks outshine ;
Yet he, the artist, from whose soul shone bright
The nobler fire of genius, God's divine
And greatest gift to man, had never cast
One ray of gratitude for mercies past.

"I have been most ungrateful, Lord," he said.
" Bound up in self, I have forgotten Thee ;
Yet now, I pray, vouchsafe me this day's bread,
And I will pay of my poor thanks the fee, ·

As I now pay for favors heretofore " —
The irreverent knocker clanked upon the door.

Marquis of Stafford entered. "Please to say
Who bought," he said, "your ' Angel Uriel.' " —
"It is not sold." — "Not sold! Then let me pay
The price you ask for it." So it befell
That friendship followed, and the artist came
To better days, and had the use of fame.

THE SINGER'S ALMS.

In Lyons, in the mart of that French town,
A pallid woman, leading a fair child,
Craved a small alms of one who, walking down
The thoroughfare, caught the child's glance, and smiled
To see, behind its eyes, a noble soul.
He paused to give, but found he had no dole.

His guardian angel warned him not to lose
This chance of pearl to do another good;
So, as he waited, sorry to refuse
The asked-for penny, there aside he stood,
And with his hat held as by limb the nest,
He covered his kind face, and sang his best.

The sky was blue and mild, and all the place
Of commerce where the singer stood was filled.
The many paused, the passer-by slacked pace
To hear the voice that through and through him thrilled.
I think the guardian angel helped along
That cry for pity woven in a song.

The singer stood between the beggars there,
Before a church, and, overhead, the spire,

A slim, perpetual finger in the air
Held toward heaven, land of the heart's desire,
As if an angel, pointing upward, said,
"Yonder a crown awaits this singer's head."

The hat of its stamped brood was emptied soon
Into the woman's lap, who drenched with tears
Her kiss upon the hand of help: 't was noon,
And noon in her glad heart drove forth her fears.
The singer, pleased, passed on, and said in thought,
"Men will not know by whom this deed was wrought."

But when at night he came upon the stage,
Cheer after cheer rose from the crescent throng,
And flowers rained on him : naught could assuage
The tumult of the welcome, save the song
That he superbly sang, with hidden face,
For the two beggars in the market-place.

THE KING'S SACRIFICE.

For seven years the drought had parched the land,
Yet day by day the sun blazed overhead,
A fire-eyed fiend of fire with flaming brand.
The stretching worm was by toothed famine fed.
No green thing grew, for starved men tilled the mold
In the dry beds where once the rivers rolled.

The fakirs of the swart, abundant gods,
And magi, the consulters of the stars,
In contrite sackcloth, bearing serpent-rods,
Cleft the close air with words like scimitars:
" The gods demand a human sacrifice —
No rain will fall until the victim dies."

The wise king sat in council on his throne,
And heard the false priests going up and down.
"A life!" he cried.   "Must ever blood atone?
I hate its clotted stain upon a crown.
Yet if I hold my peace, and, at their shrine,
A life be offered, all the stain were mine!

"Lo, it is somewhat more to be a king
Than gleam in robes of office, sit in state,
Be first in pomps, and rule in everything:
To love the people — that alone is great!
So I, to prove my love, and give you rain,
Proclaim myself the victim to be slain!"

The fancied wrath of idols to assuage,
Forth for his death they led their upright king;
Kind Time, the snail to youth, the bird to age,
Had touched him lightly with its passing wing.
Youthful in age he looked, bright-eyed, smooth-browed,
As for the sacrifice he knelt and bowed.

Then, while the headsman held aloft the blade,
A cloud, wet-laden, stole before the sun,
And on the weapon, with a hand of shade,
Laid dusky seizure; for the fates had spun
A longer, royal thread: the cloud amain
Scattered aslant its diamonds of rain.

THE CALIPH'S MAGNANIMITY.

A TRAVELER across the desert waste
Found on his way a cool, palm-shaded spring,
And the fresh water seemed to his pleased taste,
In the known world, the most delicious thing.
"Great is the caliph!" said he; "I for him
Will fill my leathern bottle to the brim."

He sank the bottle, forcing it to drink
Until the gurgle ceased in its lank throat;
And, as he started onward, smiled to think
That he for thirst bore God's sole antidote.
Days after, with obeisance low and meet,
He laid his present at the caliph's feet.

Forthwith the issue of the spring was poured
Into a cup, on whose embossed outside
Jewels, like solid water, shaped a gourd.
The caliph drank, and seemed well satisfied,
Nay, wisely pleased, and straightway gave command
To line with gold the man's work-hardened hand.

The courtiers, looking at the round reward,
Fancied that some unheard-of virtue graced
The bottled burden borne for their loved lord,
And of the liquid gift asked but to taste.
The caliph answered from his potent throne:
"Touch not the water; it is mine alone!"

But soon — after the humble giver went,
O'erflowing with delight, which bathed his face —
The caliph told his courtiers the intent
Of his denial, saying, "It is base
Not to accept a kindness when expressed
By no low motive of self-interest.

"The water was a gift of love to me,
Which I with golden gratitude repaid.
I would not let the honest giver see
That, on its way, the crystal of the shade
Had changed, and was impure; for so, no less,
His love, thus scorned, had turned to bitterness.

"I granted not the warm, distasteful draught
To asking lips, because of firm mistrust,

Or kindly fear, that, if another quaffed,
He would reveal his feeling of disgust,
And he, who meant a favor, would depart,
Bearing a wounded and dejected heart."

RALPH.

OLD, poor and alone — past seventy years.
The fire is out; there is no wood to burn.
I sit and shiver in the dreary cold,
And, through the window looking on the road,
Behold the pitiless, descending snow.
How softly fall the tender, lace-like flakes!
I wonder oft whether they come from God,
And whether He loves His creatures every one,
Or if He harshly turns to those who err,
And, to the cloud-born whiteness feathering down,
Pointing no finger, says without a tongue,
If thou art not as pure, pass on, pass on.

I had a strong, brave son before the war.
He said, "Dear mother, I am yours alone.
You need me; we are poor; but I can work
And fill your days with comfort for the past;
For I in everything will do my best
To please you, and ward off the briers that catch
And wound the passers-by in life's hard path.
I shall not take a wife till you are gone,
And death from both of us, I trust, is far."

I loved him for the sacrifice he made;
I loved him for himself, he was so true.
My love at least had likeness to the snow.
But yet a mother's love should not be weighed
Against a love of country: this I found;

For my dear, only son, to serve his land,
Forsook me in my weakness and old age.

Our nearest neighbor lived a mile away.
Our road is rough, and travelers to us
Were rarer than the eagles and shy deer.
So, seldom seeing others, we became
The closer knit together, and each day
Both found new reasons for the purest love.
We prospered, for our rugged acres smiled,
Their yellow harvests dimpling in the breeze.
Well stocked the farm was, and the hay-stacks stood
Thick as the tents in Indian villages.

My Ralph was tall, a comely man to see.
Broad-shouldered, eagle-eyed, with fine, dark hair,
Complexion clear, with gladly conscious blood
Painting his heart's thought on his handsome cheeks,
He was to me the grandest man of men.
And Ralph had honesty — a higher kind
Of beauty; nay, honesty is great!
Not all great men have fame out in the world;
For many noble, self-denying deeds
Are done in little things, and being done
Are voiceless, but are like the shining rungs
That led, in Jacob's vision, up to God.

Warm shone the sun the day Ralph went away.
With him I rode to town, and in the crowd
Stood dazed; but clung about him while I could,
And to his bearded cheeks pressed trembling lips
Wet with the boding liquor of mine eyes;
For Sorrow, drunken on the wine of tears,
Sobbed, desperate, and, sighing, drank again.
But the drums rolled and all the banners waved,
And still I think I hear them in my ears
And in my heart, the rolling, rolling drums,

While over all I see the banners wave.
In nights of storm I oft have lain awake,
And thought the wind the rolling of the drums,
And thought the snow the waving of the flags,
The silken banners which I saw that day.

Your father, Ralph, almost deserted us.
He made you do the work upon the farm,
And hung about the tavern day by day,
And in its liquid madness steeped his soul
Until he died. Then, till the war broke out,
You worked for me with patience and pure love,
And I was proud and happy with my son.
Alas! the frightful war! We might have dwelt
In peace and plenty on these Northern hills,
Nor heard the roar of battle all our lives.

There came no word from Ralph, nor any help.
For many months I waited, every day
A year, and every hour a weary month.
Sleep only bridged a shallow, murky stream,
Wherein I saw inverted thoughts and scenes
Depending fringe-like from the shores of day,
As I from waiting o'er to waiting crossed.

I sought to have the acres worked on shares ;
But men were scarce, and not a scythe opposed
The ripe and peaceful armies of the grass.
The man whom Ralph had hired to do my work,
In scarce a month, himself went off to war.
I sold the unused cattle one by one ;
The apples rotted on the loaded trees ;
The grain, my bread, upon the toothless ground
Wasted its increase ; all the crops were lost :
The leaves turned red, and naught was gathered in.

After long months of waiting for some word,
The rumor of a battle reached my ears —

"Ten thousand slain! A glorious victory!"
Little those mothers think of victory
Whose sons lie silent on the ghastly plain;
And what cares now even the splendid boy
Whose life was flashed out at the cannon's mouth?
My nearest neighbor, riding up this way,
Brought me a paper having news of Ralph —
Wounded and missing, printed next his name.
I read; the cheerless room went wildly round,
And to the floor I fell, and all was night.

Weary the months that had been, wearier still
The months that followed, with no word, no word.
I think if I had known my darling dead,
I should have felt more peace; but, oh! those words,
"Wounded and missing," kept ringing in my brain,
Like loud, wild bells of dolor and alarm.

Only a year ago, only a year,
Only a little year, it does not seem so long,
A letter came from Ralph, a few brief lines:
Freed from a Southern prison; coming home!
Home! Home once more! O Ralph, my soldier son,
How glad I was! how strong I felt! how sure
That God had crowned my waiting, heard my prayers!

A year ago, only a little year,
Ralph had not come. How could he wait so long?
When the dull light of that dark morning broke
I looked out on the fields and saw it snow,
And wondered whether Ralph would come that day,
For something said to me that he would come.
The snow had fallen all night, and it was cold,
Almost too bitter cold for snow to fall.
The fences and the road were lost in drifts.
I saw the silent orchard cold and white,
With branches thrown up like the stiffened arms

Of dead men on a battle-field.   Till noon
I kept my post, here at the frosted pane,
Watching for Ralph; but still he did not come.
At last, urged by an impulse new and strange,
And gifted with a strength not mine before,
I left the house, and struggled through the storm
Down to the road, and out beyond the hill,
But stumbled there on something in the snow;
The chilly fleece I brushed away, and found
A soldier kneeling, with his face bent down
As if he kissed an angel's flowing robe,
And not the threadless raiment of the storm.
I turned the body : it was stiff and cold ;
And in the sunken features pale and thin,
Disfigured by a scar across the cheek,
I saw my Ralph, my lifeless darling, Ralph.
He must have died almost in sight of home.
If he had only struggled to the top,
And not sunk down behind the little hill,
I should have seen him and have helped him in.

Under the arms I dragged the body back,
And chafed and warmed and bathed it; but the heart,
Whose beat had been a steady martial tread,
Moved not, and all was still.   No voice, no breath ;
Only a stony silence white and cold.
Here for two days I sat and watched my dead.
I did not eat nor sleep, but moaned alone.
I did not care to live ; I prayed to die.
I bent above the calm, unanswering lips,
And begged them speak, if naught but one farewell ;
And on the face my white hair lay like snow.

They found me thus, watching my dead brave son —
My dead son, dead for his proud bride's sake.
His country was his bride ; he loved her well.
But always they endure great bitterness

Who give themselves to high, unselfish aims;
And Ralph's distracted bride, in angry mood,
As if demanding only sacrifice.
Requited him with hunger, wounds, and death.

And now I am alone, alone. No more
Is left a hope that Ralph will come again;
Yet I may go to him and cease to mourn,
For we shall dwell where there will be no tears,
Nor cold, nor lack of food, nor any war;
And the pure Christ, who suffered wounds and death,
And knows how precious is a mother's love,
Will cleanse my lifted spirit white as snow.

HYMN FOR DECORATION DAY.

With fragrant flowers we decorate their graves,
   Who met in battle, or in prison-pen,
A fruitful death; who broke the chains of slaves,
   And crushed the might of proud and cruel men.

They broke the chains with tears of bondage wet,
   And gave their brave young lives for you and me;
For, where the slave endures, it is a threat
   Against the precious freedom of the free.

The sun of liberty dispels the dew,
   The tears, the night, and shines on near and far;
But, where it only lights the selfish few,
   It sears and blights, and sinks in clouds of war.

'T is fragrant gratitude we scatter o'er
   The graves of them that died for you and me:
Their names, their dust, their memories, once more,
   O Liberty, we consecrate to thee!

THE AUSTRIAN HUSSAR.

With sabers drawn and guidons dancing free,
And music dying in the joy it made,
In gay Vienna rode the cavalry,
The pride of Austria, on grand parade.
Like a rose-garden, with fair colors set,
Lay the wide plain whereon the host were met.

A little child — a lovely, rosebud girl —
In white attire, and ribbons green as moss,
Straying away, lost in the crowded whirl,
Into the open field she thought to cross,
Rushed out, when to the bugle's cheerful sound
A squadron of hussars came sweeping round.

From the main body of the horsemen these
Rode down to honor with their steel salute
The empress, where she sat in velvet ease,
A diamond 'midst the cluster of her suit.
She cried with horror, her delight undone,
To see the danger to the pretty one.

Directly on the child, like angry flame,
Had wheeled at headlong speed the brave and strong;
They faced the dazzling sun, and, as they came,
Carried a gust of pennant air along.
Swift as unbridled rage, they rode as tho'
In battle charging fiercely on the foe.

The poor, bewildered babe, in blind affright,
Ran toward the squadron, and her shadow there,
Hiding before her from the living light,
Flat on the grassless level dry and bare,
Moved gauntly, and it took the boding shape
And gloom of death from which is no escape.

Seeing the ill, the mother of the child
Stood spellbound in the depth of her distress.
Her gaze was set; her panting bosom wild
That she to save her babe was powerless.
So, too, the multitude stood dazed and dumb;
Alas! from them no hand of help could come.

As when, in polar regions white and still,
The compass points no longer to its star,
But downward to the ocean dark and chill,
And frost and heavy silence only are;
So now hope's compass failed, amid the drear
And pallid stillness of benumbing fear.

But Succor waits on Fortune's smile and beck.
In the front rank the holder of a rein
Threw himself forward round his horse's neck,
And bending down, under the streaming mane,
Caught up the child from frightful death below,
And set her safely on his saddle-bow.

This feat he did, and never checked the speed,
Nor changed the pace, nor to a comrade spoke,
Nor lost his hold on his submissive steed,
Nor the alignment of the squadron broke.
With modest grace, which still endears and charms,
He gave the child back to her mother's arms.

Voices of thousands to the welkin blue
Cheered the good deed the brave hussar had done;
And other thousands cheered it when they knew;
But she who fondly clasped the rescued one,
And the kind empress, in that storm of cheers,
Could only tell their gratitude with tears.

Bright as a star the moment, and how blest
To the young trooper! when the emperor,

Graciously taking from his royal breast
One of the badges that men struggle for,
Placed on the other's heart, so nobly bold,
The shining golden emblem, more than gold.

That other, then, of honor may have thought
How unexpectedly it was his meed:
He had not found it in the way he sought;
But from an unpremeditated deed
In which he saw no merit, had no toil,
The flower had sprung, and from its native soil.

THE KING AND THE NAIAD.

When the wrongs of peace grow mighty,
   They beget the wrong of war,
Whose wild night, with deeds immortal,
   Sparkles brightly, star on star.

"O king, to health restore us;
   We are besieged by thirst.
There are two foes before us;
   The unseen foe is worst.

"Lest thirst's sharp arrows slaughter,
   Yield to the open foe,
And lead us to the water,
   Tho' it in thraldom flow."

Thus to Soüs, King of Sparta,
   With parched lips his soldiers cried,
When Arcadian besiegers
   Hemmed them in on every side.

In the dry and stony stronghold
   Was no drop of water found;

But a brook, beyond the rampart,
 Lightly danced along the ground.

Lofty Soüs bade a soldier
 Wave a truce, and, with the foe,
Made a compact strong as granite,
 With one rift where hope might grow.

Sparta will yield up her conquests,
 She her claims to them will sink,
If her king and all his army
 From the nearest fountain drink.

To these terms they made their pledges,
 Whom dry thirst gave fearful odds,
And, to witness what they signed to,
 Loudly called upon their gods.

In a deep, cool glen, appareled
 In green boughs, which swayed above,
To the sunlight rose the waters,
 Soft as eyes that beam with love.

Hither came the adversaries;
 And the Spartans, as by whips,
Were ondriven to the kisses
 Of the liquid Naiad lips.

As each fever-throated fighter,
 Bending low his waving crest,
Stooped to quaff his land's dishonor,
 Him the troubled king addressed:

" If thou wilt not drink, but conquer
 This temptation of the spring,
I will give to thee my kingdom,
 And thou shalt be crowned its king!"

Heedless of him were his soldiers;
  Thirst they gave a higher rank;
By the choking captain maddened,
  All, with panic faces, drank.

It appeared not heavy water,
  But divine air, cool and thin,
Which they, freed from stifling torture,
  Now were deeply breathing in.

Lastly stooped thirst-burdened Soüs
  To the treason of the spring;
But he turned, and would not drink it,
  Being absolutely king.

Rising, as his face he sprinkled,
  With his men he marched away,
Scornful of the daunted captors
  Who in vain might say him nay.

He would yield not up his conquests,
  For himself and all his men
Had not drank the sparkling pleasure
  That allured them to the glen.

AGNES HATOT.

WHEN might made right in days of chivalry,
Hatot and Ringsdale, over claims to land,
Darkened their lives with stormy enmity,
And for their cause agreed this test to stand:
To fight steel-clad till either's blood made wet
The soil disputed; and a time was set.

But Hatot sickened when the day drew near,
And strength lay racked that once had been his boast.

Then Agnes, his fair daughter, for the fear
That in proud honor he would suffer most,
Resolved to do the battle in his name,
And leave no foothold for the tread of Shame.

She, at the gray, first coming of the day,
Shook off still sleep, and from her window gazed.
The west was curtained with night's dark delay;
A cold and waning moon in silence raised
Its bent and wasted finger o'er the vale,
And seemed sad Death that beckoned, wan and pale.

But Hope sails by the rugged coasts of Fear;
For while awakened birds sang round her eaves,
Our Agnes armed herself with knightly gear
Of rattling hauberk and of jointed greaves;
Withal she put on valor, that to feel
Does more for victory than battle-steel.

She had a sea of hair, whose odor sweet,
And golden softness, in a moonless tide
Ran rippling toward the white coast of her feet;
But as beneath a cloud the sea may hide,
So in her visored, burnished helmet, there,
Under the cloud-like plume, was hid her hair.

Bearing the mighty lance, sharp-spiked and long,
She at the sill bestrode her restless steed.
Her kneeling soul prayed God to make her strong,
And prayer is nearest path to every need.
She clattered on the bridge, and on apace,
And met dread Ringsdale at the hour and place.

They clash in onslaught; steel to steel replies;
The champed bit foams; rider and ridden fight.
Each feels the grim and brutal instinct rise
That in forefront of havoc takes delight.

The lightning of the lances flashed and ran,
Until, at last, the maid unhorsed the man.

Then, on her steed, she, bright-eyed, flushed, and glad,
Her helmet lifted in the sylvan air;
And from the iron concealment that it had,
The noiseless ocean of her languid hair
Broke in disheveled waves: the cross and heart,
Jewels that latched her vest, she drew apart.

" Lo, it is Agnes, even I ! " she said,
" Who with my trusty lance have thrust thee down !
For hate of shame the fray I hazarded ;
And yet, not me the victory should crown,
But God, the Merciful, who helps the right,
And lent me strength to conquer in the fight."

BALLAD OF CONSOLATION.

A PIOUS, Catholic woman,
　　To burdensome poverty born,
For her patron chose great Saint Joseph,
　　And prayed to him even and morn.
And when she was married a twelvemonth,
　　A rose-chain of love linked with joy,
She named in her patron-saint's honor
　　That gift of sweet heaven, her boy.

She dwelt at the rim of the city
　　In a rude cabin — her shrine;
And a frail vine bore, by the doorstep,
　　One morning-glory divine.
But the day that this trumpeter angel
　　Bloomed out in the sunlight wide,
That day the delight of the woman,
　　The flower of her bosom, died.

They bitterly mourned for their darling,
  The laboring-man and his wife;
The cloud and the storm were upon them
  In that starless midnight of life.
Their loss seemed a dolorous burden
  Sent for a cross from on high.
He went without heart to his labor,
  She turned to her cares with a sigh.

But time is a whirlpool of changes:
  Or ever another year fled,
A second man-child in the cabin
  Had taken the place of the dead;
And the trusting, affectionate mother,
  With courage too faithful to faint,
Had the second new-comer christened
  The name of her worshipful saint.

The baby grew daily, waxed stronger,
  And prattled with wonder and glee.
The heart of the mother was joyous,
  His innocent promise to see.
She fancied in day-dreams his future,
  And found, in the beautiful years,
Relief from hard toil for his father,
  And songs for her burdens and tears.

For she saw her babe in his manhood,
  Noble and rich; and again,
The crown and chief star of the city,
  A far-sighted leader of men.
But how shall love, that goes blindfold,
  Look into the future afar,
Whose heavy mists hasten, unsundered,
  Before time's radiant car?

Ripe Autumn came sighing and weeping,
  Bearing her sickle and sheaves,

And into the laborer's cabin
  Threw wildly an omen of leaves.
The pretty babe sickened and withered,
  Like leaves in the boreal breath,
And the gleaming sickle of harvest
  Preceded the sickle of death.

The hopes of the father and mother,
  Once more, in their sorrowing breasts,
Lay ruthlessly ruined and scattered,
  Like a rose that a tempest divests.
But the woman, trusting, believing,
  Exalted her spirit in prayer,
And craved of the holy Saint Joseph
  To pity her humble despair.

Three fast-flying years had vanished
  In the past's immemorial sky,
When again in the working-man's cabin
  Rose an infant's pitiful cry.
And the grateful, reverent mother,
  With faith that still fully sufficed,
Named her last-born too for Saint Joseph,
  Who tended the young child Christ.

She prayed to the saint to watch over
  And guard her own little son,
And spare him to solace her heartache,
  Till her troubled days should be done.
She thought that her prayer had been granted,
  For her soul-gemmed jewel and prize
Lived three glad seasons, and, smiling,
  Looked up, out of heavenly eyes.

Then Winter came freezing and blowing,
  His long hair streaming and hoar;
To enter the laborer's cabin,
  He tugged at window and door;

But a colder than he, and sadder,
  An entrance readily found,
And covered the babe's small body
  As the white snow sheeted the ground.

From the bed-side the mother rose wailing,
  And tore her disheveled hair,
And wrung her mute hands in expression
  · Of wordless depths of despair.
It seemed an injustice of heaven,
  The death that bereft her that day.
She prayed not; but jeered at Saint Joseph
  For taking her jewels away.

The picture of Infant and Virgin,
  That hung in the comfortless room,
Disdainfully mocked, she fancied,
  Her empty-armed, desolate doom.
Her rosary rested uncounted,
  Its crucifix broken in two,
And she blamed her patron-saint ever
  For being so harsh and untrue.

The time, rebellious and prayerless,
  Flew on into hesitant spring;
But no change in the dark resentment
  Did the mild transition bring,
Till one night, when, in vain derision,
  The woman had scoffed at prayer,
She found, in a mystical vision,
  A balm for her rankling despair.

The landscape was vernal about her,
  The soothing air fragrant and still.
She saw, with a feeling of horror,
  Three gallows set high on a hill;
But she heard glad, musical voices,
  And, turning to see whence they came,

Beheld four angels approaching,
　And each of them called her by name.

The oldest was tall and majestic,
　With wings of as radiant gold
As that in the cloud-lands of sunset,
　In splendor on splendor uprolled.
The linen of purity clothed him,
　With outlines of delicate grace,
And a halo above him enlightened
　The measureless calm of his face.

The three other angels were smaller,
　With silver-like pinions that shone
As the moon, or the pearl heart of Hesper.
　Fresh roses these angels had thrown
At the feet of the sorrowful woman.
　As they looked upon her and smiled;
And she thought she had seen their faces
　In dreams or when only a child.

The radiant, golden-winged angel
　Spoke to the woman and said:
"I am your patron, Saint Joseph;
　I foster and care for your dead.
Tho' pleased with your faith, I was troubled
　When your heart found naught of relief;
For always the angels of heaven
　Sympathize deeply with grief.

"I loved with deep joy the young children
　To whom you had given my name;
But I looked out into their futures,
　And saw that their lives meant shame.
See, yonder, alone on the hill-top,
　The three dread gallows appear,
That would have been built for the offspring
　You fondled, and prayed you might rear.

" Wherefore, I at once interceded
  To save you dishonor so sore,
And was given to choose between it
  And the early deaths you deplore.
So, guided by tender compassion,
  I took your young innocents three;
And they are these loving immortals
  Who came to meet you with me."

The angels with silvery pinions
  Embraced their own mother dear;
Their kisses made saintly her features
  That lately were haggard and drear;
And they said, " O sorrowful mother,
  Be joyful, and weep not nor sigh,
For we are all waiting and longing
  To welcome you home in the sky."

The woman rose from her vision,
  And heard the merry birds sing.
The air was sweet-scented and warmer,
  The landscape verdant with spring.
She knelt repentant and thankful,
  And from bitterness found a release;
For, as the earth was clothed in its verdure,
  Her spirit was mantled with peace.

GUYOT OF MARSEILLES.

The life misunderstood is sad as tears;
Its outer seeming courts the stab of scorn:
It sits apart, and, bearing gibes and sneers,
Feeds on the lonely hope to which 't is born.
It is a murmuring shell, whose rough outside
Shows not the beauties that within abide.

Such life was noble Guyot's of Marseilles.
By patient industry he won his way,
And from whatever quarter streamed the gales,
They blew him favor, for he worked each day,
And trenched on night for further hours to use,
Taxing inactive sleep for revenues.

The silver cord was loosed, and he was bent
Graveward; but often he himself denied
The wheaten fuel, coal of nutriment,
That keeps the hungry fire of life supplied.
He wore mere rags against the sharpest frost,
And, from his youth up, shunned the ways of cost.

His rooms were mean, and on the bare, board floor
He slept on straw, and oft the freezing air
Hissed through the dusty seams and broken door,
As if to drive his purpose to despair;
But purpose, kin to sufferance, heeds no cold,
And habits turn to needs as men grow old.

The world condemns the miser: in the street
The rich at Guyot cast an honest sneer;
Even the poor folk, whom he chanced to meet,
Hooted and scoffed and after flung a jeer,
For scorn of him who basely would withhold
The cheapest comforts for the sake of gold.

They found him lying lifeless on his straw;
And thus, or with like meaning, ran his will:
"In early youth, in fair Marseilles, I saw
The poor with water were supplied but ill;
And I trade's yellow flower have widely plucked,
And here bequeath, to build an aqueduct."

O creeping water of the mountain-spring!
O dimpled water of the laughing brooks!

O water of the river! whispering
To the low bough that on its likeness looks —
Publish in crystal, through the dells and dales,
Of Guyot, noble Guyot of Marseilles!

ONTIORA.

Moons on moons ago,
In the sleep, or night, of the moon,
When evil spirits have power,
The monster, Ontiora,
Came down in the dreadful gloom.
The monster came stalking abroad,
On his way to the sea for a bath,
For a bath in the salt, gray sea.

In Ontiora's breast
Was the eyrie of the winds,
Eagles of measureless wing,
Whose screeching, furious swoop
Startled the sleeping dens.
His hair was darkness unbound,
Thick, and not mooned nor starred.
His head was plumed with rays
Plucked from the sunken sun.

To him the forests of oak,
Of maple, hemlock, and pine,
Were as grass that a bear treads down.
He trod them down as he came,
As he came from his white-peak'd tent,
At whose door, ere he started abroad,
He drew a flintless arrow
Across the sky's strip'd bow,
And shot at the evening star.

He came like a frowning cloud,
That fills and blackens the west.
He was wroth at the bright-plumed sun,
And his pale-faced wife, the moon,
With their twinkling children, the stars;
But he hated the red-men all,
The Iroquois, fearless and proud,
The Mohegans, stately and brave,
And trod them down in despite,
As a storm treads down the maize.
He trod the red-men down,
Or drove them out of the land
As winter drives the birds.

When near the King of Rivers,
The river of many moods,
To Ontiora thundered
Manitou out of a cloud.
Between the fountains crystal
And the waters that reach to the sky,
Manitou, Spirit of Good,
To the man-shaped monster spoke :
"You shall not go to the sea,
But be into mountains changed,
And wail in the blast, and weep
For the red-men you have slain.
You shall lie on your giant back
While the river rises and falls,
And the tide of years on years
Flows in from a depthless sea."

Then Ontiora replied :
"I yield to the heavy doom;
Yet what am I but a type
Of a people who are to come?
Who as with a bow will shoot
And bring the stars to their feet,

And drive the red-man forth
To the Land of the Setting Sun."

So Ontiora wild,
By eternal silence touched,
Fell backward in a swoon,
And was changed into lofty hills,
The Mountains of the Sky.

This is the pleasant sense
Of Ontiora's name,
"The Mountains of the Sky."
His bones are rocks and crags,
His flesh is rising ground,
His blood is the sap of trees.

On his back with one knee raised,
He lies with his face to the sky,
A monstrous human shape
In the Catskills high and grand.
And from the valley below,
Where the slow tide ebbs and flows,
You can mark his knee and breast,
His forehead beetling and vast,
His nose and retreating chin.
But his eyes, they say, are lakes,
Whose tears flow down in streams
That seam and wrinkle his cheeks.
For the fate he endures, and for shame
Of the evil he did, as he stalked
In the vanquished and hopeless moon,
Moons on moons ago.

LIBERTY.

WHERE the Platte and the Laramie mingle
  With waters as pure as the dew,
Wooing down from the Rocky Mountains
  Their dreamy, perpetual blue ;
Where the wild-rose sweet and the balsam
  Scent the glad, fresh, prairie air,
And the breeze, like an elk, comes leaping
  From the sand-hills changeful and bare,

Stands a frontier fort, and behind it
  The mountains peacefully rise,
Whence, over the valley, resistless
  The whirl of the elements flies.
There the sudden storm rides madly
  On an uncurbed charger of cloud,
While it shoots long arrows of lightning,
  And utters its war-cry loud.

The Sioux were fierce, cruel, and moody,
  And hated the pale-face much
For taking the lands where they hunted,
  Which he pledged that he would not touch.
So they sought to unite all red-men
  Against their habitual foe,
And, for Indian manhood and honor,
  Strike one more pitiless blow.

The chief of the Sioux tribes was kingly ;
  He rode undaunted and free ;
He was tall, broad-shouldered, fine-featured,
  And as straight as a towering tree.
In the midst of the dusky-red council
  He rose with his harrowing themes,
And a breeze through his utterance freshened,
  With voices of forests and streams.

In the war that he fiercely incited—
　While its flying arrows increased,
And murder and fire on the border
　Angered the populous East—
Near the fort where Laramie water
　Is wed to a wandering stream,
Dwelt the Sioux chief's beautiful daughter,
　Of twilight a glamour and dream.

She was tall, and was formed superbly,
　With a face so true in each line,
That, seen looking upward in profile,
　It seemed as of marble divine.
In her eyes was a languorous splendor,
　The dawning of young desire;
For those eyes, like the fawn's, were tender,
　Yet filled with a smoldering fire.

On her forehead a beaded fillet
　Bound the trailing night of her hair,
And her shoulders, perfectly molded,
　Like her tapering arms, were bare.
The stars and the flowers in bead-work
　Were copied, her beauty to serve,
And her negligent blanket discovered
　Her bosom's voluptuous curve.

She was mistress of two white ponies,
　And, riding on either of these,
She urged him to galloping swiftness,
　And her long hair streamed in the breeze.
Then seemed she that offspring of Valor,
　Liberty, and her employ
Was only to roam her dominion,
　Embodied with beauty and joy.

Begot of the sunset and freedom,
　And rich in the Indian's lore,

She knew the antelope's hoof-print,
  The birds, and what plumage they wore.
She could throw the lariat deftly,
  And bring to the earth, at a blow,
The prairie-hen low-flying over,
  Or slay the stag and the doe.

In her voice the tongue of Dakota
  Was sweeter than philomel's song;
She spoke, too, the words that the Mayflower
  From beyond sea wafted along.
She read many books and news-letters,
  And each was a cup to her sight;
For she drank from the waters of knowledge
  With quenchless thirst and delight.

At the fort, from the homes of Ohio,
  Were volunteer soldiers that came
To cover the venturesome settlers
  From the Indian's desperate aim.
With the rest came a young lieutenant,
  Blue-eyed, handsome, and pale,
And the Sioux chief's daughter, beholding,
  Felt strong love rise and prevail.

It may be that some sense of pity
  First turned to the soldier her gaze,
For she saw a mystery in him,
  The shadow of sorrowful days;
And wherever she went or tarried,
  Albeit he was not near,
In evergreen dells of remembrance
  His image would softly appear.

She could not escape from its presence;
  It dwelt in the heart of her heart,
Tho' in bitterest moments of passion
  She ruthlessly bade it depart.

But Love is far mightier, braver,
 Than anger, sorrow, and scorn ;
He drives them back huddled and cowering
 Aghast at his arrows of morn.

Like a mountain-lake silent, unrippled,
 That glasses the bountiful sun,
And so clear that the mid-bottom pebbles
 Are countable one by one,
Was the limpid lake of this spirit,
 Where life's great day-god shone ;
Tho' the depths were yet clearer and deeper
 Than the mountain-lake's, placid and lone.

When often the comely young soldier
 Had seen the maiden, and knew
That daily she eagerly watched him
 With fond eyes wistful and true,
He spoke to her kindly, and praised her
 For her beauty so wild-like and rare,
And gave her a rose of the prairie
 To lighten the dark of her hair.

Then into his eyes far looking,
 She fancied she saw the sky
Of an infinite sadness in them,
 And answered him, after a sigh.
She set the glad rose in her girdle,
 And lovingly taking his hand,
They wandered along by the river
 That lisps to the glittering sand.

Thenceforth he turned from the maiden ;
 He felt that he could not divide
The love of his life for one woman,
 Nor find in another his bride.
This other he tortured with coldness
 And the slight of his downcast eyes ;

Yet she followed him oft, at a distance,
  Perplexed, and with tearful surprise.

On horseback they once met at sunset,
  In a wooded reach of the road,
And her heart, with its torrent of feeling,
  In words and in tears overflowed:
"Oh, why do you treat me so coldly?
  And why do you spurn a true friend?
Am I not an Indian princess?
  And what have I done to offend?"

"You have not offended," he answered;
  "I have read in your eyes, I suppose;
But to pluck a red rose, and discard it,
  Were basely unjust to the rose.
I would not be false to your kindness;
  I truly shall treasure it long;
Yet for us to be often together
  Would be unseemly and wrong."

"I know," she replied, "that the white man
  Despises the dark, red race;
He hunts down our tribes, and destroys them:
  No foot of them stays in a place.
You treat us as fanged wolf, or badger,
  Which on the plains skulkingly roams.
Is it strange that we follow the war-path
  When driven away from our homes?

"We go to the wall, being weakest,
  And die in the pools of our gore.
The path we are treading is weary;
  Our feet and our spirits are sore.
Mankind are all love-craving brothers,
  And why should they fail to agree?
Befriend us, be true to us, love us,
  And of us, oh, learn to be free!

"We can teach even that; for of freedom
  The pale-face has volumes to learn,
Still a slave to the past's rude customs,
  Which time and thought must o'erturn.
Tho' he comes to the red-man's country
  The gladness of freedom to find,
He brings his base slavery with him,
  A vassal still in his mind.

"I know that not father nor mother
  Should separate loves that are true;
Why then should an alien race-hatred,
  Which in this land no man should renew?
Break away from the bondage of custom;
  Fear not to be perfectly free.
Even I am Liberty, dearest!
  Oh, turn and behold her in me!"

He looked at the mountains majestic
  In crowns of continual snow;
He saw the bright heaven of sunset
  Along them refulgently glow;
And he answered, "O bronze-dark critic,
  The splendor of liberty flies
Before us onward forever,
  Like the west-going light of the skies.

"We follow in fetters of custom
  That we never can disregard;
For rebellion tightens them on us,
  And makes them more galling and hard.
But here is your wigwam, and by it
  Your mother, who loves you so well.
Forget me; turn from me hereafter —
  Good-night, and forever farewell!"

Forget him! Do deer of the forest
  Forget the lick or the spring?

Do eagles forget the broad sunshine,
  Or the bees where the flower-bells swing?
She could not forget him; but, sighing,
  Said softly, sweetly, " Adieu ! "
And among the trees and their shadows,
  He went as the sun from her view.

He went, but his lingering image
  Yet haunted the house of her mind;
And the longing, like thirst, to be near him,
  She had not a fetter to bind.
On her pine-bough and wolf-skin pallet,
  She soon was with him in dreams,
Where the sound of his voice was more tender
  Than the musical murmur of streams.

As a traveler, lost on the prairie,
  Gains the top of some rolling divide,
And, gazing far into the distance
  Round the level lonely and wide,
Can find neither succor nor guidance,
  But stands in the wildering maze,
And absently plucks at the sage-brush,
  Treasuring some of its sprays :

So, lost on love's measureless prairie,
  The beautiful Indian girl
Looked round on the helpless horizon,
  Her thoughts in a turbulent whirl;
And beholding no path nor assistance,
  Hopeless and deeply depressed,
She plucked at the words of her loved one,
  And treasured a few in her breast.

But day after day in the wildwood,
  Adorning her beauty with care,
She would silver her wrists with her bracelets,
  And bead her long, shimmering hair;

Then would go to the fort, and be willing
    To seek her lone wigwam again,
If she only had looked on her loved one
    Riding along with his men.

She would wait slow hours at his door-step
    To see him come out and go by,
And Pity's sweet self had grown sadder
    Watching her out of the sky.
Oft she followed the soldier meekly
    With fawn-like, inquisitive fear,
As if he might even deny her
    The gladness of being so near.

If the strong and unselfish goddess,
    That long ago tarried in Rome,
Were seeking to be incarnate,
    And to dwell in her dedicate home,
What form would she take? Whose body
    Would best with her spirit agree?
And where, in the land of her favor,
    Would her truest habitat be?

She would take the fresh form of a maiden
    Imbued with the red of her skies,
Lithe, graceful, faultlessly molded,
    And with dark and affectionate eyes.
She would choose the wide sea of the prairie,
    And the mountainous Western wild,
As the place for her life to abide in,
    And be simple and free as a child.

And would she not smile on the people
    Pursuing her over the deep,
Who fought in her cause, and delighted
    Her name in high honor to keep?
She surely would hold them the dearest
    Of all that the century gave,

And would choose from among them a lover,
  Handsome, youthful, and brave.

They told the great chief of his daughter,
  As he rode with his warrior band,
And he grieved at the lowly behavior
  Of the pride of the Western land.
He sent to her friends and her mother
  To take the sweet maiden away
To a distant vale by a river,
  Where a camp of Sioux families lay.

He bade them neglect not to cheer her,
  In hope they could lead to depart
The profitless passion that ruffled
  The innocent rose of her heart.
She went with them humbly and tearless,
  Her life, itself, beaten and cowed ;
For there settled down on her spirit
  A somber, enveloping cloud.

She silently rode her white palfrey ;
  She did not smile nor complain ;
From the cloudy, waste country of sadness
  They strove to allure her in vain.
She touched not the food that they brought her,
  Who all were tender and kind.
They reached the red camp by the river,
  But ever she sorrowed and pined.

Of all life's household, the humblest
  Is Love, the begetter of Care.
Unworldly, Love asks only likeness ;
  But, missing it, broods on despair.
As the brook by the trail, in summer,
  In the rainless glare of the day,
Runs slowly on, fainter and thinner,
  The maiden was wasting away.

At dawn, a courier, foam-flecked,
  Reached the Sioux chief's war-tent door,
And told him his daughter was dying,
  And longed to behold him once more.
Away, over prairie and mountain,
  Not pausing by night nor by day,
Sped the chief to the camp by the river,
  And knelt where his loved child lay.

Of buffalo-robes, her wigwam,
  Traced round with a sylvan design,
In a wood at the foot of a canyon,
  Stood under a pitying pine.
A pine-tassel carpet and antlers
  Embellished the softness within,
And warm was its couch of rude wicker
  With the gray coyóté skin.

The tawny-haired coat of a puma
  Before the low pallet was spread.
As the sorrowful chief knelt on it,
  The blighted rose lifted her head;
And laying her hands on his shoulders,
  To his eyes that were bending above
Looked up with unchanging affection,
  And told of her heart-broken love.

"Dear father," she said. "I am going
  Across the great final divide —
Across the dark range of death's mountains
  To the parks where the spirits abide.
We shall, in that country, be driven
  From our home of the forest no more,
But be at rest with our kindred
  Who have silently journeyed before.

"In the beautiful land of the sunset
  I shall wait for you, father dear,

Where the birds sing of love requited,
  All the snowless, celestial year.
In a little while you will be with me:
  Your burden is grievous to bear;
You are growing old, and so care-worn,
  And as white as mist is your hair.

"For a pledge of you, changeless and sacred,
  Dear father, your stricken one yearns:
Of all the chiefs you are the greatest,
  And are first when the calumet burns.
I pray you go forth on the war-path
  To cope with the white-men no more;
They are countless as leaves of the woodland,
  Or as waves on the voluble shore.

"Oh, spare our unfortunate people,
  And make the war settle and cease;
Take well-won rest from the conflict,
  Ere you go to the infinite peace.
And I would that there might be hereafter
  No serpent of discord and strife
Between our proud Sioux and the nation
  Of him I love better than life.

"When my spirit has gone. noble father,
  Take this desolate body of mine,
Discarded, heart-broken, and wasted,
  The withered branch of a vine,
And lay it to rest on the hillside
  Where the wild-vines clamber and dwell,
At the fort by Laramie River,
  Where I sadly learned to love well.

"In distant, wonderful countries
  The pale-faces thought it was good
To come to our land, seeking only
  To think and to speak as they would.

They found a true name for the blessing
　　They sought, and deem sacred and fair ;
But we have no word of its meaning,
　　Tho' ever we breathed it like air.

"The name is Liberty, father —
　　A name that is almost divine.
Henceforth call me Liberty only,
　　And make the belov'd name mine.
And when our brave people in pity
　　Chant the death-song over my head,
Let them turn to the east their faces,
　　And mourn for their Liberty dead."

In sorrow too deep to be spoken,
　　The great chief hastened to give
The wished-for pledge to his daughter ;
　　But bade her take courage and live.
He called her sweet Liberty fondly,
　　And said that she must not decease.
But in vain ; for at dawn of the morrow
　　Her lamp was extinguished in peace.

Then straightway they killed her two ponies,
　　To bear, to the spirit's dim land,
The hovering ghost of the maiden,
　　And they put some beads in her hand.
Two days and two nights they bewailed her
　　To the bluffs and the forest around,
And in buffalo-robes her body
　　They mournfully corded and bound.

The braves to their shoulders lifted
　　The burden stretched on its bier,
And they went on the fortnight's journey
　　Through winter so ghostly and drear.
Thrice a hundred dusky-red mourners
　　Rode forth in the funeral train,

And at night, round their camp-fires, the death-song
  Was a wild, uncontrollable strain.

" She is dead: the pale-face has slain her,
  Our Liberty, gentle and pure.
He spurned her who most should have loved her,
  And laid on us much to endure.
Like the traveler lost on the prairie
  Whose limits he cannot descry,
Hungering, thirsting, forsaken,
  She found naught left but to die."

They crossed the monotonous prairie,
  And the shivering blizzard blew
In that wilderness wolf-haunted,
  And the fine snow blindingly flew.
It ceased, and the silence unbroken,
  And their freezing, vaporous breath,
Made it seem to them there that they traversed
  The pale, still frontier of death.

They came to the mingling rivers,
  And saw, on the opposite side,
The fort, with its striped flag waving
  In starry, indolent pride.
They sent a young warrior over,
  To carry the humble request
That, before the fort, on the hillside,
  The chief's dead daughter might rest.

With kindness the garrison met them,
  As they, from the winter-clad bank,
The requiem mournfully chanting,
  Were solemnly riding in rank.
The soldiers had garnished the quarters
  With flags and small arms and great;
In the midst, on a flag-covered table,
  They laid the hushed burden in state.

Words of sympathy, words of welcome,
    The white to the red men said;
And the chaplain, with eloquent pity,
    Touchingly spoke of the dead.
In the vanishing tongue of Dakota,
    The famous Sioux chief replied,
And proclaimed that, with his loved daughter,
    The War, Hate's daughter, had died.

"I have given," he said, "my promise,
    From its cruel path to refrain.
Were the hopelessness of resistance
    And claims of policy vain
To make me stay firm in my purpose,
    All strife with your people to cease,
Then this pledge, that I gave to my daughter,
    Would bind me hereafter to peace."

In her praise, flocks of winged words fluttered;
    And when, out of sunset, the gold
Down the passionless mountains was streaming
    Pacific abundance untold,
The body was borne by the white-men,
    Who all in the sorrowing shared,
To the chosen repose on the hillside,
    Where stood a tall scaffold prepared.

Here gently they loosed the brown death-robes,
    For a pitying, farewell look;
And the maiden seemed peacefully sleeping,
    Like some winter-stilled, wildwood brook.
Soft moccasins, gauntlet-gloves, clothing,
    Beside her were hastily thrown,
That she might not lack on the journey
    That they knew she must travel alone.

And he whom she loved looked on her
    As she lay in the rubicund light;

IIe stood by the side of her mother,
  Whose grief was as deepening night.
A mountain-lily he nurtured,
  And other fair flowers of the West,
He laid, with regret in their fragrance,
  On the dead girl's innocent breast.

They closed the fur coffin, and raised it
  To the scaffold cheerless and high,
With the head to the east, and wrapped it
  In a pall of the ruddiest dye.
Then the red-men took up the wailing
  And the wild, sweet strain as before:
"Our Liberty, slain by the pale-face,
  Shall smile on our prowess no more."

The heads and the tails of the ponies,
  Brought sacredly hither along,
To this grave in the air were fastened,
  Each to one of the four posts strong.
And a crystalline gift of the river
  Was set before either beast's head,
That he might not thirst on the journey
  To the shadowy land of the dead.

THE PATRIOT'S COURAGE.

WHEN our free land's great captain, Washington,
Was colonel in Virginia, ere the war
He led for Independence had begun,
A passing cloud obscured his rising star:
His sometimes frightful passions woke, and they,
Then unbroke coursers, had their fiery way.

For while between opposing factions there
The bloodless battle by the ballot rolled,
Into one's pride whom he had found unfair
He plunged a speech-wrought weapon, keen and cold;
And the hurt voter, with a blow unmeet,
Stretched his insulter senseless at his feet.

Forth hied the dread news, waxing as it went,
Fed by the food it gave to every tongue;
Uprose, wild-eyed, the wrathful regiment,
And idle swords and flintlocks were unhung,
And marshaled to the drum, whose speedy call
Was like the beating of the hearts of all.

When grief has rage soft pity turns to stone.
These loved their leader as they loved their land;
Aslant, like shining rain, their muskets shone,
And harsh the voice of vengeance pealed command:
" All foully slain our colonel lies, struck down!
On, comrades! Give no quarter! Burn the town!"

Meanwhile, the stricken was made whole again,
And, hurried by the townsfolk, rode to meet
The armed, excited torrent of fierce men
Advancing toward the small, elect'ral street;
And gladly holden in their wond'ring sight,
They pressed around him with unfeigned delight.

But vengeance is so inconsiderate,
Shorn of excuse it yet pursues its prey;
And all the soldiers, filled with gathered hate,
Were willed to leave black ruin on their way.
He charged them, lest the love he bore should cease,
To bate their wrath, and turn again in peace.

So they went back; and slowly he returned,
Chastising his quick passions ruthlessly;

For who, that with a foolish rage has burned,
Knows blame as bitter as his own may be?
But when red morn rolled up its splendid wheel,
Joy followed close on Sorrow's fleeing heel.

For then betimes, a lark-blithe letter flew
Out of a heart where kindness brooded warm;
But to the voter's short and narrow view
It was the white-winged augury of storm;
It asked a meeting only, yet he heard
Of challenge and of duel in the word.

For who could know that one would be so bold,
To face and brave the time? — in that it meant
That each his honor on his sword should hold?
The voter straightway to the other went,
And Washington, with courage strong and grand,
Held forth his prudent and heroic hand.

And in his love of truth, sublime and glad,
To him who struck him down he made amends:
"If with the satisfaction you have had
You are content, oh, let us then be friends!
For, looking back on our affray with shame,
I feel that I alone have been to blame."

THE PREACHER'S DOLE.

In Edinburgh, 'mid its busy whirl,
The preacher, Guthrie, walked one afternoon,
And met a sun-browned little beggar-girl
With eyes as tearful as a clouded moon.
She sobbed and wept as if there stood across
Her dark and friendless path a giant loss.

Good Doctor Guthrie, pausing by her side,
Asked her to tell him all her cause for woe.
"My mother gave me sixpence, sir," she sighed,
"And to the baker's yonder bade me go
And buy a loaf of bread for us to eat;
But I have lost the money in the street.

"Oh, she will beat me so when I go back!
What shall I do? I know not what to do!"
And cried as if in torture on the rack.
In pity for the child, the doctor drew
A sixpence forth, and as he gave it said,
"Weep not, my lass, for I will get your bread."

He led her to a place where bread was sold,
And while he bought a loaf made free to say,
"The child was sent for this; but, I am told,
She lost the sixpence for it on the way."
The baker answered, "'T is a trade with her;
For she is always losing sixpence, sir."

No indignation looked from Guthrie's eyes,
No word of haste flashed hot from heart to tongue.
He felt a larger, braver pity rise
That such deceit should dwell in one so young;
And, bending down, said to the child that she
Was now an object of true charity —

Knowing that she a living earned by sin,
He felt more pity for her than before.
He sorrowed at the want the poor were in;
But at all wickedness he sorrowed more.
Weak charity had he if he should dole
Bread for the body and neglect the soul.

Thence to her home of squalor and decay
The awe-struck child and gentle Guthrie went:

It was a nest for wingless birds of prey —
Children that, by an old man taught, were sent
To raven on the town : the little girl
Was found a place safe from the vile, gray churl.

THE STOWAWAY BOY.

As, three days out, the swift ship cleft the sea,
There came on deck a winsome, blue-eyed boy;
Not any means to pay his way had he,
Yet looked up to the broad, free sky with joy.
His face was bright and fair, for what is good
Shines out and fears not to be understood.

But on the boy a doubting eye was cast,
And, to the question of the master's mate,
He said that his step-father, near a mast
Had hidden him, with food, and bade him wait
In the dark place until the ship reached shore,
Where a kind aunt would help him from her store.

The mate was slow to feel the story true,
And thought the sailors fed the fareless youth,
And often questioned him before the crew;
But the boy's lips were steadfast to the truth.
At last the mate avowed the glaring lie
Should be confessed, or else the boy must die.

Thereat he bade a sailor fetch a rope,
And looking at his watch, with anger said,
" Boy, in ten minutes you will be past hope,
And, from the yard-arm, hang till you are dead,
Unless you speak, before the time be spent,
And of the lie make full acknowledgment."

The boy looked up and saw the speaker's face,
And, urged by fear to call the truth a lie,
Resisted fear, and stood in bitter case,
For it was hard for one so young to die;
But, braving death, the tender stowaway
Knelt down and asked the mate if he might pray.

Above its hell of fire the tortured steam
Shrieked, hissed, and groaned in terror and in pain;
Yet worked the ship's great muscles, shaft and beam.
The vessel seemed a sea-gull or a crane,
Beating the denser air that floods the world,
And round and round her watery wings were whirled.

The sky bent over the contented sea,
And, like the upturned face, was pure and clear;
The ship's kind folk assembled anxiously,
The Lord's Prayer from the earnest lips to hear.
The mate, in tears, by trouble sore oppressed,
Caught up the boy and clasped him to his breast!

THE GALLEY-SLAVE.

THERE is no grander, nobler life on earth
Than that of meek and brave self-sacrifice.
Such life our Saviour, in His lowly birth
And holy work, made His sublime disguise —
Teaching this truth, still rarely understood:
'T is sweet to suffer for another's good.

Now, tho' at heart of diverse mold and make,
There lived in France two brothers, like in face;
One did a petty theft, and by mistake
The other was arrested in his place,

And sentenced soon to be a galley-slave —
Yet said no word his prized good name to save.

Trusting remoter days would be more blessed,
He set his will to wear the verdict out,
And knew most men are prisoners at best,
Who some strong habit ever drag about
Like chain and ball; and was content that he
Rather the prisoner he was should be.

But good resolves are of such feeble thread,
They may be broken in temptation's hands.
After long toil, the guiltless prisoner said,
"Why should I thus, and feel life's precious sands
The narrow of my glass, the present, run,
For a poor crime that I have never done?"

Such questions are like cups, and hold reply;
For when the chance swung wide the prisoner fled,
And gained the country road, and hasted by
Brown, furrowed fields and skipping brooklets fed
By shepherd clouds, and felt beneath the trees
The soft hand of the mesmerizing breeze.

Then, all that long day having eaten naught,
He at a cottage stopped, and of the wife
A brimming bowl of fragrant milk besought.
She gave it him; but, as he quaffed the life,
Down her kind face he saw a single tear
Pursue its wet and sorrowful career.

Within the cot he now beheld a man
And maiden also weeping. "Speak," said he,
"And tell me of your grief; for, if I can,
I will disroot the sad, tear-fruited tree."
The cotter answered. "In default of rent,
We shall to-morrow from this roof be sent."

Then said the galley-slave, "Whoso returns
A prisoner escaped may feel the spur
To a right action, and deserves and earns
Proffered reward. I am a prisoner!
Bind these my arms, and drive me on the way,
That your reward the price of home may pay."

Against his wish the cotter gave consent,
And at the prison-gate received his fee;
Tho' it was made a cause for wonderment,
Along the road where labor paused to see,
That one so weak and sickly dared attack
This bold and robust youth, and take him back.

At once the cotter to the mayor hied,
And told him all the story, and that lord
Was much affected, dropping gold beside
The pursed, sufficient silver of reward;
Then sought his better in authority,
And gained the right to set the prisoner free.

THE CITY OF SUCCESS.

WHERE a river hastens down,
Stands an often wished-for town,
In the azure of the mountains,
On a broad, exalted plain.
Peaks of peace above it rise
To the bland, auspicious skies,
Whose inverted horn of plenty
Pours out fruits and flowers of gain.

Round the city runs a wall
Where the watchmen clearly call

The flying hours, that speed away
　　With winged, inconstant feet;
　And, throughout the gilded place,
　The palatial houses face
On cool-fountained park and garden,
　　And on pleasure-seeking street.

With sparse population stands
　This, the pride of all the lands,
In temple-crowned magnificence,
　　The City of Success;
　For, tho' all men strive full well
In its worldly halls to dwell,
Few even reach the roads to it
　　Through bitter strain and stress.

This bold city has great gates,
　And at each a dragon waits,
With huge, unsated, open jaws
　　With sharp misfortune fanged.
　High upon the barbacan
Floats hope's banner, dear to man;
But vainly are the throng without
　　From those proud walls harangued.

Witless men the gates avoid,
　And, in wily fraud employed,
Mine under the cemented might
　　That glitters, seen afar.
　Having basely stolen through,
　They the secret passage rue,
And strive to fill and cover it,
　　And other folk debar.

Such men scoff and are ashamed
　When, around the wide world famed,
Some brave outsider scales the wall,
　　And calmly takes his place,

An exemplar sweet to men,
And most proper citizen,
Who willingly would turn to meet
His clean past, face to face.

They, throughout the toilless year,
Stand arraigned in courts of fear,
Who, using methods sinister,
Have snared the swift-winged gold;
For, if it be lost, they know
That they straightway forth must go,
And never more, but far away,
The day-dream town behold.

Once, from here remote — in truth,
Years ago — a handsome youth,
Who plodded on his father's land
Behind the toilsome plow,
Saw, tho' dimly and afar,
This proud city like a star
Across the mist that islanded
The mountain's peaceful brow.

Well he loved a maiden true,
That of his glad passion knew;
For, as he went one smiling day
Home from the furrowed field,
With her milking-pail she came,
And, with heart and lips aflame,
He met her, told her all his joy,
And to her heart appealed.

With upturned, delighted eyes,
And low, tender-toned replies,
She answered him, and plighted troth
To make her his alone.
Sweet the voices of the birds
Mingled with the happy words,

And to the pair the waiting fields
   Abroad with love were sown.

"I must hasten forth," he said;
"I shall garner more than bread,
Till up a gracious path I reach
   The City of Success;
  Then, my dearest one, with you,
  In that city old and new,
I shall abide, and naught but death
   Shall make our joy the less."

With the dawning of the day
  Fared he forward on his way,
Pursuing it undauntedly
   While year succeeded year,
  Till, among a busy throng,
  He was caught and borne along;
And one high noon he saw the town,
   For which he longed, appear.

When a gainful month had passed,
  He the city reached at last;
But nearer than the environs
   He could not force his way;
  For a selfish, struggling crowd,
  Fighting hard and crying loud,
At the bronze gates seldom lifted,
   As with scorn were held at bay.

From among the press and fret,
  By a dragon close beset,
He, seeking sylvan rest, withdrew,
   One summer afternoon,
  And, reclining in the shade,
  Saw a lovely, jeweled maid
In her pavilion on the wall
   Await the rising moon.

Thus she sang: "O moon of love!
Shine thou down, my heart above,
And light the sea that never yet
    Was cleft by any keel.
Quickly, sailor, launch and float;
Wind and tide will aid thy boat;
And let the young moon pilot thee
    To all it can reveal."

As the yearning music died,
She who warbled it espied
The baffled, youthful comeliness
    Beside a lulling spring.
To him gayly she let fall
Silken steps, outside the wall,
And beckoned him to mount by them
    To what the stars might bring.

To her heart he clambered up,
    And was asked to stay and sup
Beneath the fretted, curving roof
    Of blue inlaid with gold;
For on ebony was spread
Yellow honey, milk, and bread,
And as he ate he saw two streets
    Before his feet unrolled.

He beheld the roofs and domes
Of the envied people's homes,
And, far below, the valley
    With the river sparkling through.
Reaching fondly to the skies,
Where the river had its rise,
Stood the peaks of love, enfolded
    In their gauzy robes of blue.

Said the maiden to the youth,
"I beheld thee, and with ruth,

Among the motley, eager throng
  Who struggle at the gates;
So when thee I saw to-day
Where the woodland waters play,
For sending thee alone to me,
  I thanked the sister fates.

"I desire that thou should'st know
  What of happiness and woe
These solid walls encompass,
  And to what thou dost aspire.
If the city please thee well,
  And thou still herein would'st dwell,
My companion may advise thee,
  If thou of her inquire."

As she spoke, there came a maid,
  In a nun-like garb arrayed,
With passive face, but beautiful;
  Nay, pensive, pure, and kind.
She was dark, and down her back
  Streamed her tresses thick and black,
While amaranth around her gown
  Unfadingly entwined.

To the comely youth she bowed
  As the jeweled maiden proud
Rose and said, "Sir, this is Sorrow,
  Thy attendant in this place.
With her through the city go;
  She to thee will freely show
The elegance and luxury
  That mask its stolid face."

With a smile he bade good-night
  In the moonbeams vague and white,
Which into the pavilion strayed
  Like specters gaunt and thin:

Then with Sorrow he went down
To the streets, and through the town,
And found the house for which they sought
That he might lodge therein.

Heavy carpets spread the floors,
Noiseless were the walnut doors
Set with carven dryad panels,
    Or with stained and flowered glass;
Thick, embroidered curtains swung
From the walls with paintings hung,
And in bronze a dial'd Clio
    Marked the silent moments pass.

In Success few mornings frown;
For the youth, to view the town,
When morning came, with Sorrow went
    Through statued park and street;
And they joined a gilded throng,
As it coldly moved along
Toward the temple built to Fortune,
    Low to worship at her feet.

Up against the blue immense,
In its bright magnificence
Of pillared gold enforested,
    Of architrave and frieze,
All of yellow gold and good,
On a hill the temple stood,
And cast its splendor on the vale
    And out beyond the seas.

That proud hill was covered round,
So that none might see the ground,
With marble steps of hueless white
    That led up to the fane.
Urn of plants and fountain's jet
On each rank of steps were set,

And seemed like new spring breaking forth
　　From winter's snowy reign.

In the temple, high in place
　Stood Dame Fortune, fair of face,
Holding Plutus, god of riches,
　　In her fond and fickle arms.
　Horns of plenty at her feet
　Emptied half their contents sweet,
And winged Cupid stood before her,
　　Fascinated by her charms.

Down the checkered floor of gold
　Went her crafty priests and bold,
Swinging incense through the concourse
　　Of disdainful devotees,
　Some of whom were racked with pains;
　Few could much enjoy their gains;
In plenty doomed to abstinence,
　　They worshiped on their knees.

Some with Sorrow had to sup,
　And she gave to them her cup
From which they drank the bitterness
　　With unavailing tears;
　Some had kissed the lips of Joy,
　And had found how pleasures cloy,
And other some for greed of gold
　　Made hard and cold their years.

From a gallery was heard,
　Like the carol of a bird
That, to the heart of darkness,
　　Tells the music of its dream,
　A surpassing voice, so rare
　That it loosed the bonds of care,
And seemed a strain from heaven
　　Borne along the spirit's stream：

"Asking gifts, to thee we bow,
 Goddess Fortune : great art thou
Of Oceanus the daughter,
 And protectress of the town.
Thoughtful Hellas thee adored,
And divine libations poured,
Whilst Rome to thee eight temples built
 Lest haply thou might'st frown.

"All men woo thee, some with wiles,
 Praying for thy sunny smiles,
Chasing thee in town and village
 And across thy parent sea.
Turn thy mediæval wheel ;
 Youth and age before thee kneel ;
For they who would on roses rest
 Must be beloved by thee."

When the singing ceased, the youth,
 Holding Sorrow's hand of ruth,
Wandered forth of Fortune's presence
 To the shining portico.
Thence his glance around he cast
On the city strong and vast,
That in a stone monotony
 Of buildings lay below.

Like a belt about it all
 Ran the towered and gated wall,
A century of miles or more,
 A score of chariots wide ;
While upon a neighboring hill
Stood a temple higher still
Than this one built to Fortune,
 And a voice from out it cried.

"On the morrow," Sorrow said,
As she down the stairway led,

" To the other, higher temple
  We shall betimes repair.
 Now the placid hour is late ;
  See, my liveried servants wait
With my horses, which are restless ;
  So let us homeward fare."

" Tell me of the jeweled maid
 Who bestowed the silken aid
With which I entered," said the youth,
  " This moneyed, ample town."
 Answered thus his kindly guide :
 " Would'st thou have her for thy bride,
And dwell within this streeted wealth
  Till thy life's sun goes down ?

" She hath great possessions here ;
 Yet her days are sad and drear,
Because wan Death, in dungeons dark,
  Hath shut her dearest kin.
 Of the youth that come to woo,
 None to her seem good and true ;
But thou wok'st her admiration,
  And her love thou soon might'st win."

 All that night, in dreams of gold,
 At his tired feet lay unrolled
Two streets, two open ways, that led
  Along his future far ;
 But he wist not which to take,
 Tho' one led to brier and brake,
While at the other's slender end
  Shone bright a drooping star.

 In the morning Sorrow came,
 And they went to look on Fame
Where in her temple she abode
  Upon her sightly hill.

Many paths secluded wound
Slowly up the rising ground,
And here were highways beaten hard
    By persevering will.

Not all these to Fame upreached,
    Yet in all lay dead leaves bleached,
Tho' still the haze of summer
        Veiled the languid, dreamy air.
    Facing north, south, east, and west,
    On the high hill's level crest,
Stood the temple in the splendor
        Of Apollo's golden hair.

    Of Pentelic marble pure,
    Which forever would endure,
The fane was graven over
        With the sounded names of men.
    From it rose an airy dome
    Like the one that broods on Rome,
But vaster, and with windows set,
        And symbols, sword and pen.

    On the four wide pediments
    Were informed the great events
That change the course of history,
        And for the truth make room.
    On the west, Columbus stood
    In majestic marblehood
Forever on San Salvador,
        No more in chains and gloom.

    On the unforgetful stone,
    Many names were overgrown
With ivy green, and lichen brown,
        Oblivion's slow hands;
    But the priests of Fame benign,
    Tearing off the weeds malign,

Often made some splendid jewel,
  Thus discovered, light the lands.

This great fane, so carven on,
Fairer than the Parthenon,
Was tenfold larger, and, untouched
  By time or war, looked down.
At each entrance high and wide,
Obelisks, on either side,
In tall, Syenic massiveness
  Set forth antique renown.

Gentle Sorrow and her charge,
Entering this temple large,
Looked round the vast basilica,
  And saw the vaulted roof.
It was propped by pillars high,
Of gray gneiss and porphyry,
And in the groins the echoes trooped
  And mumbled, far aloof.

On the niched and statued wall,
On the tiles and pillars all,
They saw the biographic lists
  Of splendid names extant;
And the laurel, which without
In profusion grew about,
Within was plaited into praise
  That Fame was pleased to grant.

With her trumpet to her lips,
With her girdle at her hips,
Robed in Tyrian-dyed softness,
  Stood the goddess fair to see.
Oft her mighty voice she sent,
Through the lifted instrument,
Round the world to every people,
  And to nations yet to be.

Just before immortal Fame
Was an altar with its flame,
And a vestal guardian angel
    Who renewed the sacred fire.
Face and form with splendor shone
As she ministered alone,
Feeding full this flame of genius
    That it never might expire.

One pure crystal, man-high vase
Was the altar, carved with bays,
And, in relief, with goat-leg'd Pan
    That piped upon a reed.
There, too, Theban Hercules
Robbed the fair Hesperides —
Took precious fruit and slew a wrong,
    In one exalted deed.

From the altar's golden bowl
Flared the flame's undying soul,
And lighted up the potent fane
    And Fame's benignant face.
Other light than this was none,
Save the rays that faintly shone
In the lofty dome's void hollow
    In the distant upper space.

Entering through the slanted roof,
Ran a warp without the woof,
The wire, electric nerves of Fame,
    That sensate round the world.
On the shelves of pillared nooks
Stood a mental wealth of books,
And tattered flags of victory
    Above it hung unfurled.

Of the worshipers who came,
That had each achieved a name,

The youth beheld that some, not least,
  Tho' wise and great, were poor.
 "Tell me, Sorrow," murmured he,
 "What injustice this may be?
And why success for poverty
  Should fail to be a cure?"

"These," said she, "are they that long
  From the world have suffered wrong,
The authors and inventors
  Who have little else than fame.
 They might boast their stores of gold,
 Were it not that, dull and cold,
The people rob them statedly,
  And do by law the shame.

"It seems not enough that they,
  Who with me pursue their way
Along the crags of knowledge
  To enrich the world indeed,
 Should be troubled and depressed,
 And upon me lean for rest,
Who am alien to the comfort
  And to the peace they need."

But while Sorrow spoke, the maid,
  Who had lent the silken aid,
Approached the twain, and greeted them
  With pleasure in her grace;
 And they knew that she was fair,
 With her golden crown of hair,
And tender eyes that filled with soul
  Her oval, Grecian face.

As across the lettered floor
  They were passing to the door,
The lovely maiden, gentle voiced,
  Said, turning to her guest,

"On the wall to-morrow night
Will appear a thrilling sight,
For the horsemen with their horses
Are to race there, ten abreast.

"All the city will be there.
If to see the race you care,
Be in readiness and waiting
When the chimes are telling nine."
It would please him well to go.
And, to streets spread out below,
They loitered down a laurel path
Before the fane divine.

Him the maiden bade adieu;
Then, with Sorrow tried and true,
He rode, and came to where arose
A lilied, marble spire.
"Here," said Sorrow, "they bow down,
And shall win a lasting crown,
Who tread my path with humble feet,
And crush each low desire.

"My dark path leads up to joy
That I know not, nor annoy,
For that it lies beyond my bourn,
A lucent pearl, great-priced."
Sorrow wept, and with the youth
Entered this abode of truth,
And heard the holy story
Of the mild and patient Christ.

In the morning cool and sweet,
Up the wide, frequented street,
Alone the youth walked, seeing much
Along the paven miles.
Every house by which he went
Was to him magnificent;

Yet the fountain gargoyles only
    For the passer-by had smiles.

Here, he soon could plainly see,
    Dwelt no rare immunity
From any evil that the world
    Outside the walls endured.
    Here were sickness, pain, and death,
    Shame and crime with poison breath,
And even breadless poverty
    A dwelling here secured.

Men who never come this way
    Have as much of joy as they
Who here abide in opulence,
    Their idlest wants supplied;
    For success lies in degrees,
    And to rise to one of these,
And see the others higher still,
    Is like a thorn to pride.

Up and down throughout Success
    Sought the youth for happiness,
And saw it was an empty dream
    In foolish fashion's halls.
    Everywhere it was alloyed;
    Nothing fully was enjoyed;
For Discontent went round, or sat
    Repining on the walls.

When the rising moon shone white,
    And the city was alight,
The lady came, and took the youth
    To see the eager race.
    Up the wall ran highways wide;
    On them streamed a living tide
Skyward to the race-course straight,
    And poured about the place.

All that seven-mile course along,
On each buttress tall and strong,
That propped the wall on either side,
And past its top arose,
Stood the slanted seats, where pressed
Countless people richly dressed,
Who took their places to behold
The swift event unclose.

On the dizzy battlements
Brazen cressets burned intense,
And flushed the massive, mighty wall
With scarlet flowers of fire,
Lighting up with lurid glare
The expectant thousands there,
And beaming down the valley
With the fervor of desire.

At the goal were cressets two
Flinging up flame-arms of blue,
And, just beyond, abruptly stood
An angle of the wall.
The unmoving foot of this
Rested on a precipice,
And the pebbles men flung down it
Seemed to never cease to fall.

In the shining, jeweled sword,
Belted, with a twinkling cord,
To the thigh of bright Orion
Where he stands august in space,
Is a gulf of darkness great,
Where no sun's rays penetrate —
An awful gulf of nothingness,
A black and worldless place.

So appeared the dread abyss
Down the wall and precipice

To those who, in the night, with fear,
   Looked from the balustrade.
Even the cressets' angry bloom
Parted not the heavy gloom,
That lay appallingly beneath
   In one dense hush of shade.

Near the goal, the lady fair
And the youth she made her care
Were waiting, on the cushioned seats,
   And Sorrow sat between.
Sorrow met them on the way;
She with them had craved to stay,
And now of either clasped a hand,
   And looked along the scene.

At the place of starting stood,
Strong, and brave to hardihood,
The horsemen in their chariots,
   Their horses fiery-eyed —
Coal-black coursers curbed with pain,
Plunging, fretting at the rein,
Long of limb and shaggy mane,
   And to the winds allied.

Now they start! — a score of teams
Harnessed to revolving gleams,
And speed along the softened course
   Upon the city's wall.
Driving hard with steady hands,
One large-browed calm raceman stands,
And tho' at first he fell behind,
   Ere long he distanced all.

It was pleasure worth the view,
When the horses almost flew,
To note the rhythmic movement
   With which some strained ahead.

These were urged by men of will,
And a beauty high and still
Was in the drivers' faces
　　While they ruled the strength they sped.

As of these each horseman fleets
By the living, breathless seats,
The praise of hands and mouths and flowers
　　With bounty is bestowed.
Yet anew it makes him feel
He must prove more true than steel
To win the goal through strong restraint
　　Along the flying road.

Some gave out beside the way;
Those who in the race must stay,
With haggard looks and hideous,
　　Held slack the useless rein.
They, in pressing toward the goal,
Of their beasts had lost control,
And the dark, relentless passions
　　On to ruin dashed amain.

Only one man firm and true
Paused beyond the lights of blue;
For the rest, who were behind him,
　　Rushing by with panting breath,
From the sheer and sullen wall
Leaped, and beasts and drivers, all,
At the balustraded angle,
　　Uttered headlong down to death.

Then on every seated bank
Grew the weed, confusion, rank,
And on the wall the people streamed
　　With shouts and mournful cries.
In the pressure and dismay,
Sorrow's hand-clasp slipped away,

And the youth could nowhere find it,
  Nor the fair with tender eyes.

Back from wall and buttress wide,
  Down the highways ebbed the tide —
A saddened, shuddering, troubled thing
  Whose rose was ever thorned.
  At the goal, the youth, alone,
  Saw that all the rest were gone,
And saw, in sapphire loneliness,
  The crescent silver-horned.

Far below him, in the vale,
  Honor's river, winged with sail,
Flowed along the hazy quiet,
  Deep and strong, and sparkling bright.
  Far away the rim loomed up
  Of the massive valley-cup
That held the drowsy hydromel
  Of cool, forgetful night.

He beheld, near where he stood,
  Bathed in ruby cresset-blood,
Or the flame's glare falling on her,
  A woman quite alone.
  As she turned and beckoned him,
  Through the shadows dark and dim
He thought he there descried the face
  Of her who was his own.

But when he had reached her side,
  And her features dignified
Looked down with cold severity,
  He saw it was not she.
  With harsh voice the woman said,
  "I am Duty, and have led
Her heart to whom you plighted troth.
  Oh, turn and follow me !

" They who truly find success
Come to it through faithfulness,
And not by silken ladders let
By tender women down.
Happiness is found, good youth,
In sweet love and honest truth,
And naught suffices for their loss
In all this pleasant town."

Down a highway to the street
These two went on willing feet,
And at a gate a sentinel,
Who knew stern Duty well,
At her word advanced them through;
For the youth, to Duty true,
Followed her in weary darkness
Till they rested in a dell.

Soon the east with morning glowed;
By the road the river flowed,
And they were on their way to her
Whose love the youth had won.
From a vessel dropping down,
Laden near the distant town,
They heard the boatmen's parting song,
And watched the rising sun.

" We depart, and little care,
Gilded city high in air,
That allures the simple-hearted
From his peaceful home away;
For where honor's river flows,
And the breeze of duty blows,
We guide the prow across the night
To harbors of the day.

" We the way to joy have found;
But while sailing, seaward bound,

> We quaff the sparkle and delight
>   Of crystal depths below.
> In thee, city, shadows dwell;
>   To thy walls, farewell, farewell;
> We seek the eternal ocean
>   Where the tides of gladness flow."

A SUIT OF ARMOR.

A SUIT of ancient armor in a hall
Stands like an unopposing sentinel;
I see its past behind it, and recall
The chivalry that vexed the infidel,
That waged fierce wars and wrought of woe increase
In His mild name who is the Prince of Peace.

This unworn armor has a silent speech;
To more than steel the steel is riveted,
And, empty and forlorn, appears to teach
The patient hope that oft is felt and said,
That soon all armor to disuse shall pass,
With visored helmet, hauberk, and cuirass.

There were true knights when mail like this was worn
In the long struggle for Jerusalem.
If o'er the crescent the red cross was borne,
They died content. But fame yet lived for them,
And troubadours their brave deeds rhymed upon
From stubborn Antioch to Ascalon.

Noblest the knights while they were few and poor;
They vowed to tell the truth, to help the weak,
To flee no foe, and hold each trust secure.
They let their simple dress their lives bespeak.
Firm in misfortunes, they had strength to be
Humble and generous in victory.

But when they rose to luxury and power,
When wealth and honor, bright-eyed falcons, stood
On their triumphant armor — in that hour
Went forth from chivalry the soul, the good —
And knighthood meant a price, and turned away
From rugged duty into weak display.

For while slow progress up its path has toiled,
Who has been faithful that has touched its gains?
As the clean truth, if handled, soon is soiled,
So, good is seldom pure that long obtains;
And the great cause, which sought to help and bless,
Dies at the golden summit of success.

The spirit fled, the body is but dust;
It lingers in corruption and decay;
It may not look on favor nor mistrust,
Tho' many praise it loud who said it nay.
They are too blind to see, too dull to feel,
'T is empty as this man-shaped shell of steel.

A GUARDIAN ANGEL.

WITH wings of love as stainless and as white
As snow untracked or clouds against the blue,
Clothed with God's peace, and radiant with light
That over him his aureola threw,
An angel dwelt in heaven, and all bliss,
Unending and unspeakable, was his.

Out of God's will, to this dear angel's heart
Came in grand music what in words is said:
"To yon far sparkle of the earth depart —
That bridge the short-lived generations tread —
And I will give it thee to guard and tend
A soul untried, and be his guide and friend.

"Or guide, or friend, truth-whisperer, or guard,
Be each, and all in one, to keep him true;
Yet, if he long neglect thee, and make hard
And wearisome this duty thine to do,
Thou need'st not wait to strive against his sin,
But, at the gates uplifted, enter in."

Swift are the rays, the arrows of the morn,
That pierce the dark and shoot across the sky —
Swifter the angel who, through ether lorn,
Pierced on displaying wings, until on high
God's joy-paved city dwindled to a star,
And the small earth, a pale moon, shone afar.

Hither, in silent flight, he took his way,
And found at noon, beside a shady stream,
A youth asleep, and hovered where he lay,
Appearing to the sleeper in a dream;
And was a vision of sublime delight,
With gleaming wings and robe of snowy white.

With what regretful tears in Heaven's book,
The record of our lives is oft set down!
Filled with high hope the handsome youth forsook
His native village for the crowded town,
And met the varied shapes of vice and sin
That, clothed with soft enticement, walk therein.

He battled long their vain, misleading charms,
Helped by the angel in his troubled breast:
Arose no peal of strife, no noise of arms,
But fierce and giant warfare, wild unrest,
Raged in the soul; and Virtue's citadel,
Stormed by the lower passions, crashing, fell.

When these have sway, how dark the soul and drear!
His gentle friends, who saw with inner eyes,

Beheld the man debased, yet, ever near,
An angel following with ruthful cries,
Beseeching him his erring steps to cease,
To turn and rest upon the heart of Peace.

With holy angels there is joy in pain —
Their pain is borne for love, and love is joy.
This angel would not now return again
To heavenly doors; but he would have employ
To lead a soul to pleasant fields beyond,
From the deep slough of error and despond.

His still, small voice fell fainter — less and less —
Pleading and sad as following he went;
And the long years were one with weariness,
Till to the man life's shadow, death, was sent.
But heeding his good angel, ere he died
He worshiped Him whom he had crucified.

Bearing in arms of love the soul set free,
The angel, with God's glory on his face,
Mounted on wings outspread exultingly,
Trailing his lily robe; and as through space
Angel and soul approached the central star,
Before them heaven shone with joy afar.

Oh, happy are the meetings that await
The crossers to that star of higher powers!
The soul found that the angel was a mate
That he had loved and lost in boyhood hours.
Ah! who can tell? Belike to all God sends,
As guardian angels, their departed friends.

AUTUMN BALLAD.

How mild and fair the day, dear love! and in these
    garden ways
The lingering dahlias to the sun their hopeless faces
    raise.
The buckwheat and the barley, once so bonny and so
    blithe,
Fall before the rhythmic labor of the cradler's gleam-
    ing scythe.

Behold the grapes and all the fruits that Autumn
    gives to-day,
As robed in red and gold, she rules, the Empress of
    Decay!
Out to the orchard come with me, among the apple-
    trees;
No dragon guards the laden boughs of our Hesperides.

This golden pear, my darling, that I hold up to your
    mouth,
Is a hanging-nest of sweetness; but the birds are wing-
    ing south.
The purses of the chestnuts, by the chilly-fingered
    Frost,
Were opened in his frolic, and their triple hoards are
    lost.

Last night you heard the tempest, love — the wind-en-
    tangled pines,
The spraying waves, the sobbing sky that lowered in
    gloomy lines;
The storm was like a hopeless soul, that stood beside
    the sea,
And wept in dismal rain and moaned for what could
    never be.

THE RINGER'S VENGEANCE.

In Florence dwelt a tall and handsome youth,
Courted and praised by fashion's fickle throng,
Plighted to one he loved in simple truth —
A lady proud, whose black hair, fine and long,
Some said, was like a flag, that waved or fell
Above her heart's deceitful citadel.

The youth's days now were bright, as days may be
To all who love as lovers always should;
But one fell night a cry of dread ran free,
And one belov'd in deadly peril stood.
About her house the hot flames roared and broke
In waves of fire that dashed a spray of smoke.

Prone on the seat within her oriel
The lady sank; then he, her lover, came
And lowered her to the street; but it befell
That, as he turned back from the leaping flame,
The burning roof crashed in, and to the floor
A heavy, falling beam his body bore.

They brought him forth, all bleeding, burned, and
      crushed,
And long he lay, and neither stirred nor spoke;
Not yet by wayward death his heart was hushed,
But seemed a blacksmith pounding stroke by stroke,
And mutely toiling on from sun to sun,
Until his fateful labor should be done.

For love and youth with smiling life are fraught;
They cling to life wherein to move and dwell.
The youth came back, at last, to life and thought,
And longed to see her whom he loved so well.

"She will be true and kind to me," he said,
" And glad shall be the days when we are wed.

" Dear love ! she will behold me with her heart,
And pity me, because my lot is hard ;
She will not look on this mere outer part
That for her sake is crippled and is scarred."
False hope, poor heart ! — for, when the lady came,
She turned away with loathing, to her shame.

As one in swamps sees fireflies flare in gloom,
And fancies them the street-lights of a town
Whose spires and domes in lofty shadows loom,
Yet finds at dawn but lowland, so came down
The fond hopes of the sufferer, who found
Beneath his feet a waste and useless ground.

Yet Sorrow brings no dagger in her hand
To slay the heart with whom she comes to dwell ;
The youth lived on, and he was wont to stand
Before a church, and listen to the bell
That in a great spire, bright with golden gloss,
Laughed from its yellow throat beneath the cross.

Then loss of wealth with other damage fell,
And for a beggar's pittance he became
The ringer of the wide-mouthed, thick-lipped bell,
Whose noisy somersets he made proclaim
Vesper or mass or lovers to be wed,
Or pulled it with large pity for the dead.

And now they bade him ring a joyful peal ;
For she who once had clothed his heart with pain
Before the altar 'neath the bell would kneel,
And wed another ; then, for good or bane,
There came two spirits out of east and west,
And battled fiercely in the ringer's breast.

Hate's dark-winged spirit like a shadow came,
And carried for a shield the ringer's wrong;
The spirit's eyes burned with a quenchless flame;
His sword, revenge, was merciless and strong,
And now resembled justice, as it fell
With such swift strokes as he could best compel.

The spirit of Forgiveness was like day,
Was crowned with love divine, and for a shield
Had peace and innocence; while in the fray
The wounds he took were patiently concealed.
He strove to break his dark opponent's sword,
And save the ringer from a deed abhorred.

All the long night before the wedding-morn
The ringer in the belfry worked, dark-browed,
And, as he looked forth when the day was born,
The better spirit in his heart was cowed.
The nails were drawn, the beams made weak at last,
That once had held the great bell firm and fast.

He saw the glowing landscape, and to him
It was a cup, and there the red sun stood,
A drop of splendid wine upon the rim,
And clouds arose in somber cloak and hood,
And, with their stained lips at the far, blue brink,
Seemed evil genii that had come to drink.

Arrived in time, with followers in file,
The happy bridegroom and his smiling bride
Advanced to organ-music up the aisle,
And knelt down at the altar, side by side.
The bride looked up beneath her veil of lace,
And saw with fear the ringer's livid face.

Then sprang he to the rope to ring her knell,
With all the rage of his inclement soul;

The huge, inverted lily of the bell
Shook in the gust, and, with a last loud toll,
Fell from its place, resounding far and wide,
And gave to Death the ringer and the bride.

Alas! for her; it was her sin to feign
True love that she nor felt nor understood.
Alas! for him, that he avenged his pain;
He might have joined the noblest brotherhood;
For, wrongs that are forgiven in our sin,
Are doors where loving angels enter in.

IRAK.

My sire was Tobba-Himyar, Yemen's King,
And Arem was the center of his power.
Eastward the wide, red desert paid him tax;
For, of the Bedouin, a score of tribes
Brought lavish tribute for their vassalage.
He gave his realm such wealth of happy days
That it was called The Happy, every where.
Most generous, but for blind justice stern,
His life was such as aye befits a king.
He let no shadow swerve his steadfast will,
But stayed his mind on plain realities.

His was the actual, mine the ideal life;
For Hagi, the magician, led me on
Till oft to deaf abstraction I was rapt
By waking dreams of boundless universe,
And spirit creatures haunting every gloom.
Gray Hagi, in the midnight, when the stars
Burned with their silver splendor, in the calm
Gathered about him beings of the sky —
Alitta, Hebal with his seven shafts,

9

The seven planets' seven kindly gods,
The servants of the black and sacred stone —
And whispered with them, cheek by jowl, and reached
Far glimpses of the future's caravan
Approaching our small earth ; occurrences
Whose coming, furtive footfalls make no sound.

In those dim days the world was like a dream,
And life seemed vaster than the sandy waste
Lost in the azure solitude of sky.
When, by meek Hagi guided, I arrived
At a smooth upland of recondite thought,
He gave me this : a rhymed, time-stained divan,
By one who, writing, knew to choose the best
From infinite suggestions of the mind.
The verse was like thick, raw-silk cloth, shot through
With rare, imaginative gold, and wrought
With grotesque fancies sweetly numerous —
Weird incantations strange as death, strong spells
That swayed the genii and the monstrous forms
That scarcely leave deep darkness ; this, in might,
Roused dread revenges dealing strife and blood ;
And this, from out his mire, a dragon called,
The blear-eyed, warted offspring of disgust.
But on the margin of the final leaf
Was penned the spell of Serosch, which, when said,
Baffles the dragon and the frightful deevs.

Now, bordering these days, the King fell sick.
A black-winged spirit took him in its arms
And bore him nightward while the people wept.
I should not hear his rich-toned voice again.
An awful and impenetrable change
Mantled his features, and he passed away
Into the endless silence ; but his smile
Lighted, a space, the valley-land of death.
Then I in my great grief bowed down distraught :

I heard the wailing of the streeted woe
That once was Arem, city of delight;
I heard the harps, by sympathy caressed,
Moan musical regret down palace halls;
I heard the softened footfalls come and go;
I heeded naught: I knew that he was dead,
And clad my soul in sack-cloth, with one wish,
To dwell with sorrow till I too found rest.

Then, as the long procession of the hours,
Star-jeweled, or appareled by the sun,
Passed, with the banner of a waning moon,
Into the month that followed Himyar's death,
Rose the vast populace and crowned me King —
Me, a mere youth, an abject slave to tears.
It pleased them well to woo me from my grief:
Before the curtain of dim dusk had dropped,
They flamed the lights in red carnelian globes,
Lest gloom might foster gloom; beside my couch,
They burned frankincense in an agate vase;
And black-eyed girls, their bodies swaying lithe,
And wrists and ankles tinkling pearls and gold,
Danced to the rapture of the lute and flute,
Their long hair rhythmically undulant.
The music rose and broke like javelins
At sorrow and at silence deftly hurled
By unseen outposts of approaching joys.
For when the tenth diverted day had passed,
Lulled into slumber by the wedded tones,
I drifted duskward in a boat of palm
That, helm to prow, with mother-of-pearl was lined,
And glided down a valley's silver stream,
And paused among close-petaled fragrances
That with intoxicating gladness breathed,
Telling the love that thrilled from root to flower.
These rocked in music of the fluting breeze,
And all was music, and the dream a song.

From out this mingled melody and sleep
A memory, like the maiden from the fount,
Rose fair, and glimmered through a mist of tears,
But shaped the die that, after, molded act;
For I bethought me of my idle past,
In which, in Riad, northward situate,
I heard the tones that floated down my dream.
Then, leaving Hagi to the cares of state,
And choosing escort sworn to secrecy
That the rash step should not be jarred abroad,
We took the desert beasts, and were away.
But, as we crossed the heated Dahna waste,
Arose the slow simoom, and, by good chance,
I parted from my band, and stood alone,
And watched the crouching lion of the storm
That, maned with darkness, loomed against the sky,
And roared his arid hunger to the world.
Before the violet poison of his breath
An ostrich fled on wing-assisted feet.
My horse, my brave, sure-footed Nedjedee,
Had knelt, and lay with nostrils close to earth,
And, as the storm came near, I cast me prone
Beside him, and drew breath with lips in dust,
Till the blown whirl of sandy peril wild
Passed over me, and, moaning, went its way.
It so befell that I, of all my band,
Alone survived that lion's fatal rage.
Night after night I vaguely northward went
Without a guide except the friendly stars.
I longed for even a crust, and flag'd with thirst;
Yet, ere my strength had wholly ebbed away,
At morn I saw with doubt a distant grove;
But urged my worn horse toward it, till the doubt,
A bird of darkness, fled the light of truth.
Here, on a small oasis, near the spring,
A sheik had pitched his tent of camels' hair,
And stood before the door hospitable.

With millet-cakes, and dates with butter pressed,
And pleasant words — for he had known my sire —
He gave me entertainment three brief days;
But on the fourth, when from her slumber rose
Dawn in her gauzy raiment decked with pearls,
He set out with me, that I might not err.

He on his camel, I on my Nedjedee
For seven days, the burning miles traversed.
Then, as mild twilight, with bejeweled hands,
Came braiding her long tresses, like a star
Seen from the gloomy cave of our fatigue,
Rose Riad, crowned with turrets glimmering.
The sheik embraced me now, and said farewell;
But frowned as he my diamond gift pushed back.
The city's gates stood open: in their might,
They knew no fear; and itching-handed trade
Was trustful of the long-continued peace.
I led my horse among an idle throng
That listened to a grizzled, nomad bard
Who jingled rhymes, like silver in a purse,
In praise of princess Zayda: kind was she,
He sang; but even as beautiful as kind.
Her eyes were stars reflected in the sea,
Her breath was lovely perfume of the rose,
Her step was lighter than the coy gazelle's;
And she, that morning riding near the gate,
Gave him an opal with its heart of flame
For a smooth lyric of a kindred core.

As my forthgoing to that outland town
Was of a vagrant fancy born of sleep,
I cast aside my baubles, and put on
A plainer guise, and went about the streets.
I mingled with the common of the mart,
And heard them speak of Tobba-Himyar's death,
And of his son, a weakling crushed by grief,

Who lacked his father's force, and only knew
To rule a kingdom in the world of dreams.
For pastime with a zest of novelty,
I chaffered with the venders in bazaars;
And, buying once a turban from a Jew,
Threw down some paltry silver to a shape
That cringed before me with a hateful leer,
And begged, he said, because the king was rich;
But seeing how his pleading had borne fruit,
Exclaimed, with pleasure in his greedy eyes,
" May kiss of Zayda be thy round reward ! "

These humble days wore on ; and straying forth,
At noon, along a viny slope that trailed
Its green skirt, blossom broidered, in a stream
Whose full, suburban course curved languidly,
I on the lush bank sat, and watched below
The sword-like flash of silver scales, that shone
Where the hot sunlight, through the leafy roof,
Clasped a gold bracelet on the watery arm.
The hazy air lay on the grassy hills
Like gossamer, and thinner than the shawls
That merchants draw through ladies' finger-rings.
A listless camel cropped the verdure near.
I heard the sultry drone of pollened swarms,
And, dimly conscious that a subtle thing
Had coiled before me, saw the distance change
And rise, like incense, to the fading sun.
Then Riad, gorged by sudden ruin, sank,
Dissolved in mist, and the flat world was void.
But soon my dizzy fancy whirled with dreams;
On amber isles, in sunset's ocean, rose
Arem and Mecca armed with soaring towers,
Far-glittering Balbec whose huge masonry
Was by the unseen genii lightly reared,
And that strange City of Pillars, Shedad built,
Which, long untenanted, remains entire,

And stands mysterious, invisible
To all save heaven-favored travelers;
For men may walk its streets and know it not.
Beneath the cities yawned a murky gulf
That swallowed them, at last, and all was dark.
The night pervaded space, and had no bounds.
The stars were blotted, and the blinded earth,
By her own elements consumed, was blown
Through the dull gloom in dust impalpable.

But I with spectral glide explored those fields
Until I came to where abrupt they swept
Downward, like some great wave of deepest sea,
Into a valley cold and dolorous.
Below me, midway on the slope, there rose
A somber portal strewn with ashy bones.
I heard the hingy thunder of the gate;
And grimly issued thence the dragon, Death,
Fiercer than frothing madness, and so vast
No antique hippogriff had braved his wrath.
His eyes were sunken, and his putrid jaws,
Distending wide, red drippled of his feast.
His wings were cloud-like, and his breath a storm,
And, all puissant in his bony mail,
He came at me, a king, this monster, Death.
But I recalled the spell of Serosch, penned
On the stained margin of the old divan;
For there that angel wrote it when he paused
Once in his thought-swift, seven-fold, nightly flight
Around the sleeping earth, to guard good men.
I said his magic words as with drawn blade
To meet the dread destroyer I went down.
Escaping Death's cold jaws, beneath his wing
That, webbed with terrors, over me displayed,
I thrust at his fell heart, and saw its blood
Burst from the wound in black forgetfulness.
I felt that I had done a mighty deed,

Because with strenuous arm and eager front
I gave to his own sleep the dragon, Death.
But now rolled back the pallid sea of mist,
The curling incense swung from censer stars,
Scooped by sirocco from the under sky.
Slowly from this came out the distant view
And Riad with its cliff-like walls and towers.

Before me, severed in the glossy midst,
A baffled serpent writhed with wrathful hiss;
And bending over stood a form so rare
I fancied that the charm was still complete,
That still my brain was pictured with a dream.
The maiden bade her slave take back his sword,
And shed on me heart-sunlight with her smiles.
She led along a path to her kiosk,
And sat beside a fount, and bade me speak.
I thanked her for my life, which she had saved,
Not worth the viperine, unselfish risk.
I said I was a desert wanderer
Veered by the winds of chance, but nobly born.
Her voice was like the carol of a bird:
" The sweetest waters of Arabia
Rise in the desert: so the proverb runs,"
She said, and blushed as if the fairied air
Into a crimson rose were changing her.
The fountain plashed its crystals, each on each,
That in the pool-vase fell in showers of light.
The polished floor of tessellated stone
Lay like a ripe pomegranate cleft in twain;
A stairway with a heavy balustrade,
Wound upward to a gilded gallery
On which, at either side a curtained arch,
A statue stood as warder: one upheld
A meaning finger to the sky, and one
Maintained the gathered drapery at its breast,
And clutched a scroll, and bent the head in thought.

On golden wheels the joyful days rolled by,
And, keeping in disguise my rank and power,
I wooed and won the princess Zayda's love.
Then to the haughty King went some vile spy,
And in my ears were echoed bloody words
That craved to slay me lest I grow more bold.
At night a messenger toward Arem sped
Bearing these news to Hagi: " Swiftly send
Ten thousand horsemen, veterans of the war,
To enter Riad at its many gates,
And wait about the palace for my call,
On the first midnight of the next new moon."
But lest a secret dagger might divert
The armed arrival to revengeful use,
I said to her who loved me, that a vow
Pressed on me much to be at once performed —
That I would ride to Mecca, and go round
Seven times the Caaba's heaven-descended stone,
And then come back, to reach her ere again
The slender crescent sailed the western sky.
So I a caravan for Mecca joined,
And, on the sacred journey's living wave,
The dromedary, rocked, reached pilgrim-wise
The worshiped stone, and paid, indeed, my vow.

When on the far-off verge the faint new moon
Lifted its prow of pearl, upon the hill,
That passively looks down on Riad's towers,
I too looked down, and watched the many lights
Gleam, and the groups of buildings, shadow-like,
Join vaster shadows of dream-haunted night.
I entered at a gate that, like the rest,
Stood open wide, and reached with weary beast
The many-peopled inn. Thence, when refreshed,
I went to Zayda, who awaited me
In palace depths, and seeing me approach,
Rose from the languid cushions, crowned with joy
As with a chaplet woven of fresh flowers.

That night, to his chief officers, the King
Gave a rich banquet in his lofty hall.
The drinking-cups of gold with rubies set
Poured down the vinous riot to the blood.
The distant laughter of the revel came
To our young ears, as now to me is borne,
Down the dim length of memory's palace-halls,
The recollection of that happy time.
And Zayda's tender accents, soft and low,
Were the remembered music that I heard
When in my grief I sailed a tide of dreams.
I said that our true love was like a ship
Lashed by wild winds and cold, remorseless waves;
Yet I, the pilot guiding through the storm,
Saw Safety, in her harbor, beckoning.
Even as I spoke, the arras near me swung,
Perchance in the light breeze that floated by,
And on my ear these words fell soft as dew:
"We come: our swords are sheathed; our banners
         furled."
Then entered slaves, their gleaming sabers drawn,
And led me to the presence of the King
Who sat, above his guests, upon the throne.
He said that I must die; he so decreed;
For, by the mad presumption of my love,
I cast base insult at his royal power.
Brave Zayda on her knees implored for me,
And vined her arms about my neck, and wept.
Then waved the King his slaves to take me thence.
I brushed them off, and, high above the hush,
Voiced the alarm; and into that bright room
Rushed my fierce warriors, as I cast aside
The loose disguise that hid my royal robes,
And stood before them, while they knelt around,
Irak, the son of Himyar, and their King!

In the same hall, I made the princess mine,
And crowned her Queen of Yemen and my bride.

With flags and roses they festooned the walls,
And mirth and music reveled in the streets,
And myriad welcomes, jubilant and sweet,
Rose in the sunny air, or fell with flowers.

And since, the brittle goblets of my years,
Filled to the brim with golden honey-mead,
And handed me by the great cup-bearer, Fate,
Have all been deeply quaffed; but from these hands
Fallen away, lie shattered at my feet —
The mute mementos of a life of joy.

    1863.

FOREKNOWLEDGE.

At Pentland Frith, beside the sea-coast white,
Stood an old inn to which the young Laird came.
Rain and wild wind fulfilled the sightless night:
But good cheer laughed before the hearth-stone flame.
Well entertained, the pleased and drowsy guest,
Ere it was late, retired to dreamful rest.

His father's death had left him an estate
On Mainland of the Orkneys set in sea;
And in the Hall, now part in ruins, Fate
Had roofed and reared his titled ancestry.
To visit it the Laird was on his way,
And would embark betimes the coming day.

He felt the old inn tremble in the roar;
But soon to him all sounds became remote,
And he was walking on the island's shore;
For he had crossed the Frith without a boat,
And saw the Hall's great windows all alight
In the weird depth of that forbidding night.

He treads his hall of banqueting, rebuilt
By sleepless fancy from moss-grown decay.
It flames with wax-lights whose thin lances tilt
And splinter on the gloss of rich array.
A tapestry garden, gay with woven bloom,
Is hung around the tiled and corbeled room.

In crystal and on gold a feast is spread,
And they thereat are guests of high degree;
While he, the Laird, is seated at the head,
And wonders who the gentlefolk may be.
But as his glance from face to face is cast,
Up, at the spectral sight, he starts aghast!

He sees his ancestors! And he recalls
That often, in his boyhood, he has viewed,
Against the gallery's wainscoted walls,
Their vivid portraits from the frames protrude.
His ancestors, in order as they died,
Are ranged along the board at either side.

First of the line, and opposite the Laird,
Fierce in the tawny skins of beasts of prey,
A chieftain sits, blue-eyed and yellow-haired,
To whom the brave drank wassail in his day.
In storm of battle fell this Norse oak tree,
The sturdy founder of the family.

The late laird sits beside the living host;
His light of life went out the year before.
And next there is a fonder, dearer ghost,
Come back through sleep to be with him she bore;
Her smile, that in his heart's core has a place,
Still glorifies her mild and saintly face.

The dead, when they return to us in sleep,
Are seldom frightful and of horrid mien.

Their changeless forms the bygone likeness keep,
And give no token of the dim unseen.
Their presence seems not strange; they speak their will;
We answer them, and are familiar still.

But here the young Laird shudders to behold
His unexpected guests, and knows that they
From tombs of sculptured quiet stained and old,
Through wind and rain have found their lonely way.
They chill the lighted air; they draw no breath,
And cast no shadow in that room of death.

How long the host sits spellbound, none may know.
His stately guests, in low and hollow tones,
Murmur together of impending woe;
For each the ill, forerunning news bemoans.
Their feasting done, the wan assembly all
Rise, mingle and move round the feudal hall.

In time, the Norseman, clad in savage guise,
Glides to the door that, untouched, opens wide.
He, at the threshold, turns, and lets his eyes,
Which pierce like spears, on the young Laird abide;
Then, with a warning gesture, cries " Beware ! "
And like a vapor fades in outer air.

Thus from the hall the vague ghosts, one by one,
Slowly, in turn, depart : each at the door
Pauses, and facing, as the first had done,
The rapt beholder and the light once more,
With look and hand that warn from direful doom,
Exclaims " Beware ! " and vanishes in gloom.

So the dream ends; and when dawn, cold and gray,
Like a pale ghost, passed through its halls again,
The Laird awoke, and would not sail that day
For the dream's sake : and it was well; for then

The storm-tossed boat that to the Islands crossed
Went down at sea and all on board were lost.

SCIENCE AND THE SOUL.

I sought, in sleep, to find the mountain-lands
Where Science, in her hall of wonder, dwells.
When I had come to where the building stands,
I found refreshing streams, delightful dells,
Invigorating air, and saw, on high,
Turret and dome against the boundless sky.

Out of her busy palace then she stepped,
And kindly greeted me, as there I stood
Doubting my right, and whether I had slept.
" Welcome," she said, " and whatsoe'er of good
You find in me, you have full leave to take
For warp and woof of verses that you make."

That these, her words, for more than me were meant,
I felt, and thanked her as seemed fitting then ;
While, in her looks, I saw that she was sent
To lighten work and knit together men ;
And that with patience such as hers could be,
The coral mason builds the isles at sea.

Servant of Use, upon that mountain wise
Was the plain title she was proud to own,
And, clearer than her penetrating eyes,
The light of Progress on her forehead shone.
Her smile the lips' sharp coldness half betrayed,
As if a wreath upon a sword were laid.

But now, about her palace everywhere,
She led my steps, and often by her side

A lion and a nimble greyhound were.
The swifter to a leash of wire she tied,
And made a messenger of good and ill;
The stronger with white breath performed her will.

She traced the lapse of awful seas of time
On fossil limestone and on glinting ore;
Described wild wonders of the Arctic clime,
And of all lands her willing slaves explore;
Opening laboratories to my view,
She showed me much that she could skill to do.

Then, down a marble stairway, to her bower
Was led the gracious way. "And here," said she,
" I meditate beyond the midnight hour;
Invent for peace and war, for land and sea;
Read the round sky's star-lettered page, or grope
In the abysses of the microscope."

But, while she spoke, there stood another near —
The fairest one that ever I beheld;
I fancied her the creature of some sphere
Whence all of mist and shadow are dispelled.
Her voice was low and gentle, and her grace
Vied with the beauty of her thoughtful face.

A clear, unwaning light around her shone —
A ray of splendor from a loving Source —
A light like sunshine, that, when it is gone,
Leaves darkness, but sheds glory on its course;
Yet, in my dream, her footstep made me start,
It was so like the beating of my heart.

I turned to Science, for small doubt had I
That she best knew her whom I deemed so fair,
And asked, " Who is she, that so heedfully
Waits on you here, and is like sunny air?

In her all beauty dwells, while from her shine
Truth, hope, and love, with effluence divine."

Then Science answered me, severe and cold:
" She is Time's brittle toy: the praise of men
Has dazed her wit, and made her vain and bold.
With subtle flattery of tongue and pen,
They title her the Soul: I count it blame,
And call her Life, but seek a better name.

" Alone, in her gray-celled abode, she dwells,
Of fateful circumstance the fettered thrall,
The psychic sum of forces of her cells,
Molecular and manifold in all;
But æons passed ere Nature could express
This carbon-rooted flower of consciousness.

" Life, from the common mother, everywhere
Springs into being under sun and dew;
And it may be that she who is so fair
From deep-sea ooze to this perfection grew,
Evolving slowly on, from type to type,
Until, at last, the earth for man was ripe.

" But like a low-born child, whose fancy's page
Illuminated glows, she fondly dreams
That hers is other, nobler parentage;
That, from a Source Supreme, her being streams;
But, when I ask for proof, she can not give
One word, to me, of knowledge positive.

" Wherefore, regretfully I turn away,
In no wise profited, to let her muse
On her delusion, now grown old and gray.
It is a vain mirage that she pursues —
Some image of herself, against the sky,
To which she yearns on golden wings to fly."

What time I left that palace high and wide,
She followed me, whom I had thought so fair,
To guide me down the devious mountain-side,
Speaking with that of sorrow in her air
That made me grieve, and soon a tear I shed
To think that here she is so limited.

"Oh, I am life and more, I am the Soul,"
She said, "and, in the human heart and brain,
Sit throned and prisoned while the brief years roll,
Lifted with hope that I shall live again ;
That when I cross the flood, with me shall be
The swift-winged carrier-dove of memory.

"I shall have triumph over time and space,
For I am infinite and more than they.
In vain has Science searched my dwelling-place ;
For, delve in nature's secrets as she may
For deeper knowledge, she can never know
Of what I am, nor whither I shall go."

THE CITY OF DECAY.

I.

Where a river and a highway
    Running side by side together,
Lead along through pleasant queendoms
    To a peaceful, ancient town,
Once a bent and wrinkled Graybeard,
    Brave and true in every weather,
On the road pursued his journey,
    Autumn's fruitful land adown.

He had left Spring's balmy country,
    He had passed through that of Summer,

And through Autumn's bronze dominion
    Was advancing on his way,
When a bird of sweeping pinion,
    To the kindly-hearted comer,
From the topmost bough of knowledge
    Caroled forth a welcome lay.

Dragging from this boat of music
    His close net of recollection,
Went the Graybeard's thought, regretting
    One great pearl that he had lost.
He beheld again the country
    Ruled by Spring, and clear reflection,
In his spirit's limpid waters,
    Of the star-like pearl of cost.

Then the Truthsayer, far-sighted,
    Found the long-sought Graybeard dreaming
In the thoughtful, wayside shadow
    Of the vocal, golden tree ;
And he said to him, " O brother,
    Would'st thou find thy pearl, whose seeming
So enchants thy soul with beauty
    That thou think'st no more shall be ?

" In the ocean-bounded city,
    Whither thou art tending surely,
Undissolved thy pearl awaits thee
    By the darkly silent shore.
Do thine alms-deeds ; follow mercy ;
    Hold thy hand from wrong securely ;
When thy pearl again elates thee,
    Thou shalt have it ever more."

To behold the Prophet fully,
    Turned the traveler sedately,
Tho' doubt and hope, alternate,
    Were reflected in his face ;

But the Sayer had departed,
  And the other wondered greatly
That a stranger, kingly-hearted,
    Should regard him aught with grace.

All one way the folk were going,
  On that highway by the river,
In their journey daily nearing
    Rest and quiet by the sea.
Long the Graybeard searched among them,
  With his thankful lips aquiver,
For the Prophet glad and cheering,
    Who foretold the joy to be.

But he found him not, and sadly
  Down the road his course pursuing,
Saw the wizened leaves whirled madly
    And bestrew the crystal stream ;
He beheld the air-like current
  Making haste to its undoing,
And, on birds that dipped and skimmed it,
    Watched the sunlight's silver gleam.

Often ships of cloud sailed over,
  With their wingy canvas lifted,
Or they lay becalmed or anchored
    In the portless, circling blue.
In a small, frail shallop nightly
  On the silent stream he drifted,
Till bright Lucifer had fallen,
    And the victor drank the dew.

Then on wakefulness he stranded,
  And took up his onward journey,
Thinking deeply of the promise
    That so graciously was made ;
While the winds, like knights of terror,
  Round him whirled in joust and tourney ;

But of gusty doubt and error
   His belief was not afraid.

For through these he went undaunted,
   And, one afternoon, when brightly
Shone the sun, by clouds unhaunted,
   At his feet a valley lay.
He was standing on a hill-top,
   And below him, wide and sightly,
Where the river cleft the sea-coast,
   Rose the City of Decay.

Far beyond it, black and silent
   Stretched Oblivion's deep ocean
Fog-confounded, thick and waveless
   To the rim of western sky.
Time's replenished river emptied,
   With a never-ceasing motion,
Into these relentless waters
   And unfathomed mystery.

Often vessels, steered by Circé,
   Down the ebbing river sailing,
Ventured boldly out, and vanished
   In the mute deep's heavy gloom;
But not one came back, or wafted
   Sounds of laughter or of wailing,
From Persephone and Pluto's
   Dimly-lighted land of doom.

Down the highway to the city
   Came the Graybeard through the valley,
While its sunset skies were glossy,
   And approached the crumbling wall.
At the gateway, high and mossy,
   Soon he paused, his strength to rally;
And expectancy allured him
   With the joy that would befall.

II.

Wide the rusty gates stood open,
  For they long had been unguarded;
And perforce the foot would enter,
    That the weary road had come.
In the passage, half imbedded
  Lay the heavy bolts discarded,
And therethrough went Echo, wedded
    To the twilight gray and dumb.

Here the air was damp and chilly,
  And, with pencil chaste and rimy,
Drew the arabesques of Winter,
    On the stones that arched the way;
But in the vast metropolis
  The walls with dew were slimy;
Tho' it was the land of Autumn,
    It was like the home of May.

Tho' the border-hills of Winter
  To the city were adjacent,
Up the dreary, sullen ocean
    Came the sultry, panting South;
And it fawned on beldam Ruin,
  That, in pride of dress complacent,
Sat attired in grass and ivy,
    And concealed her gaping mouth.

On the city wall grew poppies
  Red as wine, or white as lilies;
And so drowsily they lifted
    Their full faces to the sun,
That the saffron-vested robin,
  Proud, erect — a winged Achilles —
Sang no more with wakeful rapture
    As he in the Spring had done.

In the city dwelt in plenty,
  In a mansion quaint and olden,
One who was a lady truly,
    For she doled the poor her bread.
Gentle charms of face and manner
  Hid her years in glamour golden,
And her hair of silver brightened
    To a halo round her head.

She was once superb in beauty,
  And a handsome youth true-hearted
Had desired of her this duty,
    That she love him all his years;
But too late — her troth was plighted;
  Yet with soft regret she parted
From the youth, the unrequited,
    Who had turned away with tears.

Now her husband and her children
  Under church-yard turf were sleeping;
She, with Kindness to attend her,
    Down life's western slope made way;
But she watched the couch of sickness,
  Calmed the bitter voice of weeping,
And enlarged the paths of mercy
    In the City of Decay.

Haply hearing of her goodness,
  That it was a potent essence
To revive the weary stranger,
    Or to heal misfortune's sting,
The Graybeard sought her dwelling-house,
  And, standing in her presence,
The diminished star discovered,
    Whose full orb he loved in Spring.

Having given his name, he briefly
  Sketched their early, tender meeting,

And the after-years — these chiefly
    For the star's projected beam.
The woman smiled, and took his hand
    With kindly words of greeting ;
Her eyes were memory-vistas,
    And love was like a dream.

Then he told her of the wonder,
    Long in Summer his possession,
That had slipped from him asunder
    Into Time's elusive tide ;
And anon of that Truthsayer
    Who had warned him from transgression,
And who promised that the jewel
    With its owner should abide.

Glad the woman was, and said she,
    " Whatsoe'er my friendship chooses,
That it likes to do — would aid thee
    Till thy perfect joy thou find.
He achieves no Alpine summit,
    Who to take stout help refuses ;
And not yet have line and plummet
    Gauged the sea-depths of the mind.

" Come, Kindness, near, and speak him fair,
    That once was my true lover,
And, up and down this crumbling town,
    Assist him in his quest,
Searching daily, rising early,
    Till, at last, he shall discover
That great virtue pure and pearly,
    Which aforetime he possessed."

So with soothing hand came Kindness,
    And reposed it on his shoulder ;
But he dazedly, as with blindness,
    Pressed his palm upon his brow.

And bethought him of his sister,
　Who to memory seemed older —
A beloved and holy maiden
　That abode in heaven now.

The woman spoke: "Across the way,
　There stands a monastery,
Where, within a darksome cloister,
　Dwells an abbot sad and pale.
I know him well; he lives alone;
　But many folk, once merry,
To have him pray their sins away
　His heavy doors assail.

"Bide thou with him hereafter;
　For I shall reward him freely.
But to-night he shares our table;
　Nay, he even now is here!"
Thereupon, the abbot entered,
　And his restless eyes and steely
On the woman quickly centered;
　But she gave him gracious cheer.

Low his monkish garb depended
　With a cross and beaded cable.
As if but his cowl offended,
　He removed it from his head.
The abundant, girdled habit
　Heightened whitely, with its sable,
His dull, hollow-cheekèd pallor;
　But his lips were full and red.

The Graybeard, bowing coldly,
　Touched the abbot's hand extended,
And, beside the board, more boldly
　Showed his liking scant and small;
But when rising for departure,
　He was to the monk commended;

And they crossed the street, and lingered
      In the monastery hall.

Seated here beneath the flicker
      Of a lamp hung from the ceiling,
Said the abbot, "Worthy senior,
      Doth thy heart not know me yet?
Hast forgot?   Thou thought'st me sainted,
      In the wayside shadow kneeling:
Who with me is unacquainted,
      Seeing that I am Regret?"

Past midnight lone, the guest was shown
      Where he might sleep and slumber,
As, on before, the abbot bore
      A bronze, Pompeian lamp.
The Graybeard saw long rows of lore
      The echoing halls encumber,
And, on windows mediæval,
      Heavy night-dew trickle damp.

Thenceforth he scarce elected
      To behold the monk, who, hidden
In his cell, with soul dejected,
      Brooded palely on the past.
There was a trusty servitor
      That took him food when bidden,
And the guest's lone board replenished
      With profusion to the last.

But that night the Graybeard's spirit
      Anchored in the Indian Ocean,
Off Ceylon, in oystered waters
      Where, with sudden plash and swirl,
Swarthy divers darted under;
      And, with weltering commotion,
From the breathless fields of wonder
      Brought the harvest of a pearl.

III.

Early service swift to render,
  Came the woman's placid maiden,
And led on through morning splendor
  To a ruin old and gray.
It was of an arch, or grotto,
  That, with heavy mosses laden,
High upon it bore the motto,
  Only truth shall not decay.

Near the arch had stood a temple
  Where an oracle was spoken
On the sea of truth men worshiped
  For a meaning all their own.
Now about the sward they dented
  Lay the fluted columns broken,
And the thought they represented
  Was as mythic error known.

Each belief is truth most holy
  To the holder — is eternal —
Tho' beliefs are birds that slowly
  Hatch their broods and fly away.
Ammon, Isis, Auramuzda,
  Jove and all the gods supernal,
Had the ruins of their altars
  In the City of Decay.

Carefully round arch and column
  That had been to Truth erected,
Went the Graybeard, meekly solemn,
  Seeking out his one desire.
He had fondly hoped to find it,
  By the love of Truth protected,
Somewhere hidden here, denuded
  Of the restless river's mire.

But it had his search eluded,
  And from that sad place he wended
Through a street of tombs and willows,
    Nor believed the jewel there;
Tho' far and wide on either side
  The monuments extended,
And birds with heaven flooded sweet
    The unregretful air.

Ruined castles slowly crumbled
  Here and there within the city;
Their high battlements had tumbled,
    And their grassy moats were dry.
Gone every knight and lady dight,
  For no more the love-lorn ditty
Rose beneath the listening window,
    In the moon's enamored eye.

There have been, in Spain, great castles
  Of the nimble mason-wizard
That, with neither square nor plumb-line,
    Ever rears a chinkless wall.
Once as great were these now broken,
  Where abode the bat and lizard,
And where just a word, loud spoken,
    Sometimes caused a tower to fall.

Haply, Kindness and the Graybeard
  Reached a magic castle olden,
That was standing draped with ivy
    Like a goddess with her hair;
But the cross-barred gate of iron,
  All so rustily was holden,
That they pushed it down, and wandered
    Through the stillness lone and bare.

From the ample space allotted
  Towered the thick walls skyward grandly,

Tho' the floors and roof had rotted,
  And in dust had disappeared.
Overhead a light cloud drifted,
  And an owlet, resting blandly
In the shade, to where it shifted,
  Nestled closer, as they neared.

That this dusky bird Minervan
  On the corbel-mask was perching,
Now the Graybeard thought an omen
  That herein his quest would end;
And his hope would fain accord him
  That the castle they were searching,
Or one like it, must reward him,
  And his master-wish befriend.

For he knew that in the ruins
  Of men's high anticipations
There are pearls of greatest moment
  Found in wiser after-years;
But no joy for his anointment
  Here was vased, and sad libations
Poured he out to disappointment,
  From the brimming cup of tears.

Kindness, quick to calm and cherish,
  Homeward then his steps directed,
Shunning streets where daily perish
  Hopes of wealth and high renown.
But her words, that sweetly fluttered,
  Told him of a world affected
By the influence that uttered
  From the portals of the town.

As the sun his blue path travels,
  Highest minaret and steeple
Toward him lean; the sweet bud ravels
  Into flower, and toward him blows;

And throughout the ages hoary
  Have the ever-restless people,
Westering and migratory,
    Followed his unfading rose.

To this wide-spread sunset city
  Thus are drawn the generations;
Youth, and middle-age, and ancient
    Hither stream in swerveless tides.
Here life centers; gay youth enters
  Crowned with Spring's associations;
But decrepitude, so childish,
    Often longest here abides.

While true Kindness thus was talking
  To her charge, they passed by slowly
Thronging counter-currents walking
    In the sunny, spacious way.
He, with alms-deeds oft appeasing
  Want with palm outstretched and lowly,
Found its gratitude as pleasing
    As violets are in May.

IV.

The Lady and the Graybeard,
  Drawn by horses black and prancing,
Down the morning-streeted valley,
    Rode to Retrospection's halls.
There was not a court or alley
  Where the dancing sunbeams, glancing,
Lighted not unfading pictures
    Hung upon interior walls.

Everywhere, in grandeur dusky,
  Rose, to Retrospection builded,
Palaces with hinges husky
    Opening backward in review —

Lofty halls like Spain's Alhambra,
  Ceiled with frost-work forms, and gilded —
Buildings like the Doge's Palace,
  Glassed in depths of dreamy blue.

All faced one way; all looked eastward
  Up the road, and up the river,
Peering over roof and ruin
  Into Summer's land and Spring's.
Some by fountains were surrounded,
  In whose crystal toss and quiver
Humming-bird-like sheen abounded,
  Burnished blue and twinkling wings.

There in grass the long-thighed hopper
  Clicked his castanets in measure,
An unrecognized Tithonus,
  And old, crabbèd Pantaloon;
While the almond-tree in blossom
  Dropped its snowy petal-treasure,
And the windows of the buildings
  Dimmed and darkened all too soon.

The abodes of Retrospection
  Separately were divided;
Like the Cretan Labyrinthus
  They were doored from hall to hall;
But no artful terror thundered,
  Nor were prisoners there misguided;
For to each his rooms were secret,
  But he knew them scarcely all.

Of these palaces, the pictures
  Bore one master artist's *fecit;*
For the Angelo of Memory,
  Whose brush is never still,
Did the work alone, and daily
  His delight was to increase it,

Till of spaces left in places
    None remained for him to fill.

When from halls deceased a tenant,
    He would take his painted story
On his starry journey with him,
    To declare his place and age ;
But History, backward glancing,
    With her stylus dipped in glory,
Likenessed all the greater pictures
    On her scant but deathless page.

Many deeds of noble daring
    And of patient self-denial,
That alone were worth the caring,
    In what yet was left to tell,
Had survived the heel of silence,
    Cheered the world in every trial,
And of Love's broad ocean murmured
    In Expression's rhythmic shell.

Having briefly on their way fared,
    To a House of Retrospection
Came the Lady and the Graybeard,
    Where, to old-time words, the door
Opened for them ; and they wandered
    Through the halls in each direction,
And, before the canvas, pondered
    On its reminiscent store.

Lighted corridors retreating,
    Through the woman's past descended ;
And their calm research completing,
    Saving that of but a few,
She would not stay, but turned away
    With him that she befriended,
Knowing well his spirit's compass
    Had to Heaven and her been true.

For he led her through his smiling
  Halls of manhood, now resounding
To their footfalls on the tiling,
    Where lay broken cups of joy.
In pictures wide, on either side,
  His life arose, abounding
In the painter's richest colors,
    Which the grave can not destroy.

When day with his life-giving torch
  Was to the sea descending,
Came out upon the building's porch
    The wand'rers sere and gray;
Then as heavy-uddered cloud-herds,
  Trampling loudly, were impending,
Homeward hied the couple quickly,
    Down the dream-dispelling way.

Against the west the clouds up-pressed
  In blackly moving ledges,
But in a rift that seemed to lift
    A splendid rainbow shone.
This climbed and kissed an ebon mist
  High up with pallid edges,
Toward whose craggy shore a vessel,
    The freightless moon, was blown.

Soon the crystal keel encountered
  Its mirk doom, and crashing, sinking,
Left the sky to darkness dreary
    Pierced by lightning, wind, and rain;
Yet that night the Graybeard weary,
  In his sleep's disordered thinking,
Deemed the vanished moon the jewel
    He was seeking to regain.

Through the hopeless night and morrow
  Poured the gray rain sobbing, sighing,

While its gusty breath of sorrow
    Tossed the dead leaves to and fro.
Looked the Graybeard from the casement
  On the leaves and rain-drops flying,
And a wind of self-abasement
    Through his spirit seemed to blow.

She to whom he was beholden
  Sent him fruit for toothsome pleasure,
Apples crimson, apples golden,
    Ripe as Juno's and as sweet.
Truths he thought them ; Kindness brought them,
  And, with hope of his lost treasure,
Sunned away his rainy feelings,
    Seated humbly at his feet.

v.

The defeated clouds retreated,
  And the flushed, exultant morning,
With shields that shone and banners blown,
    Advanced above the hill.
And divine, reviving roses,
  The metropolis adorning,
Looked up to greet the victor,
    Sweet with fragrance they distil.

The Lady and the Graybeard,
  Urged by Kindness, their attendant,
Rode to see the lofty palace
    Where the Emperor abode ;
For Decay was chief of cities
  That upon him were dependent,
And within its grassy quiet
    His unfailing bounty flowed.

" Gray Time, the Emperor, lately,
  To display his might and splendor,

Has proclaimed a triumph stately,"
  Said the Lady to her guest.
" Vast his recent conquests tragic ;
  But, as did the witch of Endor,
He will raise the dead by magic
  From their melancholy rest.

" He will break their vaulted slumber,
  Bring again their absent features,
And advance their sea-sand number
  In diversified array.
Them, that erst were his possession,
  He will show to us, his creatures,
And re-lead them in procession
  Through his capital, Decay.

" He, besides his scion, Winter,
  Has three pure and loving daughters :
Proud, bright-eyed, fruit-bosomed Autumn,
  Summer dark with sun and dew,
And young Spring with eyes of blue.
  These, along the ebbing waters,
He has given each a country
  Good to dwell in, fair to view.

" No Lear he among his children ;
  He is yet their ruler rigid.
Tho' at times they seem to brave it,
  They his will have aye obeyed.
Its still chains with might environ
  And constrain the kingdom frigid ;
For his scepter is of iron,
  Tho' with velvet softness swayed."

On the way, the simple Graybeard
  Cheered his tender heart with flowers,
Whose rare beauty rose exultant
  From the black and humid soil.

Dark decay is beauty's mother;
  And the daughter turns to bowers,
Ruins gray, and decks their towers
  With a tendril-twining toil.

Every form is matter's dwelling,
  And, as soon as one is wasted,
From decay another rises.
    Changing like the forms of truth
Matter round the bent world wanders;
  It of every joy has tasted,
Finding in decay renewal,
    And the fresh delights of youth.

Through the city, in profusion,
  Danced, on wings like flakes of color
From the painter Nature's palette,
    Nectar-fed gay butterflies.
Even a woodland fairy-ballet
  To the sight were less and duller;
For the hue of their seclusion
    Is the fairies' only guise.

On the faithful Graybeard brightly
  Burst the view of Time's great palace,
In the distance rising lightly
    From the hill's enameled crest.
Arm-high, near the site commanding,
  Every lily raised its chalice,
As if at a banquet standing
    In the honor of a guest.

Somewhat like the regal dwelling
  That enroofs the crowned Castilian,
And is life to sunny Madrid.
    The impassioned heart of Spain,
Stood the Emperor's white palace
    Hung with banners of vermilion,

And a clock-tower rose amidst it,
   With a bell of solemn strain.

In a meadow near the ocean
   Trod an old man mowing, swaying
With the keen scythe's crescent motion,
   As he laid the long years low.
In the stable where he shut them
   Stood the sun's black horses, neighing
For the provender he cut them,
   Which not otherwhere would grow.

Like the Halls of Retrospection,
   Facing mornward, up the river,
Stood the palace, and behind it
   Ran the city's mighty wall.
This with towers and bastions bristled;
   But no soldier emptied quiver
While its barbed death sped and whistled,
   When a tower would sway and fall.

Where it fell, it formed a passage
   For the troops of vegetation
To attack the standing rampart
   With triumphant shields and spears.
Kindness and the Graybeard clambered
   Over débris to a station
On the wall, and wide before them
   Lay the city worn with years.

Far as the eye could aught descry,
   The town stretched, quilted, seamy,
Toward Winter's star; and eastward far,
   With pagan, pillared fanes.
The castle towers and palaces
   Hung in the distance dreamy,
And ancient baths and aqueducts
   Were traced in arched remains.

Along Time's hill, which bordered
  On the ocean black and lonely,
The high wall ran whereon the man
    And Kindness gazed around.
Far below them, on the waters
  That were gloom and silence only,
Lay a twilight that to midnight
    Deepened westward, vapor-bound.

VI.

On another day came Kindness
  With the Graybeard, and, descending
To the dismalest of beaches,
    By the dark sea walked a while.
In the shallow, marshy reaches,
  Where white ibises were bending,
Grew the lotus and papyrus
    That have vanished from the Nile.

In the hillside steep and rocky,
  Vined with paths of deep reflection,
Countless tombs were hewed, whose mummies
    Were in life to Horus true.
He, to perished lives he cherished,
  Brought fresh bloom and resurrection,
Son of Hathor, golden goddess
    Of the heavens soft and blue.

Egypt thought that, with life brutal,
  Souls departed were encumbered ;
But again they would be human,
    After three millenniums fled.
With their self-renewing beetles,
  Long the mummies here had slumbered,
And beyond the time appointed ;
    Yet they woke not from the dead.

As if tomb or beach enshrined it,
  Sought the Graybeard for his jewel.
He was sure that he would find it
    By the dateless, dusky shore;
For his failures ever straightway
  Gave his flame of hope new fuel;
Yet he clambered to a gateway,
    Unrewarded as before.

On the arch an unknown motto,
  In the weedy stones and rotten,
Was engraved, and gave its token
    To the blind and voiceless deep;
While inside this coastern entrance,
  Busts of great men long forgotten,
And their statues, marred and broken,
    Lay unvalued on the steep.

But behind the stagnant ocean
  Glowed bright-arrowed day, declining;
Yet no shaft of all his splendor
    Pierced the dull deep's mail of night.
All the city towers, like tapers,
  With his level rays were shining;
But the waters and their vapors
    Were the darker for the light.

On the coast the wall was weakest,
  Holding up a slight resistance;
For a tidal-wave incoming,
    At a blow, had dashed it down.
But it showed the thin partition,
  And how perilous the distance
Between dead inanition
    And the retrospective town.

VII.

With his lovable companion
  Went the Graybeard on the morrow,
Toward the quay along the river,
  And the rotting, wooden piers.
He was swiftly growing older,
  And her strength he had to borrow;
For he leaned upon her shoulder
  With the trembling weight of years.

It was beautiful to see them
  As they through the old streets wended.
Her eyes were mild, and when she smiled
  Some heart with joy was filled.
She was fair, and her complexion
  With the open lily blended;
But her words set roses blooming,
  And the raging tempest stilled.

Many a time some mildewed building,
  Bat-frequented, long neglected,
Would, with sunken roof and doorway,
  Fall across the empty street.
On the mound it thus erected
  Outlaw briers and weeds collected,
To cut and try the passers-by,
  And often cause retreat.

But from out a lofty gateway
  Of the wall beside the river,
Came the gentle couple straightway
  To their quest along the quay.
They beheld the dead leaves, drifting
  In the black, thick water, quiver
And eddy near some slimy pier,
  To ebb away to sea.

All the commerce was departed;
  And tho' deeply laden vessels
On the wide, straight river started,
    To discargo at the town,
Few arrived to cheer and richen;
  None the tempest longer wrestles;
For all lie half-sunk, unpitchen,
    By the piers, and there go down.

Patiently the Graybeard hunted
  For his mystic pearl delightful.
On pier and hulk and round each bulk
    He looked to see its gleam.
For he fancied, as he sought it,
  That for him, the owner rightful,
Some kind riverman had brought it,
    Having found it in the stream.

Baffled still, the Graybeard lifted
  His calm eyes to scan the distance,
And a bulged sail growing larger
    Watched till it beside him moored.
Men make faith of what is hoped for;
  And, that his foot-sore persistence
Soon would clutch the gem it groped for,
    By his faith he was assured.

Forthwith went he toward the master,
  Who upon the prow was standing,
And exclaimed, with heart-beats faster,
    " Tell me of my pearl, long lost! "
Then the other, as a brother,
  To the Graybeard on the landing
Kindly said, " Describe this jewel,
    Which must be of heavy cost."

When the Graybeard had outlined it,
  As he might some fading vision,

He whom he besought to find it
    Blankly stared, as in a swound.
"Vain is search," he answered slowly;
   "Yet, within my thought elysian,
One abides whose name is holy;
    She a pearl like yours had found.

"She the winsome jewel lost not;
  In my heart she has it ever;
Only there can I restore it;
    She who wore it was my bride.
Woe befell me: bride and jewel,
  In the swift, onflowing river,
In the silence cold and cruel,
    Sank, in darkness, from my side.

"She was hurried to the waters
  Where the dream called life forsakes us —
Dream, or glimpse, that Nature gives us
    Of her many-featured face.
To the sea she sweeps the nations;
  Thence she brought us, thither takes us,
And we lose the limitations,
    Time, causality, and space.

"More we see not, nor this plainly;
  For our knowledge here is blinded,
And it gropes and searches vainly
    Out beyond life's final breath.
Doubt not of it we shall profit,
  Tho' the creeds were other minded,
If it be a fact in nature
    That the soul lives after death."

Oh! never more along that shore
  This riverman went sailing.
No breeze might waft his wingless craft,
    That all dismantled lay.

Nor was he met thereafter
  By the Graybeard, who, fast failing,
Deemed the quest was unavailing
    In the City of Decay.

VIII.

Day by day the Graybeard wasted,
  Scarce from his apartment going,
Till he turned from food untasted,
  And lay ridden on his bed.
Kindness and her friend, intently
  To his care themselves bestowing,
Smoothed his patient pillow gently,
    And their comforts round him spread.

But when, like May, the triumph day
  Came balmy-aired and splendid,
They moved him to a broader view,
    And swung the window wide.
To every space the populace
  Their waiting sea extended,
And by-streets nigh and housetops high
    Were blackened with its tide.

Down the way came heralds riding,
  Through their silver trumpets crying,
"Time is passing! Time is gliding!
    Live the Emperor! He is here!"
Countless pretty baby children,
  Laughing, sighing, running, flying,
Led the pageant; while sweet music
    From a distance charmed the ear.

Naked were the infant Moments,
  But with fruit-tree blossoms belted,
That were ever snowing petals
    And bestrewing all the ground.

Then came lissome older children,
  By the flying blossoms pelted —
Graceful Hours, and twelve were rosy;
  Twelve, dark-veiled, with stars were crowned.

Then the Days came, budding maidens:
  They had hair of morning brightness,
And about with night were skirted;
  Some Days dark and others fair.
At their heels the Months close followed:
  In their steps was less of lightness;
On her arm a shield of silver
  Each Month lifted high in air.

Spring came smiling, showered with praises,
  Crowned with violets and arbutus,
Robed in woven flowers and fragrance,
  Crocuses, anemones,
Tulips, hyacinths, and lilacs,
  More than all the wealth of Plutus;
And of marigolds and daisies
  Hung her tunic to her knees.

Round her flew the birds, and uttered
  Her full soul in warbled wooing:
All her blossomed promise fluttered
  With the blithe surprise of song.
Fell her hair of gold supernal
  To her feet; their touch renewing
Waking Love, whose laughter vernal
  Followed after and along.

Swarthy Summer was next comer:
  Dowered with beauty Cleopatran,
Fervid, full of storms and sunshine,
  And with bosom deep and round.
Like a ruby shone the dog-star
  On the forehead of the matron,

While her gown, her form revealing,
 Trailed with roses on the ground.

With a sickle for a scepter
 Autumn followed, luscious, mellow,
On vines that groaned and sheaves enthroned,
 And under boughs of fruit.
Loud the flail announced her progress,
 Thudding on her grainy yellow,
While her sober verdure lightened
 To a gold and crimson suit.

Winter came with freezing bluster,
 In an icy chariot riding,
Drawn by northern, snowy horses,
 Each with long and streaming mane.
Crowned with icicles whose luster
 Sparkled, he, in ermine hiding,
Sat and frowned, his body palsied
 By his breath's benumbing pain.

But the Graybeard paled and shivered
 In the breath so sharp and stinging,
Like a clinging leaf that quivered
 In December on a tree.
He could feel the years encroaching;
 He could hear far, sweet bells ringing,
And the Emperor, approaching
 With his horses, he did see.

These, in maned and fiery splendor,
 Never man beheld correctly;
For inadequate and tender
 Is the eye, and deemed them black.
They the sun-god's were, and coldly
 Glanced at Winter indirectly;
But they drew the monarch boldly,
 With the scythe hung down his back.

Of him heedless, scant devotion
  House or street would show this mower
Of the meadow by the ocean,
  For his passing won no cheers;
Yet his chariot resplendent,
  Moving swifter, never slower,
Scattered blessings, some transcendent,
  From its stopless wheels of years.

The Emperor, tall and meager,
  Had a forelock thin and snowy,
Of which the bold have taken hold,
  And gained the thing they would.
He wore no crown; his scepter
  Was a clock-hand gilt and showy;
And the sands he held were running
  Toward the promised Age of Good.

In the chariot, with the ruler,
  Rode three stated creatures duly:
One, the woman, was his consort,
  And was of divinest mold.
Of her lord she much demanded,
  Tho' she loved that niggard truly;
But, with folly open-handed,
  Spent his momentary gold.

She was Life, and gave the lowest
  Often overflowing measure,
While withholding from the dearest
  What she spared to bird and beast.
In her hand she held her goblet,
  Bitter-sweet with pain and pleasure,
Quaffed with bacchic joy by matter
  At the outset in the East.

She the Graybeard at the window
  Saw, and toward him reached the chalice.

Smiling on him with a glory
 That outbeamed the light around;
But the figure like a shadow,
 Hooded, mantled — as in malice —
In the splendid chariot riding —
 Dashed the goblet to the ground.

This was Death, Life's dread companion,
 Bound to Time by icy fetters;
But between Death and the woman
 Stood her slave, a comely youth.
He could sweep the keys of feeling,
 Read the earth-book's rocky letters,
And in cloistral conscience kneeling
 Face to face commune with Truth.

Like the genii so potent,
 In the story of Aladdin,
That were faithful in the service
 Of the egg, the lamp, or ring,
To the human clay enchanted,
 He was slave, and strove to gladden
Life, at whose warm touch it panted:
 What she asked for, he would bring.

It was he that built the cities,
 Wielded nature's restless forces,
Led the arts, delved mine and quarry,
 Bridged the rivers, sailed the air,
Tamed hot steam to fetch and carry,
 Traced the dim stars in their courses,
And from the sky brought Mercury
 Labor's yoke to don and wear.

Of obtrusive foot elusive,
 To the wise and gentle-hearted
He was ever welcome, being
 Slave and king whom men call Thought.

High of forehead, pale and silent,
  With a smile his lips were parted,
And his eyes, large, dark, and dreamy,
  From the skies their ardor caught.

Close behind Time's chariot followed
  Earliest men, the club-armed savage
Of the geologic epoch
  When grim Winter plowed the earth.
With the mammoth and the great bear,
  Which at will were wont to ravage,
These men met in hasty warfare,
  And were brutal from their birth.

From this shaggy strife and grewsome,
  Each was in his trophy girded.
Fierce his beard swept down his bosom,
  And his long hair flag'd behind.
Reared in caves where day scarce shimmered,
  He with mimicked sounds was worded;
Yet from even him outglimmered
  Dawnings of prescient mind.

Then came those who toiled in Shinar
  To upbuild sky-seeking Babel,
With Noah bent — who eastward went,
  And founded China's power —
And with Misraim, Nile's lord, Misraim,
  Son of sable Ham in fable;
For Misraim fared to Egypt
  From the folly of the tower.

After these came gods, or rather
  Famous folk of mythic story,
Who, for beacon deeds or passions,
  By mankind were deified.
Zeus, Latona, and Apollo,
  Venus fair and Neptune hoary,

Thor, the hammerer, and Odin,
   Glided by with stately pride.

Into view upon the way rose
   Many purple heads of nations,
All the shepherd-kings and Pharaohs,
   With gray Sidon's kings, and Tyre's —
Nay, Nineveh's and Babylon's;
   While their subject populations
Hung about them, kindred vapor
   Filled with often-flashing fires.

And the Graybeard at the window
   Saw the colony Egyptian,
Who, in Attica, the rugged,
   Added grace to art and lore.
Then not surprised he recognized,
   By Homer's clear description,
All the heroes that for Helen
   Raged with battle-joy of yore.

In that ever-moving pageant,
   Far surpassing every other,
He beheld the prince Æneas
   On his exiled, Idan prow;
Saw great Romulus and Remus
   With their lupine foster-mother;
Saw dictator Cincinnatus
   Standing humbly by his plow.

With his army, Alexander,
   In bright armor and regalia,
Preceded Afric Hannibal;
   And high in pomp and state
Sat the mighty leader, Cæsar,
   At the feast of Lupercalia,
Pushing back the golden bauble
   That aroused the dagger's hate.

Darkness came; the land was shaken,
  Fanes and castles waver'd falling,
Graves were of their dead forsaken,
  And the risen gibberers pale
Down the way moved whitely, fleeing
  In the mid-day night appalling,
On whose stream each ghostly being
  Seemed a tempest-driven sail.

Then the Graybeard at Death's window
  Saw a sight that deeply thrilled him:
Three dead bodies on three crosses
  On dark Calvary lifted high.
But the Central Face with rapture
  And with glad amazement filled him;
For with joy he cried, *The Truthsayer!*
  Then fell backward with a sigh.

Through the gloom a wan ray glinted
  As the woman found his pillow,
And, in benediction, printed
  On his lips a sacred kiss.
He was dead : a shadow horrid
  Had engulfed him, like a billow.
Cold he lay, from foot to forehead;
  But his hands were clasped in bliss.

IX.

With a foot that rested lightly
  On the wall that girt the city,
Where the masonry looked seaward
  Near the palace-towers of Time,
Robed in splendor stood an angel
  With benignant arms of pity —
Wings like gleams of morn outspreading,
  And face and mien sublime.

12

His stature was colossal;
  He was taller than the tower
Of an organ-voiced cathedral;
    Yet most beautiful his form,
Rising worshipfully Godward,
  Calm, august with sacred power —
His serenity more awful
    Than the grandeur of a storm.

Just above him, back a measure,
  On a level with his shoulder,
Stood a lofty, equal pleasure,
    Like a brother to the first.
Over him a third joy hovered,
  Then a fourth, till their beholder
Knew a hundred, glory-covered,
    On the raptured vision burst.

Thus the great seraphic stairway
  Reached far out above the ocean,
Step by step, to dim dominions
    Of the sapphire-vaulted sky.
In the light the argent pinions
  Beat the air with gentle motion,
And the robes of brightness fluttered
    Trailing downward from on high.

As the angel stairs ascended,
  To the vision they diminished,
Tho' they all were like, and blended
    As one ray their wisdom shone.
They looked down with calm indulgence
  On the pageant still unfinished,
Waiting, in their winged effulgence,
    To receive and crown their own.

Now, the freed soul of the Graybeard
  In her bosom bearing gently,

Came dear Kindness to the seraph
   With his foot upon the wall.
Into his soft hands she gave it,
   And he looked on it intently ;
For to him it was an infant
   New-born, helpless, frail, and small.

To the angel next above him
   He upheld it when he blessed it,
And that splendor took the spirit
   And bestowed it on the third ;
To the fourth the third joy raised it,
   And it grew as each caressed it,
For young wings upon its shoulders
   Started out as on a bird.

Upward, onward borne and lifted
   To the tenth seraphic whiteness,
There the spirit fair was gifted
   With a spotless robe of truth,
And was crowned with his lost jewel —
   Nay, a star — a dream of brightness —
The beatified renewal
   Of the lustrous pearl of youth.

Gentle Kindness, gazing upward,
   Saw the radiant youth ascending,
Far along the wide-winged stairway,
   Toward the glory-parted skies.
He had spread his sweeping pinions,
   Filled with love and peace unending ;
And she watched his heavenward journey
   Till he vanished from her eyes.

Yet she heard the music tender
   That adown the stairway sounded,
And beheld the blessèd splendor
   When high heaven's gates were raised.

But with rhythmic wings and voices,
　Her the seraphim surrounded,
And, beseeching her to join them,
　They upon her beauty gazed.

But Kindness yet would rather
　Bide within Time's breathful portal,
Knowing that she has a Father
　In the purer world above —
Love unselfish, universal,
　Truth celestial and immortal,
In the city built of jewels,
　Whose foundation is of Love.

BELLEROPHON.

THERE lives a creature of a dreamer's brain,
That strove by charms, and with the aid of ghosts,
Of making gold to find the secret out;
That drew a magic ring about his crucible,
And, while the spirits worked at alchemy,
He, to beat back vast, adverse ghosts essayed.
But soon, within the circle he had drawn,
Was set a monstrous Foot, so large, his face
Was level with the instep: all in vain
His puny efforts to drive back the Foot.

Oh, hard for him who, having once let in
On the charm'd circle of the golden good
The first advance of error, strives to oust
The evil, and make clear the round again.
Not often will the giant Foot retreat.

And I bethink me him who, in the past,
Before Christ's passion ransom'd man from sin,

And in a land that did not know of God
Forced back the Foot of one remorseful crime,
Walked silently beneath the silent stars,
And gave his heart to cogitation thus:

"Anteia, wife to Proitos, tempted me:
She, in the palace where the fountains are,
Met me at twilight as she walked alone,
Clad with uncinctured robe, adorned with gems,
Perfumed with all the spices of the East.
She made her arms a wreath about my neck,
And, lifting both her small, gold-sandal'd feet,
Hung her full weight upon me; her mouth's closed
      bud
Burst into honey'd flower against my lips.
With warm cheek pressed to mine, she, in my ear,
Exhaled the poison whisper of her love.

"I drew back scornfully surprised, and hissed
Between set teeth a menace at all sin.
She left me thus, and went to him, her liege,
And with the broken fragments of her speech —
Bits of the jar that could not hold her tears —
She let it fall that I had wronged her much.

"In swift, deep wrath the fierce king called for me,
And on a tablet writing fatal characters,
With them he sent me forth beyond his realm
To Lykia, to the king thereof, who met,
And, by the stream of Xanthos, welcomed me.
Nine days of feasting passed, and on the tenth
The tablet was unsealed, its purport known —
And its base appetite is gorged to-day.

"Th' unconquerable Chimaira first I slew.
She was in front a lion, and behind
A serpent, and in the middle a goat.

Her breath was blazing fire, with which, in rage,
She burned the drought-parched forests in her path.
And her, by winged alliance with the horse,
I slew, indeed, and gave to rigid death.
I overcame the far-famed Solymi,
I smote the man-opposing Amazons,
I turned to naught the well-armed ambuscade,
And made illustrious my bitter name.

"But what if I had yielded to the queen,
And from the king had stolen that which she,
Tho' offering, had yet no right to give?
I hold, the soul is like a piece of cloth
That, being stained, can be made clean no more—
That nothing can erase the stain of sin.

"Picture that I, having passed safely through
The darkness that is seen by dying eyes.
Have reached the light beyond, and see the gods
In synod throned, and hear Zeus speak and say:

"'We serve no law, yet bind the steadfast earth
And all the ways of men in chains of law
Harmonious with good and linked thereto.
The blinded mortal lured to break one chain
Makes discord, stains the fabric of his soul,
And brings dire retribution headlong down.'

"Then I, in meek abasement kneeling there
Upon the low, first step of Zeus's throne,
Hold up my shameful soul, a piece of cloth
Through fault of Queen Anteia doubly stained,
And say:

"'O Zeus, accept this humble gift!
Thou wroughtest it: the texture is as fine
As the loose wool of clouds, or the worm's silk.
These blots and stains are most like roses strewn.'

" His calmness rippled by slight breeze of scorn,
The great cloud-gatherer would answer me :

" ' O fool ! and blind, to mock the mighty gods ;
For, on the mystic texture of the soul,
Only a noble deed shows like a flower.'

" Well, whoso wills shall ever have his way,
And what was right, that I had willed to do.
So, haply, I on Pegasus shall scale
White-crowned Olympus to the brazen halls,
If I may keep the path of righteousness
That the strong gods ordained."

       Thus mused he then,
Unmindful that great zeal for any good
Begets a narrowness that leads to ill.
The heaven-sent gad-fly stings the flying horse,
And hurls the rider back to common ground.

THE HERMIT.

The holiday was azure-domed and fair,
And to the Coliseum thronged again
Blithe children, fresh and pure as morning air,
Fond, tender women, and rude, brawny men ;
And all gaze centered in the ring below,
To view once more a gladiatorial show.

The late few days had been to waning Rome
A giddy wine in pleasure's brittle bowl.
There had been pomp of legions marching home,
And civic games, and races to a goal ;
There had been fights with beasts ; and now all breath
Served expectation at the show of death.

This was the triumph that had been decreed
To Stilicho, who, on an Easter-day,
Had met the Gothic hordes, and made them bleed,
And turned invasion into wild dismay ;
But with drawn swords the gladiators came
To end the pleasures with a deed of shame.

Feeling the weight of eyes upon them rest,
They came undauntedly, for often pride
Shuts up the dens of fear within the breast.
These men were bold to battle till they died,
But lacked the fortitude, uncommon still,
To show resistance to the public will.

For it is less to face soon-ended death
Than to oppose a great and popular wrong.
But he was bolder, armed with fearless breath,
The white-haired hermit, broad of soul and strong,
Who in that deep arena dared intrude,
And raise his voice against the multitude.

"This is not pleasure — it is shame !" he cried.
"O people, let these public murders cease !
Here let them end, and now, lest we be dyed
In guiltless blood again, and mar our peace.
Oh, let us not with sin God's grace repay,
Who gave us might to drive the Goth away !"

Bareheaded, and with naked feet, he stood
Between the fighters in the open place,
Clothed in plain garb : his face was mild and good,
And beautiful with kindness to his race ;
For there are June-like souls so warm and free
That love blooms in them for humanity.

But round him loud the Coliseum rang
With disapproval of his kind appeal ;

The populace, exclaimed, "On! on! Let clang
The sharp contention of exciting steel!
Fight, gladiators, fight! Nor heed nor look
Give to the movement of this froward brook!"

Enraged that still he stayed the swordsmen back,
True as an arrow to his heart's good aim,
The whirlpool of the people in attack
Surged down resistless, hissing as it came;
And, buffeted and trampled on, he died,
And was as drift ingulfed in that round tide.

For when the living whirlpool ebbed away,
And cleared the barbarous arena's space,
Stretched on the ground the hermit-martyr lay,
A smile of triumph on his peaceful face;
His long white hair was clotted with his gore,
And marks of feet were on the garb he wore.

Great is the martyr's blood, for it can gain
Its owner's cause, and surelier than he!
For when the people saw the hermit slain,
And through the storm-spent cloud the sun shone free,
They loathed what they had done, and from that day
The shows of gladiators passed away.

A MORNING PASTORAL.

IF some way Bichat's theory be true,
That animal and all organic life
In man combine and culminate — the brain
The animal, the heart the organic life —
I know wherefore my love unasked goes out
To meadows, trees, clear brooks. and distant hills,
For thus I am their fellow and their kin.

I chiefly like, while yet the day is new,
To walk among the fields along the road,
And brim my heart with Nature as I go.
The hoarse grasshoppers soon begin their drone;
But on a leaf, one here appears to drowse —
A sleepy sailor in an open boat,
Rocked on uneasy billows of thin air —
A Palinurus, who, while piloting
The Trojan galleys on disastrous seas,
Drowsed into death, among the Siren rocks.
Here, on a cliff, a noisy brook gets force,
And, plunging under alders, leaps along
Down to the fallow, rioting like a boy.
Anon I start a thrush, and up he wings,
And with a trail of music darts away,
Seeking the old republic of high woods,
Where he is citizen, but where his kind
Use melody for speech, and have no flag
Save the waved leaf above each wicker home.
Over the tree-tops yonder flies a crow
That boldly vents his unpopular caw,
And breasts the stubborn wind to gain the shore,
And cram his crop with what the tide brings in.
All flowers along the way are friends of mine,
And once I knew a meditative rose
That never raised its head from bowing down,
Yet drew its inspiration from the stars.
It bloomed and faded here beside the road,
And, being a poet, wrote on empty air
With fragrance all the beauty of its soul.
I pause beneath an overhanging elm,
Where, cut in granite of the vine-grown wall,
The wide mouth of a quaint, conspicuous face
Speaks to all thirst with visible eloquence.
Beside it sits a beggar on its trough,
Who craves with quivering lip an alms from me.
I give him from my earning, and go back
Toward the loud city with a lighter heart.

STORM.

THE pale day died in the rain to-night,
  And its hurrying ghost, the wind, goes by;
The mountains loom in their silent might,
  And darkly frown at the sea and sky.

The petrel wings close to his surging home,
  And stabs with a shriek the shuddering night;
The mad wave beckons with hands of foam
  Dipped in the blood of the sea-tower's light.

So, in my heart, is a storm to-night,
  Storm and tumult that will not cease;
And my soul, in bitterness, longs for the light,
  For the waking bird and the dawn of peace.

VANDERLYN.

THE man who, with a single aim, sailed forth
From doubting Spain toward the unknown West,
I would so paint that men in after-years,
Like me, long sick at heart with hope put off,
Seeing his lifted and prophetic face
That fronts the fact and substance of his dreams,
Shall look not only on Columbus there,
But see themselves in him, and each one feel
That he, too, with persistence, shall set foot
On the firm border of his hope's new world.

How weak our hands to do the work of thought
That flies before! Here, after thirty years,
I am again in Rome: now on the quest
To find a portrait of my hero's face,

And fill one panel at the Capitol.
With failing force — weary, broken, old —
How shall I say in color what I feel,
Or make stand out the picture seen within?

'T is well that doting retrospection comes
To help us bear the burden of disuse,
When little light is left wherein to work,
If so be any more may still be done.
I, looking back, see that my work is true —
At one with truth, and wrought with humble love.
Men come and go; but truth shall ever be.
It does not fade, nor rust, nor waste away;
But, like the sun, endures: forgetting this,
We painters miss the heights we might attain
In feeling that the truthful work we do
Will live and speak when we are silentest,
And strongly plead for us against neglect,
The dull, cold-shouldered mother of regret,
That in our hopeful faces shuts the door.
For merit scorned may safely laugh at scorn,
Because the common heart by nature turns
And to the truth despised does reverence.
But whether scorned or praised, good work abides,
And, praised or scorned, the undeserving dies;
And who is he, so short of sight, so vain,
That is content to have his poor work live?

Painters there are who never touch a brush:
The founders of my country's government,
Upon the ample canvas of their hope
Painted a great republic that to art
Should be most bountiful, should wed no creed,
But be fast bound to honor in all ways,
And free to peaceful feet from every shore.
Thus clear was their exemplar: it is strange
The work itself is so lamentable.

How long before the outlines that are left
Shall be defaced by shamed experience?
Munificent to art! — its artists starve.
Art does not thrive without encouragement,
Which follows surelier beneath a crown,
Where titled wealth and taste are often joined,
Than from republican ingratitude.
For how shall art have that which is its due
Where every nerve strains in the race for wealth,
Which, being won. is not laid out for art
Nor aught that will ennoble, but for dress
And gay equipages — mere brainless show,
Incongruous with true democracy?
Nay, how shall art receive its just reward
Where honest worth, willing to serve the state,
Spurns the political and slimy rungs
That lead up to a short authority? —
Where foul corruption, listless to rebuke,
Veiled by the shadow of the Capitol,
Stains weak hands with dishonorable gold,
And so makes law?

       It has been truly said
That, lacking art, no nation can be great;
But yet one wholly given up to it
Is a top-heavy ship, not ballasted,
And helpless in the fury of the storm.
But in a baser, more ignoble case,
A nation of mere dollar-getters, warped,
Narrow, sordid — a people such as mine,
Who left me to stand waiting through life's noon,
Through life's high noon, that never comes but once,
And when my sad and only day is spent
Give the commission twenty years delayed.
Why not have handed it forthwith when asked?
Then I had ringed the whole Rotunda round
With painted history, and from the past

Called back a silent Congress to look down
On men — the immortal on the mortal.

But now, too late! The studio is cold,
The landscape on the easel rent across,
The palette broken, the last brush worn out.
All colors fade; for night we know not of
Soon, soon will close the brief, regretful day.
Too late! too late!

DANDELION AND TIGER-LILY.

I.

THE gentle slope of a meadow
　Lay mantled in spring-time green,
And beyond, in the glare of sunlight,
　The sky-rimmed ocean was seen.

A rocky ledge in the meadow
　Towered up with a lichened face,
And a lonely, oft-sighing pine-tree
　Shadily rose from its base.

The meadow was jeweled over
　With the dandelion flower,
And under the boughs of the pine-tree
　There grew a natural bower.

From the distant, spire-crowned village,
　A man in life's young prime
To the rocky, green-roofed seclusion
　Came seeking rest for a time.

A breeze from the lulled Atlantic
　Swayed the grieving pine-tree's bough,

And, caressing each dandelion,
    Kissed softly the comer's brow.

And a breeze from a sea of sorrow
    Swept over his inmost soul:
To branch and flower of his being
    The sighing tenderness stole.

This waft from the isles of music
    Was yearningly sad and sweet;
It murmured along till he voiced it in song
    For the flowers that grew at his feet.

He sang to the dandelions
    That covered the meadow fair,
And they lightly leaned and listened
    To the words of his pale despair.

THE DANDELION.

Dear flower, so meek and humble,
    Most kindly I behold
Thy slender stem and leafless
    Upbear thy yellow gold.

Sweet day-star of the meadow,
    The languid lily knows
The weariness that closes
    Thy petals for repose.

The stars that watch thy slumbers
    Helped warm thee into bloom;
Haply of them thou dreamest
    When curtained in thy room.

Thy room hath silken curtains
    Wherein thou dost abide

When Sleep and Night come sailing
  Across the darkling tide.

Thou lack'st the soul of fragrance
  That hath the rose, thy queen;
Thy soul is globed and downy,
  And at thy death is seen.

Death ends not life, thou showest;
  For thy white, mist-like ghost
Is blown abroad, and wanders
  To distant field and coast.

Yet not beyond the border
  Of this round stage of strife
May thy wan ghost be wafted
  And dwell again with life.

But man has faith, whose pinions
  The starry depths divide,
That he, in worlds he knows not,
  Shall be revivified.

O flowers! O dandelions!
  The flower I love is dead.
Beneath the dandelions
  They made her lonely bed.

I could not see her spirit
  As I might look on thine,
That, soft and light as zephyr,
  Floats in the air divine.

But she is yet before me
  In beauty rich and fair;
Her face is bending over
  Amidst her golden hair.

Her eyes, in depth and luster,
   Outrival star and gem;
She is more lithe and graceful
   Than thou upon thy stem.

She, too, a golden day-star,
   Dreamed of the stars on high,
Closing her jealous curtains
   When Sleep and Night came by.

Alas, the flower-like maiden
   Whom I have loved so well!
Too soon her white soul ripened,
   Too soon life's petals fell.

Yet when the flower had faded,
   And all was tears and dole,
Poised on its stem a moment
   The sphered, departing soul.

A wind of night came sighing,
   And bore the soul afar,
Beyond the world, to waken
   On some seraphic star.

No more my arms enfold her;
   In grief I bow my head.
O flowers! O dandelions!
   The flower I love is dead.

II.

Near the foot of a lofty sierra,
   Whose peak was bound in snow,
Lay a dreamy town of adobé
   In the summer noontide glow;

And in one of the sunny plazas,
  That boasted the city's name,
Was a well in the midst of cacti,
  And hither some maidens came.

Up-drawing the pleasant water,
  That sparkled as winter stars,
On their heads, like Syrian women,
  The bevy set it in jars.

One rose of the dark-eyed garden
  Was lovelier far than the rest;
She bore no jar, and a jewel
  Heaved on her tawny breast.

With her night-like shawl she hooded,
  For a traveler wandered near;
But, out of the folded darkness,
  Upon him she looked with cheer.

"Sweet maid," said the handsome stranger,
  Dismounting at the well,
"Beneath which roof in the plaza
  Does the good alcaldé dwell?"

With a graceful, languid gesture
  That bore an unconscious charm,
She drew the long hood backward,
  With the glimpse of a rounded arm.

She stood, an embodied twilight,
  With fading sunset skies,
And the moon of love, and the star above,
  In the depths of her dusky eyes.

She answered the simple question
  With utterance soft and low,

And the gentle intonations
  Had a longing, melting flow.

"My father is the alcaldé;
  And, if the stranger please,
I will lead the way to the mansion;
  It is yonder, among the trees."

The traveler walked with the maiden,
  And led his dusty beast;
And first to meet them and greet them
  Was a long-robed shaven priest.

The maiden smiled at the omen,
  As it seemed to her throbbing heart;
But was grieved that the manly stranger
  Moved from her slightly apart.

She felt he had read the meaning
  Of her smile and every look,
As if they were lines red-lettered
  In some old, familiar book.

He was tall and of graceful carriage,
  And had black-lashed, deep-gray eyes,
That under his wide sombrero
  Looked eager for bold emprise.

Reproachfully went she nearer
  And glanced at his face above;
For the summits of admiration
  Were touched with the dawn of love.

The stranger entered the mansion
  And its court of tropic green,
Where a warm New-Mexican welcome
  Was given with stately mien.

For the much-beloved alcaldé
  Was glad, he said, to behold
The son of a faithful comrade
  In the wandering days of old.

Dull gray were the walls of the building;
  But white were the rooms within,
And a crucifix over a mantel
  Was hung for the healing of sin.

While Hospitality, sitting
  In the midst of a lavish store,
Filled the house with her plenteous sunshine
  That had lighted it oft before.

And the joy of the good alcaldé,
  Her thoughts not daring to phrase,
Disclosed to the guest her favor
  In tenderly winning ways.

That night, on his arm close-leaning,
  In the moonlit garden air,
She rested against his shoulder
  Her crown of lustrous hair.

But a vision rose before him
  Of the love that used to be,
With the form so fair and the golden hair
  That he saw by the distant sea.

And tears in the blue eyes gathered,
  That drew him reluctant away
From the breathing flower of enchantment
  That close to his shoulder lay.

For his cold good-night was spoken
  At once, with a shrinking start,

And the maiden still lacked a token
  To gladden her loving heart.

But he dreamed of her long black lashes,
  And the gloss of a raven tress ;
For the dream was veined with the love contained
  In the soft, repulsed caress.

III.

He rose in the sultry weather ;
  The sun was soaring high,
And the pathed court under his window
  Lay smiling up at the sky.

There glistened a spraying fountain
  With green luxuriance round,
And tiger-lilies were blooming
  In a beam of the star-shaped ground.

They lifted their red-gold trumpets
  As they stood in close array,
And with swarthy silence saluted
  The ruler of shining day.

The guest, beholding their splendor,
  By the voice of his heart was told
That more than the dandelion's
  Is the tiger-lily's gold.

For he saw in the tiger-lilies
  The gracious similitude
Of the tawny, motherless maiden.
  Whose favor had come unwooed.

At eve she came from vespers,
  With her prayer-book, like a saint,

And, alone in her room in the twilight gloom,
  With tears made mute complaint.

While they yet fell salt and grievous,
  A curtain was drawn aside,
And the frank request of the favored guest,
  To speak, was not denied.

His kiss on her hand brought succor
  To the hopes that had fought her fears,
And she brushed away the uncounted
  Pearl rosary of her tears.

The young man spoke: "Senorita,
  'I love you' is simply said;
As I say it to one that is living,
  I said it to one that is dead.

"Far away where the wild Atlantic
  Rolls white on New England's shore,
In a kindly village I met her
  Whom morning shall waken no more.

"Green, green lay the earth about us,
  And the meadow with flowers was fair;
For the gold of the dandelion
  Was like my loved one's hair.

"Her eyes were the skies of azure,
  Her voice was the woodbird's song,
And the radiant love she gave me
  Was a river deep and strong.

"But she faded away to a spirit
  That often I yet behold;
Her eyes are upturned and peaceful,
  Her hair is fluttering gold.

" She dwells on a star, and softly
    Descends on its limpid ray,
To float as a song where I journey along
    The irretraceable way.

" From the scene of my Eastern passion,
    The prairie wilds across
I came to forsake my sorrow,
    The shadow of bitter loss.

" When first I beheld you I loved you,
    And the shadow was turned away;
But what of my dead love's spirit?
    Must I bear its scorn for aye?

" Will it scorn me, and harm you for taking
    The place in my life it possessed?
It may be that my love brings sorrow;
    But here it shall stand confessed.

" I warred at first with its coming,
    And bade it forever depart,
Lest a shaft from the quiver of evil
    Might find its way to your heart.

" For if *she* had lived on, and *my* spirit
    Kept watch and ward of her life,
Would *I* be content and unangered
    To see her another's wife?

" I know not. I know that I love you."
    As her hand in his own he pressed,
Her arm round his neck stole fondly,
    And drew his head to her breast.

And she said, with a voice whose music
    Flowed clear as a rock-sourced stream,

"The living should live for the living,
    For the dead are a fading dream.

"The living should live for the living,
    For the dead, on the further shore,
Are filled with joys immortal,
    And think of this life no more."

IV.

Again queen Sleep ascended
    Her sable, starry throne,
And her heavy, indolent empire
    About its base lay prone.

She lifted her downy scepter
    With closed and weary eyes,
And opened the gates of dreamland
    Where her poppied meadow lies.

The elves and fairies came tripping
    Across the fantastic green;
The clown and harlequin jested,
    And columbine danced between.

The dead with the living mingled,
    And time was rolled away;
For in dreamland is no to-morrow,
    Nor yesterday, nor to-day.

Thus rapt, the town of adobé
    Lay shut in the hand of night;
And the moon's impalpable silver
    Clad roof and wall with white.

All deeply dark were the shadows,
    And, like another of these,

A Nav'ajo lithe, broad-shouldered,
  Crept onward by sure degrees.

He stole along through the plaza
  Till, the door of the mansion found,
His summons startled the echoes
  That loudly repeated around.

He said to the proud alcaldé,
  "One day my life you saved.
Your mercy to-night I come to requite,
  And much for this have I braved.

"As glad to reward a kindness
  As I am to avenge a wrong,
My arrows are swift and deadly,
  And the love in my heart is strong.

"Twice a hundred fierce Apaches
  On the war-path start to-day,
And are coming down the canyon
  To rob your people and slay.

"The Utes and Navajos promise
  To meet and battle the foe,
That will hasten back, as a frightened pack
  Of howling coyotes go."

In the dusk of the day that followed,
  The red-skinned allies came ;
And their camp-fires, round the plaza,
  Were a girdle jeweled with flame.

Three hundred armed and painted
  Were mounted at break of day,
And the Navajo with the white guest
  Rode in the van away.

Three hundred dusky allies
  Rode out in the dewy morn,
And many an Indian maiden
  Was doomed to live forlorn.

The good alcaldé's daughter
  Sat at her window alone,
And, seeing the armed departure,
  Drooped with a piteous moan.

But the Utes and Navajos, valiant,
  Rode onward till lost to view,
And came to the silent canyon
  Where the sensitive aspens grew.

The fir and the pine cast shadows
  Down the slopes of the great divide,
While a sorrowful wind, like a soul that had sinned,
  In the resinous branches sighed.

All the lonely length of the valley
  A stream of melted snow
Wound gulfward. a pale-blue ribbon,
  With a silken sound and flow.

Between white-hooded sierras
  The awful canyon lay,
The bed of a mighty river
  Whose waters had shrunk away.

Two days the leader-like pale-face
  And the warriors followed the trail,
And they reached the sides of the canyon
  That it seemed no foot might scale.

Here the frightened stream rushed toward them
  As white as the face of fear;

And an eagle, in widening circles,
    Flew up from his covert near.

At the mouth of the league-long narrows,
    Like a dragon's out-thrust tongue
Stretched a plain, where, in deep, lush grasses,
    The bells of flowers were swung.

The trail led up the canyon
    And clung to its rocky side.
What was it thereon descending
    That the pale-face first descried?

He looked from a jutting bowlder
    And knew the Apaches came.
The westering sun was sinking
    Like a giant world aflame.

The Ute and the Navajo allies
    Returned from the open space,
And in a gorge of the mountain
    Encamped in a hidden place.

They saw the distant Apaches
    Arrive on the flowery plain,
And betimes for the night in the shadowy light
    A restful bivouac gain.

How soothingly thou dost silence,
    O Night! the discord and jar,
And manacle with thy darkness
    The violent hands of war.

Give sleep to the seeker for glory,
    And dreams that angels devise;
For a night that is deeper than thou art
    To-morrow may darken his eyes!

v.

Ere from the dim horizon
    The darkness had yet withdrawn,
The day like a bride forthcoming
    Was seen in its veil of dawn.

The Ute and the Navajo army
    Moved down, in the early breeze,
To the green plain's southerly border
    Of rustling cotton-wood trees.

Therein a watchful Apache
    Fired an echoing shot of alarm.
With fierce surprise in their fearless eyes
    The camp awoke to arm.

They ran for their tethered horses,
    Tho' flying arrow and ball
Fell'd some of them near, while other
    At the neighing goal must fall.

Yet the many in safety mounted,
    And, swarming like angry bees,
Charged, yelling and whipping with fury,
    On the deadly cotton-wood trees.

But, meeting a flight of arrows,
    The squadron divided in twain;
For some of the steeds were wounded,
    And some of the riders slain.

Each brave bore a petted rifle,
    A steel friend true and tried;
And he fired it with deadly damage
    As he rode on his horse's side.

Each face was striped with vermilion,
　And plumes and trappings were red;
The sun rose savage and fiery,
　And dark as the pools by the dead.

But the Utes and the Navajos fiercely
　Resisted the charge of the foe,
Tho' the sting of Apache rifles
　Laid many a warrior low.

Wherever the war blazed densely
　The pale-face battling rode;
His roused, swift blood was a risen flood,
　And his gray eyes burned and glowed.

Two frowning storm-clouds, meeting
　With volleying bursts of fire,
Clash loud with bellowing thunder,
　And the strife is vivid and dire.

So clashed the band of defenders
　With their fell Apache foe,
And the rifle-shots rolled and thundered
　Through the canyon to and fro.

Now, from her heights descending,
　Came Victory, flushed and proud,
And hovered over the battle
　Like sunshine over the cloud.

She led the charging Apaches,
　As if fain to become their guide;
But, when doubting they stood at the verge of the wood,
　She ran to their enemies' side.

Long, long in the wood raged the battle,
　For the foemen fought hand to hand.

When the Navajos once retreated,
  The unyielding Utes made a stand.

They pressed the baffled Apaches
  From the wood to the open plain,
And fired at the red invasion
  From ghastly ramparts of slain.

The pale-face, as in a vision,
  Saw Victory waiting near,
A brilliant, masterful goddess,
  Majestic, brave, and austere.

She carried the branch of a palm-tree,
  And laurel leaves wreathed her head;
There were praise and joy in her coming,
  But her steps with slaughter were red.

Her sandals were gold, and her garment
  To the movement of limb was free,
While her face for its firmness and patience
  Was honor and glory to see.

The pale-face glanced at his shoulder,
  And knew for the first that it bled;
But he still to the foe dealt carnage and woe,
  Tho' his steed at his feet lay dead.

He cheered as he saw the Apaches
  Disordered flee to the plain;
Yet they turned, with a desperate rally,
  And wildly re-charged; but in vain.

For the Utes and their allies, maddened,
  Were tireless to do and to dare,
And hurled, from the steeds advancing,
  The might and main of despair.

The pale-face saw Victory running
  From one to the opposite side,
As if at a loss, in the turmoil and toss,
  With whom it were right to abide.

But while the few scathless Apaches
  Still doggedly held to the fight,
Above and between the two forces
  Victory paused in her flight.

She stooped, her sandal to fasten,
  And her right hand reached and found
Her raised right foot; but the movement
  Had swerved her body around.

Thus postured, staggering, falling,
  Her form on the balustrade
Of the temple, Athena Nike,
  The Greeks in marble displayed.

And now, when she lost her balance,
  As on one foot poised she had stood,
She fell as a gift to her lovers
  That fought on the edge of the wood.

Giving palm and crown to the pale-face,
  He felt on his cheek her breath;
But he sank to the earth in darkness,
  And lay by the river of death.

O sister to Strength and Valor,
  And daughter of Titan and Styx,
Was it well, with this draught of thy nectar,
  So bitter a potion to mix?

Was it done to avenge the spirit
  With golden semblance of hair,
For that the new love of her lover
  Was more than her heaven could bear?

VI.

The guest of the proud alcaldé,
  That fell in the surly fray,
In the weird and ghostly silence
  On the shore by the river lay.

No light in the night about him
  Showed either earth or sky,
While beneath was a deeper darkness,
  With darkness weltering by.

It seemed to him there by the river
  That a thousand years had passed,
When, dim and afar, a glimmering star
  Pierced the black shadow at last.

The star waxed larger and brighter,
  And shone in one broadening ray
That sharply parted the darkness,
  But scattered it never away.

As the light of a boat on the water
  Sends down a dagger-like gleam,
The light of this boat of heaven
  Pierced deathward its silvery beam.

And a spirit of light and beauty,
  Appareled in sanctified white,
Emerged from the star, and descended
  The depths of the desolate night.

She came on the ray, with no movement
  Of wing, or of foot or hand,
And was borne, by her calm volition,
  From the bright to the shadowy land.

She was white as the downy spirit
  Of the dandelion flower,
And seemed as if lightly wafted
  From the lonely Atlantic bower.

About her head a nimbus
  Of golden, floating rays
Was the glorious hair that the angels wear,
  To the dreamer's enraptured gaze.

That templed and palaced city,
  Her thoughts, with her past in fee,
In her soft blue eyes was mirrored,
  Like Venice in azure sea.

The spirit stood over the dreamer
  In the glow of the star-sent light,
And tenderly low was her voice, and its flow
  As a song's on the water at night:

"O loved one that still dost wander
  The whirled earth's dreary round,
I lament thee here by the river,
  Life's uttermost mundane bound.

"I lament thy painful danger
  And the ebb of thy fearless blood,
And grieve that thy fate hath brought thee
  So close to the sorrowful flood.

"I looked from the star and beheld thee
  With the maiden of midnight hair,
And to see thine arms enfold her
  Was a bitterness hard to bear.

"To see thine arms about her
  To thy troth and my love seemed wrong;
    14

While the feeling that I was forgotten
  Trailed like a serpent along.

" By thee, whom I love, I was wounded,
  Tho' the suffering left no scar ;
But I wished thee to die, and to meet me on high
  In yonder luminous star.

" Experience broadens forever ;
  And the selfish dross and the clay
In the crucible of that moment
  Were purged from my love away.

" For soon I fully forgave thee ;
  The love that is pure is wide ;
And I know that my joy will deepen
  When thou art wed to thy bride.

" But the Powers of the Universe ever
  Hold the cause of the wronged in trust,
And repay with an equal evil
  Whatever they deem unjust.

" Yet fate, that I fought, to save thee
  From the path that thou would'st pursue,
Hath carried thy life through the perilous strife,
  And given thee victory too.

" Thy hurt is the retribution
  For that I was wounded sore ;
But thy fate now draws thee backward
  To life and the light once more."

Thus she spoke, and ascended softly
  The silvery path of the ray,
As the soul of the dandelion
  At a breath is lifted away.

And the star and the darkness faded
  In light that seemed suddenly born,
As the orbs of the firmament vanish
  In the opulent gift of morn.

VII.

Looking down on the tiger-lilies
  That grew in the court beneath,
Sat the joy of the kind alcaldé,
  Twining a delicate wreath—

A wreath of love for her lover,
  Of endearing thoughts and dreams,
The redolent flowers that the sunniest hours
  Bring forth with their ardent beams.

For the faithful Navajo wildly
  That day appeared at the door,
And told, to the pale astonished,
  His tale of battle and gore.

There had been, of the Utes and his people,
  A daring moiety slain;
But never a score of Apaches
  Escaped from the canyon's plain.

The pale-face fought like the giants
  That, of old, hurled bowlders down,
And he with his brave, red comrades
  Was riding back to the town.

But he and others were wounded,
  And some of them scarce alive:
It might be midnight or morrow
  Ere the burdened troop would arrive.

The good alcaldé's daughter
  Sat rapt in a waking dream,
And was borne, in her song of the brave and strong,
  On melody's plaintive stream :

THEY ARE BRINGING THE WOUNDED HOME.

They are bringing the wounded home
  From the field of havoc afar ;
The feet of the horses are slow ;
  But my love is the light of a star,
And crosses the distance between.
  I look on my loved one's face,
That is paled by a crimson loss :
  If he die, I would be in his place.

They are bringing the wounded home ;
  But Victory's glittering wings
Enlighten the honored return,
  And the heart in my bosom sings ;
For my lover is brave and true,
  And fought like a king in the fray :
He rose as the sun in his might,
  And the battle-mist vanished away.

They are bringing the wounded home ;
  But the print of the hoofs is red.
O steed of my lover, be strong,
  And warily, tenderly tread.
Bear him safely home to my arms,
  As lightly as waves bear the foam.
To healing and waiting and hope,
  They are bringing my hero home.

The loving melody ended
  In the low, dim glow of the west ;

But the singer's fears, like darkness,
　Gloomed in her passionate breast.

A trample of hoofs at midnight
　Was heard in the plaza below,
And the town, for the fortunate victors,
　Was quickly with welcome aglow.

The jubilant bells rang music
　From the belfry holy and high,
And waves of huzzas surged upward,
　While bonfires lighted the sky.

For the guest and the tiger-lily
　Soon came betrothal and feast,
And the service was said, when the lovers were wed,
　By the bride's good omen, the priest.

THE GIANT SPIDER.

PART FIRST.

OF the strict god called Science, in my youth
I had enthusiasm and a gift.
About the lives of winged and creeping things
I was most curious; and having heard
That in gray Caffa, or its ancient tombs,
A giant spider balked the snares of men,
Thither I went, and in the city dwelt.

The simple folk wagged heads incredulous
Of what I asked to know; but ere the moon,
A crescent at my coming, changed to full,
I chanced, at sunset, on a fisherman
Leaning against his stranded prow: he looked

As gray and melancholy as the sea.
In answer to my question, which had trod
On smiling salutation's awkward heels,
He said that he had seen my quest's desire.
He thought the spider larger than a man,
And that the cord it spun might serve for rope
To hoist the boat's lateen impatience with.
At night belated on the tumuli
That make the hillside sloping to the shore
A page of raised, archæological words
For the blind gropers of to-day to read,
He entered wearily an empty tomb,
And slept therein, until defeated night,
Warding the thrown spears of advancing day
With the round world's upheld, emblazoned shield,
Retreated, facing its continual war.
So seemed the conflict in his dream: he woke,
And found that in thick cords he lay ensnared;
But reached his knife, and slowly cut them through.
Then, from the lighted outlet of the tomb,
A horror fled on sideways-working legs.

Back from the beach, and nestling in a glen,
A vine-clad cottage, under heavy eaves,
Looked seaward with a set, expectant gaze,
As some lone watcher with hand-shaded eyes
Looks thither for the unreturning sail.
Here dwelt my helper to the spidery news.
Trees, and a varied garden full of flowers,
Sequestered and perfumed the verdant cot.
Like Ahab in his house of ivory,
Dining on tasteful pleasures rich and rare,
The bee, in casual pollen robed and crowned,
Sipped in the snowy lily's palace hall.
And there lay yellow lilies strewn about,
As if the place had been the banquet grove
Of Shishak, king of Egypt; for the flowers

Were like the cups of gold that Solomon
Wrought for the service of the only God.
Out of the cottage, through the garden came,
Like spring, but breathing a diviner air,
A maiden with a violet in her hand.
" This is my daughter," said the fisherman.
Her jacket glistened with a golden fringe ;
The hound-like sea-breeze, romping by her side,
Caught up her sash, and let it fall again ;
Her broidered skirt drooped loosely to her knees ;
The silken, Turkish trousers hung below,
Their fullness at the ankles gathered in ;
But the red, toe-curved shoes betrayingly
Left her arched insteps naked as the moon.
A scarf enswathed her head, and masked her face ;
But large, dark eyes looked forth, and in their depths
I viewed a soul of tenderness and truth.
So first I met this unexpected May,
On the Cimmerian Bospore's fateful shore.
I saw light laughter dancing in her eyes
At my mistaken uses of their tongue.
We lingered round the cot a flowery hour,
Then entered, and, refreshed with grateful fare,
Made music an occasion for delay.
We parted in the garden under boughs,
And as I hurried homeward, light with hope,
I still beheld her softly-speaking eyes,
Which in my heart shone down like two clear stars
Set in the boundless heaven of her soul.

Thenceforth, day after day, I went to meet
The dark-eyed daughter of the fisherman.
She welcomed me beneath her trustful roof ;
The scarf, that veiled the splendor of her face,
She drew away, and laid her hands in mine.
Her eyes were diamond portals arched and pure,
And Sleep their silken latches softly closed

When, couched beneath his poppy parachute,
He wooed her, leaning from his dusky car.
As angels issue out of heaven's gates,
So, swift and bright, her glances, full of love,
Streamed from the sunny portals of her soul.
If painter or if sculptor should behold,
Upon a summit of that spiritual world
He treads with visionary, faltering feet,
Faith, Hope, and Charity in outward forms,
And give them concrete likeness in one face,
I know that it would be a face like hers.

Yet she at times was sad when I was near,
And when, embracing her, I asked the cause,
She said she sorrowed at their low estate,
At fortune dwindled low, and at the yoke
Their people chafed their necks in, on the hills.
Her father was a great Circassian chief;
But here, in dress and work, he dwelt disguised,
Till he again could lead his tribes to war,
And raise the heel that ground them to the dust.
To confidence there was, in my reply,
A silken clew: on this at once she seized,
And said that unknown evil threatened her.
Forerunning shadows of approaching doom
Darkened the parks and gardens of her mind,
So late familiar with the feet of joy.
She felt she was entangled in a web;
For tightening cords were drawn about her life,
And not on any side would give release.
I tarried late, and told her of my past,
And of the monster I had come to find;
But now, even she, of whom I had not dreamed,
Around my heart had cast a web of love.
She said that she too in this web was bound,
But could escape not from that darker web
Woven about her by the spider, Fate.

Our hearts renewed, we parted ere the dawn,
And, at our lips, love met deliciously
His clinging counterpart. the answering love.
As from the garden shore I homeward went,
I saw against the sky a distant hill,
Whose outlines, merged in darkness, took the shape
Of an immense black spider : its raised arms,
That I remembered were by day two trees,
Caught vainly at a gleaming, firefly star.

PART SECOND.

An early knuckle smote against my door.
I rose and opened to the fisherman ;
For it was he — his face as white as death's,
His eyes insanely glaring, and his hair
Tossed up as if abhorrent with his fear.
"Come, hasten with me," were his boding words.
We ran along the morning road and shore,
And breathless reached the silence of his house.
He led me to his daughter's vacant couch.
The single window of the favored room
Was open, and I looked out to the ground.
On the low cottage's gray, crannied side
A vine with tapering fingers clung and crept,
And, latticing the window, curtained it
With drooping, heart-shaped leaves. But what was this
That, fastened to the ledge, trailed to the earth ?
A glutinous rope, twisted with five strong strands.
Fright, like a wild wind, rushed on me, and whirled
And bore me like a leaf, as I, with bloodless lips,
Gasped out, " The Spider ! "

                    What was best to do ?
We saw strange vestiges along the beach ;
But these were lost beside a marshy dell
Where all trace had an end. The long day through,

Up from the dell we searched among the tombs;
But unrewarded, 'when the sun was quenched,
Sat wearily down, and gave ourselves to tears.
Then by a slender thread the darkness dropped,
And, like an awful spider, o'er the earth
Crawled with gaunt legs of shadow : soon we rose
And sought our homes, to meet again at dawn.

The night was warm, and with the window raised,
I sat, and Job-like cursed my natal day
And, filled with grief and horror, wrung my hands.
Without a light, the house in darkness stood.
My back was toward the window : something shut
The puny sheen of starlight from the room.
The Thing, a monstrous shape, was with me there;
Its two hard arms were thrown about my waist,
And in them I was carried lightly forth.
Benumbed, I had no voice to make a cry,
Nor moved to cast my foe off, bound by fear
No less than by the giant spider's arms.
Then I grew glad thinking I should be borne
To the dull creature's web, and there, mayhap,
Learn the dread fate of her I loved so well.
Ere long we neared the hill whose two tall trees,
Like spider's arms, clutched at the fire-fly stars.
Up the stark cliff we went, and crossed the web
Just as the full moon bloomed upon the verge,
And lilied white the Panticapean vale.

The funnel of the web was in the mouth
Of a vast tomb, whose outside, hewn on rock,
Outlined a Gorgon's face with jaws agape —
Medusa, Stheno, or Euryale,
Changed to the stone that, in the elder time,
She changed the sons of men who looked on her.
Then, through the funnel, into the tomb we went.
Round me the spider quickly drew his cords,

Binding my arms, while I resistlessly
Drooped on the rock, inured to ugly fear.
I fancied that I now was safe till dawn.
If I could use my hands, I might lay hold
On club or stone, and wield a chance for life.
Pinioned, I drew my arms along my sides,
And struggled till at last I wrenched them free ;
But both hung harrowed by the twisted bonds
That with my blood were wet.

                    The dread night drag'd ;
But at the glimpses of auroral gray,
A faint moan woke an echo in the tomb.
The echo, like a pitying answer, came
For solace to the moan ; the light increased,
And I descried, not far from where I lay,
A maiden sitting : of her thick, long hair
She made a raven pillow, as she leaned
Against the gloom of that memorial wall.
My heart threw wide to her its doors, my arms.
She too, as I had been, was closely bound ;
But I undid, in part, her sticky cords.

The sun came up and spread his cloth of gold
Over the world : we saw the vale and sea,
And there the ancient city's skeleton
Protrude, with rib-like columns, from its grave.
We watched the folk, mere ants, move here and there
Within the modern town, and pointed out,
Not knowing we should enter it again,
The billowy grove wherein her cottage stood.

Two thousand years ago this outspread sea
Was whitened by the snowy flakes of trade
That fly from land to land along the tides.
When Athens was, and when her scholars cut,
With thoughts unrusting, their exalted names

On the stone tablet of slow-footed fame,
A city flourished here, and from the gates
Its thrifty, wheaten surplus sent abroad.
For centuries, like some majestic star,
The city waxed and waned; now shining large
With Eastern splendor and magnificence,
Now into occultation fading back,
With naught but ruins of its greatness left.
It felt the undermining wrongs of peace,
And was acquainted with the wrong of war,
And these destroyed its power; for all wrong
Crawls like a giant spider through the world,
And blights the cities where it weaves its web,
And buries men in tombs of dark despair.

While we looked forth on this past-haunted view,
We saw the subtle spider throw his cord
Over an eagle tangled in the web.
With what of strength was left, the eagle fought,
And spread one wing, and darted its sharp beak.
At last the spider seized it by the neck
With his serrated claws, which grew like horns,
And bit it dead; then plucked the vanquished plumes,
And sucked the warm blood from the sundered ends.
This showed us that the monster brought us here
To be a hideous banquet, and that one
Must needs be near and see the other slain.

The web was like the sail of some large ship,
And reached out from the Gorgon's open mouth
To boughs of blighted trees on either side.
Birds were caught in it: and, about the place
Wherein the spider hid to watch for prey,
Their bones lay bleaching in the fervid sun.
On the strong web the winds laid violent hands,
And tugged amain; but had no sinew knit
To tear it, or divorce it from its place.

The rain left on it, when the sun came out,
Dyed the vast cloth with gay, prismatic hues,
And made it glitter like the silken wings
Of Cleopatra's barge.

                We felt quite sure
The eagle's death bequeathed us lease of life.
In hope to find an object of defense,
We closely searched about: the tomb was strange,
And secret save to the spider and to us.
A rich sarcophagus stood in the midst,
Of deftly inlaid woods, or carved, or bronzed;
Within, a skeleton (its white skull crowned
With gold bestarred with diamonds) chilled my blood.
A bronze lamp, cast to represent a beast,
The triple-polled conceiver of the Sphinx,
Lay on the floor, and from its lion's mouth
The flame had issued like the flame of life
That flickered and went out from the grim king.
A target hung above. and on it clashed
Trojan and Greek, adverse as right and wrong.
About lay cups of onyx set in gold.
On conic jars were bacchanalian scenes:
Nude, chubby bacchi, grotesque, leering fauns —
All linked beneath the cluster-laden vine;
And in the jars were rings and flowers of gold.
We found twin ear-drops, sapphire Gemini,
Metallic mirrors, and a statuette
Of amorous Dido naked to the waist.
All these we found, but nothing for defense.
A club had been of greater worth than these.
On desert sands a crust is more than gold,
In peril arms, and on the sea a plank;
The moment gives the value to a thing.
Hopeless of any weapon to repel
The loathsome, crawling danger, we embraced,
And kissed with silent kisses mixed with tears,

And waited for the end. Then, for light things,
Like gnats that dance in air before a storm,
Rise in the mind in moments of suspense,
I thought of Italy's tarantula
Whose bite is cured by music, so they say,
And wondered whether love, which ever seems
Like tenderer music than sweet sounds afford,
Had power to heal us from this spider's wounds.

As day was sinking to his crimson death,
With back to us, the savage monster crouched
Upon the cliff at our pale prison's mouth.
His hateful body was a fathom long;
Two parts it had — the fore part, head and breast,
The hinder part, the trunk: the first was black,
The last was furry with short, yellow hair.
Eight sprawling legs to the tough breast adhered;
Eight eyes, that never closed, stared from the head,
Behind their windows of transparent nail.
His pincers stood between his foremost eyes,
Were toothed like saws, were sharp and venomous,
And on their ends had claws; two arms stretched out
From the mailed shoulders, and with these he caught
His tangled prey, or guided what he spun.
Slowly about he turned, and glared at us,
Working his arms, and opening his claws,
Then suddenly moved toward us in attack.
Dismayed, we fled to the sepulchral depths
Where darkness dwelt, and where, as Heaven willed,
My foot on some hard substance struck surprised.
Stooping, I grasped, and found with boundless joy
That sharp, unpitying fang of war, a sword!

I rushed upon the spider as he came,
And with one blow cut off his baneful head.
Awhile he writhed, but, at another stroke,
Drew up the eight long legs and two thick arms,

And, rolling over on his useless back,
Gave up to Geryon his Hadean ghost.

The treasure of the tomb soon brought us wealth,
And the great Tzar, hearing our story told,
Sent us rich wedding-gifts of silk and pearls.

POPLICOLA.

WHEN Roman virtue was aroused,
  And had deposed the kings,
Looking on all their pomp and pride
  As unbecoming things;
When lustful Tarquin's might was crushed
  By all-avenging Fate,
A consul named Valerius,
Wise Publius Valerius,
  Became the head of state.

Against the sky, upon a hill
  Before the forum, rose
His ample, lordly dwelling-house,
  In marble's white repose.
Rome's grave assembly, gazing up,
  Soon made of it a foe;
For, tho' mistrust may not be wise,
They thought the house cast jealous eyes
  On what was done below.

To see come forth Valerius
  With his attendant train,
Their potent rods and axes borne
  As if in high disdain;
To see them then descend the hill
  Before the forum wide,

To doubt and fear, that prate of woe,
It was an ostentatious show
  To regal pomp allied.

It was indeed a stately sight,
  Of which a bard might sing;
But men would have that it was meant
  To shadow forth a king.
They said, too, that the dwelling-house,
  The robed hill's showy crown,
Was lordlier than the palace,
That the consul, out of malice,
  Had sternly leveled down.

Love's shadow is dark jealousy,
  And jealousy knows fear;
For men who love their country much,
  And hold their freedom dear,
Are jealous of the tendencies
  In him they trust with power,
And mark them in his acts, lest he,
On their devoted liberty,
  Should bring a trying hour.

But when the wise Valerius
  Knew what suspicion said,
And that the people, whom he loved,
  Upon him looked with dread,
He sent for many laborers,
  And, in a single night,
Pulled down that pale magnificence,
His stately, marble-walled offense,
  And blotted it from sight.

The people in the morning came,
  And saw that it was gone,
The dwelling-house an architect
  Had lavished beauty on;

And when they knew it was destroyed
  For words that they had said,
They truly mourned, as if it were
A vestal, or a senator,
  That lay untimely dead.

The sight of it was lost to them
  They felt with sense of shame,
And for unfounded jealousy
  They held themselves to blame.
Through these light mists of kind regret
  Their consul's rising star
Shone in the Roman mental sky
Like daily Phœbus mounting high
  In his triumphal car.

Valerius now owned no roof;
  But dwelt with gentle friends
Until the people, with respect,
  Had hewn him stone amends.
They built the doored and windowed gift
  To lodge their servant in,
All seemly to their rigid will;
But not upon the haughty hill
  Where his offense had been.

They bear the palm and rule the best
  Who wish to truly serve,
And nothing from this meek intent
  Could make the consul swerve.
He hoped to found a government
  Men would not overturn,
And that to virtue would be dear:
He made it pleasant, pure, and near;
  Not distant, proud, and stern.

He mingled with the people all
  To learn the common will,
15

And ever deemed its finer sense
  His duty to fulfill.
He was familiar, kind, and true
  To every one that came ;
He strove to mete out justice due;
And all the winds of heaven blew
  The trumpet of his fame.

Surrounded by his civic guard,
  He to the forum went,
Whenever the assembly met
  For acts of government.
On entering he bowed his head,
  And, to the left and right,
His axes parted from his rods,
And homaged, as it were the gods,
  The sovran People's might.

Yet was the man's humility
  The noble means he took,
Not, as men thought, to dwarf himself
  For reputation's book ;
But to disarm their doubts and fears,
  So quick to rise and frown —
To give the factious murmur sleep,
And, by a wise forbearance, keep
  The dragon, envy, down.

For envy comes from ignorance,
  Which sees the outward show,
And lightly thinks of heavy cares
  That with high office go.
Hence bad men climb to power, and glut
  The ways that lead to it.
With venal hands they foul its stream,
And cause reproach to make it seem
  For moral health unfit.

The honor of Valerius
　　Was sweet to every lip.
He gave the right to citizens
　　To sue for consulship;
Yet ere he would a colleague take,
　　Lest one might thwart the cause,
Or bring delay where none should be,
He built a house for Liberty,
　　Of just and equal laws.

He made it death to seize on power
　　Without the people's leave.
He raised offenders one more hope
　　Their freedom to retrieve;
The sentence that the consuls gave
　　The people might relax;
And, brave with either sword or pen,
He freed the poorer citizen
　　Of an excessive tax.

What thus from his authority
　　He wisely took away
He added to his real power,
　　Which in the people lay;
For they submitted willingly,
　　And showed their happy state
By naming him Poplic-ola,
Republican Poplicola,
　　Or People-lover Great.

Poplicola! Poplicola!
　　Reëchoes in the air.
Across the silent centuries
　　I hear fame's trumpet blare;
Across wide wastes of slavery,
　　Time's dusty deserts vast,
Across the heat, the dearth, the shame,

Comes sounding down the honored name,
  From out the ruined past.

I see its way along the years;
  I see how pomp and pride
Have robbed the people of their rights
  And turned the truth aside.
In crowned oppression's bloody work
  To rivet servile chains,
I see the fight for freedom sway,
I see the triumph and dismay,
  The losses and the gains.

What wonder that when, sere with age,
  The grand old Roman died
The people deeply felt the debt
  They owed this faithful guide?
The flowers he found on freedom's heights
  They scattered round his bier.
The shadow of their loss was dark,
For, as his special honor-mark,
  All women mourned a year.

He slept entombed in Velia,
  Within the walls of Rome;
And when, of his posterity,
  One reached the common home,
The mourners set the body down
  Where its great kinsman lay,
Then held a torch the bier beneath;
And with this flower from honor's wreath,
  They bore their dead away.

They showed that honor follows not
  From sire to son along.
Few men can rule by love and truth,
  The most have ruled by wrong.

Not birth, but nature, makes men great;
   True greatness is divine.
It bursts the bars of humble blood,
And streams not in a constant flood
   Along a royal line.

O Liberty! that on our land
   Hast seemed to kindly smile,
Oh! let not wealth and pride of place
   Men's hearts from thee beguile;
But make our rulers each like him
   Who knew thy way to plan,
Poplicola Valerius,
Republican Valerius,
   In very truth a man!

THE EMPEROR'S MERCY.

WHEN Theodosius, who ruled the land,
Had laid exactions, deemed too hard to bear,
On Antioch, angry revolt was planned,
And, hoarsely surging to the public square,
The folk dashed on the statues of the crown,
The ruler's and his wife's, and broke them down.

But when the tide of fury ebbed away,
Upon all hearts there lay a stranded dread;
The people sorrowed for their deed that day,
And on thought's canvas saw their danger spread.
A somber painter, born of fault, is fear,
That magnifies the ills it makes appear.

So Bishop Flavianus, strong of pen,
In truth a poet, but who humbly found
That he of greater use could be to men
In preaching Christ than if with laurel crowned,

Left Antioch, and hasted on his way,
The ruler's wrath to soften and allay.

He reached Constantinople, and was led
Before the emperor, who heard his plea:
"We place a wreath on even the wicked dead;
Since wrong, repented of, no more can be,
On our dead wrong let now thy pardon rest,
Like wreathen roses on a lifeless breast."

With darkened look the ruler made reply:
"In breaking down the statues, your mad throng
Have reared another to the angry sky —
The black, colossal statue of a wrong!
This shall abide the fury of my hate!
I am resolved: my word is law and fate."

With saddened soul the bishop turned away;
But, knowing that, of boys with harps, a choir
Before the emperor made glad the day,
While he reclined at meat, there came desire,
Through these, the singers, to renew his plea,
And with a song the threatened city free.

Straightway, with loving care, he wrote an ode —
Glad that, at last, to turn the wheel of use,
The sparkling brook of his clear numbers flowed.
"That art is best," he said, "which can induce
To serviceable ends: of old, art's kings
Were fain to do good work on useful things."

The rhyme was finished, and the gliding words
Launched on a sea of music, whose sweet tone
Was like the twilight notes of woodland birds;
And when from off his golden-curtained throne,
The ruler came to feast, like seraphim
The choir with harps took up the song for him.

They sang the wrong and fears of Antioch,
And of the might that mercy gives to kings;
They woke, with fingers swift, a flying flock,
The fine compassion of the trembling strings.
The ruler cried, " Oh, cease your plaintive song,
For I forgive the city of the wrong ! "

LOW LIVES WE LED OF CARE AND SIN.

Low lives we led of care and sin,
And had no aim but that to win
  Our brown and bitter bread.
Beside a mountain, at its base,
We dwelt, and saw its passive face,
  A sphinx's, overhead.

We could not read a meaning there.
To our dull eyes, what rose in air
  Was naught but rocks and trees.
We had not climbed the cloudy height;
Enough for us the small delight
  To sit betimes at ease.

What good were ours, if we should stand
Upon the wind-swept table-land,
  And look on fields below?
We sneered, contented in the vale;
We had nor will nor wish to scale
  The cliffs where cedars grow.

But haply on a genial day,
A neighbor, plodding on his way,
  Saw, at the sunset hour,
The day-god on our mountain high
Rest, like a golden butterfly
  Perched on an azure flower.

Our least impressions have their use;
The good or ill that they produce
  Must soon or late befall.
And our observant neighbor said,
"It may be fertile overhead
  Upon the mountain-wall."

Forthwith we climbed the flinty crags,
And boughs and vines hung like the flags
  Of welcome in a town.
On vernal plains we wandered by
Clear lakes wherein the bending sky
  Narcissus-like looked down.

Even the grass beneath our feet
Was somewhat greener and more sweet
  Than that which grew below.
We breathed a purer, better air;
Our lives seemed wider and most fair,
  And earth with love aglow.

O ye, long used to care and sin,
Look up! take heart! and strive to win
  A high and noble ground!
Think not that Virtue sits alone,
Withdrawn on peaks of ice and stone
  Where only thorns abound.

She rather has the mountain dells
Where, with her kin, in peace she dwells.
  Her sky is ever fair;
And in her pleasant, quiet meads
The flowers of fragrant thoughts and deeds
  Enrich the healthful air.

THE HOST'S HUMILITY.

HUMILITY is the excess of love
We have for others — if that be excess
Which He, who for our help came from above
And wore our humbler nature, loved to bless;
But Envy is the coward side of Hate,
And all her ways are bleak and desolate.

Nathan, a wise man, who had nursed with care
A tree of trade that bore sufficient coin,
Lived not alone for self, but thought to share
His wealth with others; so at once to join
His thought to action, where two highways crossed
He reared a palace, fair and white as frost.

Here, food he laid, and smooth wine made to flow
For all who came from either east or west;
Beggars were not too base for him to know,
And each was served as an invited guest;
And when at last there came the parting day,
He gave them gifts, and saw them on their way.

From these mere springs, his fame in rivers flowed,
And proud Mithridanes, not taking heed
That charities, when done for praise, corrode
And lose their virtue, thought that each good deed
He too might do and win as high renown,
For Nathan's name was better than a crown.

So he too built a palace, wide and high,
And clad it with the banners of his land;
The prosperous towers touched the golden sky,
The cooling fountains tossed on either hand:
And this, and Nathan's palace, seemed to be
Let down from heaven for works of charity.

But proud Mithridanes was envious still,
As Nathan's name was held above his own;
And soon he willed to go to him and kill
The generous man, that he, and he alone,
Through the broad world might win the fame he could
For hospitality and doing good.

See how vile Envy may mislead our hearts,
And feed us with unpalatable sin!
Mithridanes for Nathan's door departs,
And, reaching it, with peace is welcomed in;
Even a parrot, up a stairway heard,
Stabs at his envy with a friendly word.

But ere he gained that house munificent
He overtook a graybeard on the road,
And said to him, as by his side he went,
"I go to Nathan and his praised abode."
"I am his servant," said the old man gray:
"I will ride forward with you on your way."

This man was Nathan, tho' unknown to him
Whose deadly purpose slumbered in his breast;
And often in the park, at twilight dim,
They met thereafter, one with gloom oppressed,
And dealt in words so pleasing and so true,
That, from the commerce, wealth of friendship grew.

Here, in the green seclusion of the wood,
The proud guest told the frost-beard that he came
To slay his envied rival great and good —
That, furled by death, the banner of his name
No more should over hill and vale be sent
As the most noble and benevolent.

"That you may do the deed and not be seen,"
Meek Nathan answered, "at the bud of day

Your foe will walk beneath this covert green,
And you may fall on him, and be away
Before his death is bruited: lest in wrath
They should pursue you, flee the mountain-path."

At morn, to slay the host, went forth the guest,
And saw the old man walking 'neath the trees,
The friend that he of all men loved the best.
"Lo, I am Nathan! great Mithridanes;
Here, where the heart is, pierce me to the hilt;
Pause not with fear, but slay me if thou wilt."

Then at his feet the guest fell prone, with tears:
"My dearest father, I was proud and base;
Forgive me, for remorse in after-years
Will rack me, when I think upon thy face!
No more my envy makes a foe of thee,
For I behold thy vast humility."

"Arise!" said Nathan. "Tho' I do forgive,
I need not; for, in wishing to excel,
You have done nothing wrong; proud monarchs live
Who, to be great, have thought it wise and well
To slay whole armies on the field of strife;
But you have only sought my humble life."

The pleasant jewel of good Nathan's face
Shone with the inborn luster of his soul,
As round the other's neck, with loving grace,
His friendly arms in full forgiveness stole;
While coward Envy, as she turned to fly,
Envied the triumph of Humility.

TO RICHARD GRANT WHITE.

ON READING HIS LIFE OF SHAKESPEARE.

I READ your life of Shakespeare late;
  The clock, swift-handed, showed the hour
Of midnight on the numbered plate,
  And yet your cultured page of power
Held my attention captivate.

I seemed to be in Stratford town,
  Our Shakespeare's English Nazareth.
I saw the houses thatched and brown,
  The street whose squalor brought it death.
To my own time the past came down.

I saw the Avon wind and glide,
  And Sir Hugh Clopton's bridge across,
With fourteen arches cool and wide,
  Deep-shadowed in the water's gloss,
Like care that spans some pleasure's tide.

And still the present seemed to me
  The age of Queen Elizabeth.
And on the wall of Trinity
  I saw the painted shape of Death —
The rude, tho' strong, Dance Macabree.

To Shottery I seemed to stray,
  And to the house where Shakespeare went,
In idle hours of youthful May,
  To wed himself to discontent
And that fair shrew Ann Hathaway.

I saw his lampoon on the gate
  Of proud Sir Thomas Lucy's park,

And knew he thus would irritate,
  More than deer-stealing after dark,
The pompous village potentate.

Boy-husband, scarcely twenty-one,
  Yet with three children round his knees,
It was full time the poet won
  From Fortune's wheel the bread for these;
For mouths must eat, and work be done.

And by the magic of your book,
  Which was like something seen, not read,
I saw our Shakespeare as he took
  The road for London from the stead,
And his want-shadowed cot forsook.

And from the Aladdin's lamp he bore,
  I saw his wondrous dramas rise —
Vast palaces of precious store,
  Perfumed with flowers, adorned with dyes
Of thoughts that no man had before.

At Globe or Blackfriars, in his play
  Of "As You Like It," him the part
Of faithful Adam, sere and gray,
  I saw impersonate, with art
As fresh and beautiful as May.

I saw him when he meekly wrote
  With Greene and Marlowe and the rest.
Of his own power he took no note;
  For wounded pride within his breast
He sought a simple antidote —

And that to dwell in Stratford town,
  And live at ease, a gentleman,
By poverty no more held down,

No more beneath that dreadful ban
The village great-man's stony frown.

And so through life the poet passed,
To win a goal of poor pretense;
Like that old sculptor, who once cast,
For low and paltry recompense,
A statue deemed divine at last.

THE PICTURE.

A WIDOW by her landlord was oppressed
To pay at once her backward coin of rent;
For he, cursed by the wealth that should have blessed,
Forgot that he, too, in a tenement
Dwelt, with unpaid arrear; and surely he,
More than the widow, lived in poverty.

For they alone are rich who have obtained
The love of God, for which no gold can pay.
Blind to the peaceful joy he might have gained,
The craven landlord, on a winter's day
That pierced with cold and wind-thrust snow and sleet,
Drove forth the widow to the roofless street.

Her clinging son, with elfin prattle, sought
To charm away her grief; yet, in his heart,
By the indignant pencil of his thought,
The shameful scene was drawn in every part.
There lived the widow's tears, and hard and base
Stood out the likeness to the landlord's face.

Like breaking waves, year after year rolled up,
And in their tide the widow's son became
A truthful painter, in whose life's bright cup
A thankful world dissolved the pearl of fame.

Then, with his brush, which spoke in every hue,
The picture in his heart he strongly drew.

Near to the landlord's home the painting hung,
As at his threshold, in a public place;
To view it came the townsfolk, old and young,
And said, " This is our neighbor's ruthless face,
And this the cruel deed that he has done
To the poor widow and her artist son."

The landlord brought temptations coined and **vast**,
And would have given half the wealthy town,
To lay the brush-raised specter of his past:
No gold availed; the specter would not down;
But haunted him thereafter till he died,
In looks and words and deeds, on every side.

FLOS MORTI.

IN MEMORIAM H. E. O., ÆT. XVII.

MAIDEN, whom I so briefly knew
    That unto me thou art a dream,
A lovely vision lost to view
    Across the dark, relentless stream,

They bring thee final gifts, and one,
    A broken lyre of fragrance deep,
Is symbol of thy life, undone
    By that cold hand whose clasp gives sleep.

They bring thee flowers, who wert a flower
    Above the lily and the rose.
The fading tribute of an hour
    I also bring to thy repose.

This flower of rhyme, this petaled song,
  I give to death, I bring to thee
Whose soul was raised and borne along
  By mystic tides of poësy.

Thou wert thyself a poem true,
  A lasting joy to know and read;
The manuscript is torn in two;
  The rhythmic strain is mute indeed.

So oft, through flowery paths of song,
  Sweet angels led thy thoughts to range
The immaterial world along,
  That heaven can not to thee be strange.

For not to verse wert thou impelled
  By love for praise; but by the stir
Of voices that within thee welled,
  And by thy strength of character.

O loveliness with eyes like night!
  We should not call thee to return
From out the darkness that is light,
  To where our lamps of being burn.

For long and thankless is the path
  Wherein thy tender feet were set;
Thou shalt not know the briers it hath
  On heights beclouded with regret.

On thee Old Age shall lay no hand,
  Friends shall not turn from thee away,
Nor shall Temptation near thee stand,
  Or Disappointment say thee nay.

From Life thou took'st thy rose of youth,
  Which at the beaker's brim was hung;

And in the Heart of love and truth
   Thou shalt abide, forever young.

Not less with us thou still shalt dwell;
   For it is beautiful to be
Enshrined in hearts that love thee well,
   A blest and grateful memory.

THE JEW'S PIETY.

DANGER ennobles duty simply done.
Nicanor, an Alexandrian Jew,
Had traded honestly with every one
Until his spreading tree of fortune grew
Beyond the small, dwarfed stature of his needs,
And each bent bough bore reproducing seeds.

And then, like him who, walking up the way,
Turns round to question him that comes behind,
He, turning, faced his heart and asked one day,
" What shall I make my duty? Fixed, my mind
Demands its aim must now be understood,
For every man should live for some set good."

Thereto his heart made answer, " Lips are fair;
Make two vast doors for lips, and go with them,
And hinge them on the Temple's mouth, that there
They long may name thee to Jerusalem:
With lily-work and palm thy doors be made,
And both with beaten copper overlaid."

In time the lips were wrought, and, with much gain,
He stowed them on a bark, and sailed away,
And saw the land fade forth from off the main.
Beneath the sun, the rippled waters lay

Like the great roof that Solomon of old
Built on the Temple, spiked with goodly gold.

When certain days flew west a storm came up,
And night was like a black and fearful cave
Where Powers of Awe held banquet ; as cloud-cup
Struck waved cloud-cup, the clash deep thunder gave,
And spilled the wine of rain : the thrilling gloom
Was filled with loud but unseen wings of doom.

Then said the master of the worried keel,
" Vile Jew, thy doors are heavy : they must go ! "
Nicanor cried, " Here, at thy feet, I kneel,
And crave of thee to spare them : I will throw
My goods away and gold, my proof of thrift ;
But spare the doors — to God my humble gift.

" Despise me not ; for he that scorns a Jew
Without just cause, himself shall be despised."
Thereat his gains he gathered up and threw
Into the sea, till all were sacrificed
Except his gift ; but still the Pan-like blast
Piped on the reed of each divested mast.

Up spoke the sailors to their master dark :
" We late made mention to our gods of this,
And they require we shall unload the bark
Of the vile Jew and all that may be his."
As the dread judgment meek Nicanor heard,
He radiantly smiled, but said no word.

Into the deep the lofty doors were thrown.
Nicanor prayed, " I put my trust in Thee ! "
And sprang out to the storm, and scaled alone,
'Gainst Death, the rolling rampart of the sea.
He sank and rose ; but, going down once more,
His guided hand seized on a drifting door.

Dripping and weak, he crawled upon his float,
And heard the cry go by, "The ship is lost!"
Then shrieks, death-ended. Swords of storm that smote
Were now soon sheathed, while flags of foam that tossed
Were furled in peace, and good Nicanor found
The lip there kissed the sweet and certain ground.

A cape ran out, a long, rock-sinewed arm
That buffeted the sea, and this had caught
The Jew and both his doors; and free of harm
He stood in dawn's gray surf: stout help he brought,
And going safely inland far and fast,
The gifts were on the Temple hinged at last.

Long centuries succeed, and Herod, king,
Rose to rebuild the Temple: for rough stone,
He reared stone snow, white marble; each pure thing
He beautified. Nicanor's doors alone
Were left. "These," said the wise high-priests, "shall be
For a memorial of piety."

WINTER DAYS.

Now comes the graybeard of the north:
    The forests bare their rugged breasts
To every wind that wanders forth,
    And, in their arms, the lonely nests,
That housed the birdlings months ago,
Are egged with flakes of drifted snow.

No more the robin pipes his lay
    To greet the flushed advance of morn;
He sings in valleys far away;
His heart is with the south to-day;
    He can not shrill among the corn.

For all the hay and corn are down
  And garnered; and the withered leaf,
Against the branches bare and brown,
  Rattles; and all the days are brief.

An icy hand is on the land;
  The cloudy sky is sad and gray;
But through the misty sorrow streams,
  Outspreading wide, a golden ray.
And on the brook that cuts the plain
  A diamond wonder is aglow,
  Fairer than that which, long ago,
De Rohan staked a name to gain.

IN HANGING GARDENS.

In an old city, so the Rabbins say,
Lived a fair lady having youth and wealth,
Who in the hanging gardens, day by day,
Moved through the noiseless paths as still as stealth —
The lofty paths that climbed, the sun to kiss,
Above the pinnacled metropolis.

Here stair on stair with heavy balustrade,
And columned hybrids cut in rigid stone,
And vase, and sphinx, and obelisk, arrayed,
And arched, wide bridges over wheelways thrown.
Valleys of heaven the gardens seemed to be,
Or isles of cloud-land in a sunset sea.

The lady, daughter of some prince or king,
Was sued in love by one of lowly birth.
He gave her gems inclosed in toy or ring,
Trifles of cost, of value for their dearth;
But she was used to greater gifts than these,
And their small beauty failed her heart to please.

She turned away : she did not love him less
For that he gave her what to him was rare ;
She only felt its total nothingness
Beside the jewels she was wont to wear.
She turned, and in the hanging gardens strayed
By drippling fountains in the palmy shade.

The Soul is child of God, and when the World,
Her lover, brings his presents, wealth and fame —
Wealth, a bird jeweled ; fame, a ring impearled —
She is not satisfied : she bears no blame ;
But turns from them to gardens hung in bliss,
The untempled calm of heaven's metropolis.

VERSES IN MEMORY OF GENERAL GRANT.

WHITE wings of commerce sailing far,
  Hot steam that drives the weltering wheel,
Tamed lightning speeding on the wire,
  Iron postman on the way of steel —
These circling all the world, have told
  The loss that makes us desolate ;
For we give back to dust this day
  The God-sent man who saved the state.

When black the sky and dire with war,
  When every heart was wrung with fear,
He rose serene, and took his place,
  The great occasion's mighty peer.
He smote armed opposition down,
  He bade the storm and darkness cease,
And o'er the long-distracted land
  Shone out the smiling sun of peace.

The famous captains of the past
  March in review before the mind ;

Some fought for glory, some for gold,
  But most to yoke and rule mankind.
Not so the captain dead to-day
  For whom our half-mast banners wave;
He fought to keep the Union whole,
  And break the shackles of the slave.

A silent man, in friendship true,
  He made point-blank his certain aim,
And, born a stranger to defeat,
  To steadfast purpose linked his name.
For while the angry flood of war
  Surged down between its gloomy banks,
He followed duty, with the mien
  Of but a soldier in the ranks.

How well he wore white honor's flower,
  The gratitude and praise of men,
As General, as President,
  And then as simple citizen!
He was a hero to the end;
  The dark rebellion raised by Death
Against the Powers of Life and Light,
  He battled hard, with failing breath.

O hero of Fort Donelson,
  And wooded Shiloh's frightful strife!
Sleep on! for honor loves the tomb
  More than the garish ways of life.
Sleep on! sleep on! Thy wondrous life
  Is freedom's most illustrious page;
And fame shall loudly sound thy praise,
  In every clime, to every age.

PHILIPPA.

In praise of Queen Philippa — in her praise
Who, while the king, her husband, fought with France,
Beat back at Neville's Cross the sturdy Scots,
And from the grape of their invasion pressed
The wine of victory.

                  A manly deed
Befits a woman, as, in truth, no less,
An act of gentleness befits a man.

But when the Scots were scattered on the hills,
And nursed defeat, Philippa crossed the sea
Between the island and the continent,
And, in the camp besieging Calais' gates,
Was welcomed by the army and the king.

Upon the wall of Calais, which, howe'er
Impregnable to savage force of arms,
Was stormed and scaled by Famine gaunt and thin,
Stood up the governor in sight of all,
And waved for parley to his English foe.
The king sent forth to him an officer,
Who, when arrived, look'd up, and asked his wish.
"Brave knight," exclaimed the governor, "my king
Intrusted unto my command this place.
Nearly a year you have besieged us round,
And I, with these about me, as we could,
Have done our duty in the town's defense.
But now we are reduced by that lean foe
Invisible, more pitiless than war,
And deadlier than its missiles; for, alas!
We yield to famine, and to thee who art
Its officer and representative.

But, ere the gates be opened, I require
This one condition, that thou wilt insure
The lives and liberties of these brave men
Who have with me borne peril and fatigue."

The knight made answer to the governor:
"I know the will of Edward, England's King.
Enraged at Calais, that so stubbornly
It has resisted him, he has resolved
To put it wholly to the sword, and make
A red example for succeeding wars;
That henceforth when he stands before a town
And calls for its surrender, those within
Will blanch and tremble with the ague, fear,
If in defense one dare to raise a hand;
For all will think of Calais, and so yield."

"Consider," said the governor. "Is this
Such treatment as the brave accord the brave?
The blinded victor shows the basest fear,
Belittles his own deed, and conquers not,
Who grants no mercy to a fallen foe.
Were I an English knight, and this a town
In sea-girt England, what would'st thou expect
Save that I should be valiant to resist?
The men of Calais did that for their king
Which merits the esteem of every prince,
Much more of one so gallant as thine own.
But now I make to thee no idle boast;
If we must perish, thou shalt buy our lives
With heart's-blood of thy ranks; for, tho' not strong,
We are not yet so weak that we will die
And leave unstruck a blow for hope forlorn.
But these are desperate and wild extremes
To which thou should'st not drive us; but we trust
That thou, brave knight, wilt kindly interpose
In our behalf thy gentle offices,
And thwart the vain continuance of war."

The knight went back, and on his loyal knees
Raised meek petition to the warlike king
To make his rigor less, and so revoke
The doom that threatened Calais. To the prayer
The angry monarch yielded, but required
That six of Calais' noblest citizens
Should be sent forth to him, without delay,
That he might treat them after as he willed ;
They must come barefoot, and bareheaded too,
With ropes about their necks, to hang them with —
Must bring the keys of Calais in their hands,
And lay them at his feet : if this were done,
The people in the city should be spared.

When these ill news were bruited through the town,
Fresh consternation wanned the hollow cheeks.
Who were the six to be? To send them out
To fall on certain and ignoble death
For signal valor in a common cause
Seemed as severe as that they all should die.

As when a vessel beating 'gainst the wind
Changes her course, and for a time drifts back
As if irresolute which way to turn,
Her white sails flapping, trembling in the gust,
So were the men of Calais, in that hour,
White, shaking, fearful, and devoid of will.

But soon brave Eustace de St. Pierre stepped forth
To show his willingness to suffer death
For safety of the populace ; and then
Another, by his lofty action roused,
Made a like offer, till the needed six
Stood up before the people, whose wet eyes
And trembling lips made manifest the grief
Felt for the martyrs to the city's cause.

At the high gate the doomed went calmly out,
As malefactors clad, bearing the keys,
And laid them proudly at the conqueror's feet.
He, hard and cold, and heedless that his steps
Went down to infamy in such a deed,
Ordered that these heroic burgesses
Should be removed and quickly put to death.

Then she who won the day at Neville's Cross,
Philippa, saved her husband's mighty name
A blotch beyond time's healing; for, with tears,
She threw herself before him on her knees—
Nay, England in the person of the queen—
And begged the lives of these brave citizens.

Obtaining her request, she led the six
Into a tent where rich repast was served,
And giving each silk clothing and red gold,
Dismissed them all in safety to their homes.

THE FISHER-MAIDENS.

NORMANDY.

WE two are fisher-maidens, and we dwell beside the
        sea
Where the surf is ever rolling, where the winds are
        blowing free;
And we loved a youth, the bravest that had ever drawn
        the seine,
And for comeliness and honor he was fit to wed a
        queen.

We loved him, and we hated one another for his love
That he never showed for either. Could he toss it like
        a glove?

But one day the sails were hoisted, and he left the
    loving shore,
And we saw him in the beauty and the pride of life
    no more.

For the tempest broke upon him as at night he ven-
    tured back:
All the sea was frothy madness, all the sky was wild
    and black;
But we combed the drifted sea-weed from the sable
    of his hair,
And the day that he was buried seemed too much for
    us to bear.

We two are fisher-maidens, and we hold each other
    dear;
We are wedded by a sorrow, we are very fond and
    near;
For the love we lost unites us — is a bond between us
    twain,
And in tears we clasp each other in the nights of wind
    and rain.

BY HUDSON'S TIDE.

WHAT pleasant dreams, what memories, rise,
    When filled with care, or pricked in pride,
I wander down in solitude
    And reach the beach by Hudson's tide! ·
The thick-boughed hemlocks mock my sigh;
    The azure heaven is filled with smiles;
The water, lisping at my feet,
    From weary thought my heart beguiles,
        By Hudson's tide.

I watch a slow-wing'd water-fowl
  Pursue her finny quest, and bear
The gasping silver of her prey
  Far up th' untrodden heights of air.
In quiet depths I note the course
  Of dreamy clouds against the sky,
And see a flock of wild-ducks float,
  Like water-lilies nearer by,
      On Hudson's tide.

The mullein lifts, along the bank,
  Its velvet spires of yellow bloom;
And there a darting humming-bird
  Gleams in the cedars' verdant gloom.
By basins of the brook that flings
  Its dewy diamonds far below
Into the ripples' pigmy hands,
  Sweet maiden-hair and cresses grow,
      By Hudson's tide.

I wander on the pebbled beach,
  And think of boyhood's careless hours
When, in my boat, I used to float
  Along the bank and gather flowers;
Or catch the wind, and swiftly dash
  Across the white-caps in their play,
And feel their wet resistance break
  Against the prow in pearly spray,
      On Hudson's tide.

And once, in those lost days, I lay
  Becalmed with limp and drowsy sail,
And drifted where Esopus Isle
  Mid-stream reclines in rocky mail;
And up he rose, and stood erect
  In leaf-trimmed armor wrought of stone,

And cast his eyes, as from the skies,
  On me that drifted there alone
      On Hudson's tide.

Only his feet were lost to view,
  And cleft the current ebbing down;
His ridgy helmet, plumed with trees,
  Propped the blue zenith with its crown.
The river's self was but his lance
  That lay neglected on the ground;
Upon his greaves were grass and leaves;
  His breastplate sparkled far around,
      Like Hudson's tide.

I had not been surprised if he
  Had mounted on some thunder-cloud
And charged at Ontiora's knee,
  With sudden war-cry sharp and loud.
But he was mild, and blandly smiled,
  And spoke with accents sweet and low.
His words with kindness glanced and fell,
  And seemed like music, or the flow
      Of Hudson's tide.

"Enjoy the river and thy days,"
  He said, "nor heed what others say.
What matters either blame or praise,
  If one in peace pursue his way?
The river heeds not; heed not thou:
  Cut deep the channel of thy life.
Thou hast a fair exemplar there:
  With what serene indifference rife
      Is Hudson's tide!

"How level lies its changeful floor,
  Broad-sweeping to the distant sea!
What Titan grandeur marks the shore!
  What beauty covers rock and tree!

What ample bays and branching streams,
 What curves abrupt for glad surprise!
And how supreme the Artist is
 Who paints it all for loving eyes
   By Hudson's tide ! "

I woke; and since, long years have passed;
 By Hudson's tide my days go by:
Its varied beauty fills my heart.
 Of other scenes what need have I?
And when my boat of life and thought
 Shall quit the harbor of my breast,
And seek the silent, unknown sea,
 I trust this dust in peace shall rest
   By Hudson's tide.

INVOCATION TO THE SUN.

O Sun, toward which the earth's uneven face
Turns ever round, strong Emperor of Day,
To thee I bring my tribute of large praise;
And yet not I; but that which in me is,
The life in life, conscience, suggester, muse.

Not as to Quetzalcoatl came of old
Fane-climbing worshipers with trump and drum,
And human victims bared for sacrifice
On dizzy Aztec altars; nor, indeed,
As to Apollo of the golden hair
And fiery chariot, who darted war
Against the lords and following of Night,
Come I, O Sun, to thee.

    Nor like the Gheber throngs
Who on the eastern shore of ocean bow,

Kissing the trail of thy departing robes,
Do I, to thy down-going, offer prayer.

I, worshiper no less, but not of thee,
Rising at cool-breathed, night-releasing dawn,
Thank the unseen All-Giver for thy day,
And see in thee a ray-strung instrument
Swept by His hand for harmonies of life.

Not I alone salute thy springing beam;
The mountains do thee homage first of all,
And hinder, with their bold and rocky brows,
Thy swift, protracted ray.

      Thou callest up
The blooming new from out the withered old,
And givest consciousness to soulless things.
Thou sendest forth the lightning-arrowed cloud;
And the coy breeze, a wordless whisperer,
Doth interchange the breath of man and tree.
Thou dost invite the robin from the south;
Thou whitenest 'the harvest for our need;
Thou fillest out the youthful cheeks of fruit
With sappy wholesomeness, and dost, at last,
Print one broad sunset on autumnal woods —
In rubricated letters making known
A sad and sylvan moral of decay.

To tread where populations that are dust
Eked out their changeful lives, and left behind
Little beyond a ruin and a name,
Men trust the brief forbearance of the sea;
But thou, above, silent, immutable,
Art long familiar with the scenes they seek,
And hast beheld all times and nations fade.

Tho' like the leaves the generations die,
And tho' the ages in the past recede,

Spun by this pendulous swift wheel of earth
In its fixed orbit by thy influence,
Thou makest man endure; he ceases not;
But stands with steadfast feet upon all time;
Nor shall he cease while yet to-morrow holds
Its one remove away.

       Our yesterdays
Are like a lonely and a ruined land
Wherein a breeze of recollection sighs —
A fading land to which is no return.

Uncertainly we bode the life to come,
Yet deem we stand upon the topmost height
Material; but this, that thinks and dreams —
This many-tided vaster sea within —
Baffles itself, and knows not what it is,
Save that its being is enlinked with thine.

And thou, O Sun, dost look on many worlds —
On eight-mooned Saturn with his shining rings,
On Jupiter, on Venus, pearl of dusk —
Thou dost behold thy worlds, and lay on them
Thy ray's restoring finger: they receive
Their sight, and go rejoicing on their way,
Changing, we think, thy light and heat to life.
But we, bound down, shut in on one small star,
Shall not know fully of those other spheres
Until the soul, up-drawn by rays Divine,
Out of this seed-like body blooms on high.

DELAY.

Aware that, in the warp and woof of fate,
 Delay's long threads are seen to be sublime,

Till even hope was dead I learned to wait,
  And waiting donned the foolishness of crime.
How often, in the bitter words, "Too late!"
  Delay gets back the slight it gives to time!

AZOAR.

My loved and beautiful bride, Azoar,
  Stooped to drink at the wayside spring
When, riding up from the wooded shore,
  Garbed as a hunter came the King.
He begged, with a smile, to quaff the bowl,
  And ever his heart to her eyes would cling —
Those sea-blue boundaries of her soul.

A cry went out o'er the land for war —
  You who have heard it know how it thrills!
Low on the verge burned my rising star.
  There was breath of hope in the wind of ills.
Feeling that life was shut in no more
  By the blue impervious haze of hills,
I bade farewell to my bride Azoar.

Pointing to cliffs in the wilderness,
  I said, ere weeping I turned away,
"Lo! the years their saddened lips shall press,
  And mark their progress in sure decay,
On these; but not on my love for thee."
  Then the clouds loomed up across the day,
Like bergs of ice in a polar sea.

So, for the rights and the hopes of man,
  An eager host, tho' weary and sore,
Marched southward far. I was in the van.

17

We pitched our tents on an alien shore.
Soon, with iron lips and flaming breath,
  Gage of battle was cast, and we bore
The shock and brunt in the teeth of death.

And it chanced that men unfurled my fame
  Like a thousand flags in the joyful air.
The deeds I did as the sun became
  And shone with my glory every where.
The army moved at my sole command;
  All opposition put on despair,
And I was lord of the conquered land.

Yet with an uncertain sense of loss,
  I went to embrace my home once more,
And peace, like a great white albatross,
  Passed over the realm from shore to shore.
The King gave honors that might be seen,
  And down to greet me he led Azoar —
My bride no more, but Azoar, the Queen!

Honors of Satan! Glory of shame!
  Dishonor smiting true honor's face!
To fight to victory, win a name,
  And meet, at triumph, the name's disgrace!
"I will not brook it!" I fiercely said.
  Then insurrection made head apace
And crowned me King in the false King's stead.

It struck him down as he sat enthroned;
  It slew Azoar as she hied away;
For mine was the cause the people owned,
  And death and vengeance were of the day;
Since there never fails to come the hour
  When trampled honor begets dismay
And mounts again to the seat of power.

FAITH'S VISTA.

When from the vaulted wonder of the sky
  The curtain of the light is drawn aside,
  And I behold the stars in all their wide
Significance and glorious mystery,
Assured that those more distant orbs are suns
  Round which innumerable worlds revolve, —
  My faith grows strong, my day-born doubts dissolve,
And death, that dread annulment which life shuns,
Or fain would shun, becomes to life the way,
  The thoroughfare to greater worlds on high,
The bridge from star to star. Seek how we may,
  There is no other road across the sky;
And, looking up, I hear star-voices say :
  "You could not reach us if you did not die."

A DREAM FROM SONG AND VAIN DESIRE.

In the amber haze of a tropical land,
  A giant lily — I saw it grow —
Spread its white pavilion, cool and bland,
  And cast its shade in the path below.

A large, slow serpent in emerald coil,
  Waiting for aught that the hour might bring,
Lay 'neath the lily, half hid in the soil,
  And death forgetful was in his sting.

So sweet and drowsy the scent of the flower,
  On all volition it turned the key ;
For, pent in fragrance, I had no power,
  Nor scarce the purpose, to set me free.

The lily's stamen of vivid gold
  Stood, to the middle, in floral snow.

Was it hair or pollen, in fold on fold
    Around the stamen ?   I questioned so.

It was hair, long hair, disheveled quite ;
    Its arrested sunshine glinted there —
The hair of a maiden in gauzy white —
    A graceful maiden most strangely fair.

A sudden gust bent the lily down
    To the toppling grass at my listless feet,
And lightly forth with her waving crown
 . The maiden stepped from her pale retreat.

As the flower swung back and her glance met mine,
    I sighed for the heaven of her embrace ;
For love's divinity seemed to shine
 - From her lily beauty of form and face.

The cloven wave of her bosom heaved
    With passion so deep that it bordered pain,
And, mad of the joy which it had received,
    The quick blood danced in my heart and brain.

Her magic loveliness thrilled me through ;
    It fixed on my being's inmost core,
And I reached out longing arms to woo
    The breathful life that the lily bore.

The vision was fruit of a vain desire,
    Or ever the loveliness moved a pace,
The dreaded serpent, with eyes of fire,
    Wound swiftly forth from his covert place.

My bondage ceased as he reared his head
    To deal me death with the joy denied ;
And the maiden's voice, as I turned and fled,
    Flooded the air with a blissful tide.

A voice of melody, full and clear,
　Repeating a tender, love-sweet cry:
Return, my belov'd.　Why winged with fear?
　Return, my belov'd, lest I fade and die.

Or was it a songbird high in the pine
　Warbling his love in the moonbeams white?
I heard him singing his song divine,
　And woke from my vision of crossed delight.

Oh! wild the song and supremely sweet
　In that noon of night and the light thereof,
And waves of ecstasy through it beat
　On shores of sorrow from depths of love.

Vanished were maiden and serpent, all;
　But loud, from his perch in the tassel'd choir,
Was the wakeful nightbird's rapturous call, —
　The longing voice of a vain desire.

GARNET-SHIRLS.

ONE quality your beauty has, no less
　Than your supernal soul: it is a rare
Unvarying note of delicateness.
　The lily has it too; she is so fair,
She seems the very angel of the flowers —
　So pure and holy that, across the seas,
They pluck her gladly from the willing bowers
　To deck the Christ with, at solemnities.
The doubter likes his mission, and will say
　That delicacy is ripeness soon to fall,
A frost-work fairy-palace, or a ray
　Of lace-like moonlight on an ivied wall;
　But that oft stays to be the last of all,
Which ever lifts its wings to fly away.

Oh! might I praise your beauty as I would
　With splendors of the high, descriptive pen
That touches all the salient points and good,
　And in the likeness makes them live again!
So Dante wrote of Beatrice divine,
　So Petrarch wrote of Laura, and so he,
Vast-minded Shakespeare, in many a sonnet-line,
　Wrote of some beautiful, mysterious she.
Had I the gifts these master poets had,
　I should compose a ring of golden verse
And in it set you, Diamond, — all too glad
　Such jeweler to be, — and thus rehearse
To the whole world, and for all time renew,
The excellence that sways me and is you.

WHAT DO WE PLANT?

WHAT do we plant when we plant the tree?
We plant the ship, which will cross the sea.
We plant the mast to carry the sails;
We plant the planks to withstand the gales —
The keel, the keelson, and beam and knee;
We plant the ship when we plant the tree.

What do we plant when we plant the tree?
We plant the houses for you and me.
We plant the rafters, the shingles, the floors,
We plant the studding, the lath, the doors,
The beams and siding, all parts that be;
We plant the house when we plant the tree.

What do we plant when we plant the tree?
A thousand things that we daily see;
We plant the spire that out-towers the crag,
We plant the staff for our country's flag,
We plant the shade, from the hot sun free;
We plant all these when we plant the tree.

February, 1890.

TO BAFFLE TIME.

To baffle time, whose tooth has never rest,
  And make the counted line, from page to page,
Compact, fulfilled of what is apt and best,
  And vibrant with the keynote of the age,
This is my aim; and even aims are things;
  They give men value who have won no place.
  We pass for what we would be, by some grace,
And our ambitions make us seem like kings.
But never yet has destiny's clear star
  For aimless feet shed light upon the way.
So have I hope, since purpose sees no bar,
  To write immortally some lyric day,
  As Lovelace did when he informed the lay
Inspired by his Lucasta and by war.

A COLONIAL BALLAD.

It was winter in New York and the British held the
    town;
For the Colonies, in arms, were inflamed against the
    Crown.
There was danger in the air, and it frowned on either
    side;
But the city, ne'ertheless, had of gayety a tide.
Officers, in coats of red, lightly butterflyed about,
Flitting round the human flowers at reception, ball,
    and rout.

Miss Van Steenbergh, Kingston's belle, and of urban
    fair renown,
Paid a visit's flying gold, at the season's height, in
    town.
She had charms of grace and wit; she could feign a
    pretty sigh
For a hapless lover's case, with a twinkle of the eye.

"Sweetest girl that I have seen, and as beautiful as
    dawn,"
Looking on her at a ball, said the British General
    Vaughan.
At a formal word or two, soon their hands and glances
    met,
And he led her, like a king, in the courtly minuet.
Many candle-groups of wax lighted up the tripping hall;
Flutes and viols, perfumes, dress, swayed the senses,
    raptured all,
But the music of one voice, and one face, too soon
    withdrawn
From his dazzled, ardent eyes, filled the heart of Gen-
    eral Vaughan.

When the winter days were past, and the spring and
    summer spent,
Up the Hudson General Vaughan for a vengeful deed
    was sent.
In the mid-October haze boding leaves were fiery red.
Up the river sailed the fleet and the doughty Friend-
    ship led.
She had twenty guns and more. Friendship? Such
    we found indeed!
News about the coming fleet spurred ahead with anx-
    ious speed.
There were seven ships in all, and of galleys just a
    score;
There were sixteen hundred troops whom the ships and
    galleys bore.

Kingston, "nest of rebels" bold, heard the certain
    news with dread.
That the place was doomed to burn, gadding Rumor
    grimly said.
There could be but slight defense, well the menless
    village knew.
They must flee with what they might, Duty's trumpet
    harshly blew.

Fresh with morning came the fleet to the mouth of
    Rondout creek,
Which. with two redoubts, like tongues full of rage
    began to speak.
From the decks flashed swift replies, scarcely more
    than fume and threat.
Nothing hushed the loud redoubts but the charging
    bayonet.
As when some undaunted bird on a flock makes wild
    attack,
And the ruffled leave the flock, overpower and drive
    him back,
So a patriot galley now, that against the fleet made
    war,
Adverse galleys turned upon — up the Rondout har-
    ried far.

Then began the British march, guided by a captured
    slave,
To malign, with fire and sword, Kingston folk for
    being brave.
Up the hills, across the plains, with the Catskills look-
    ing down,
Into Kingston marched the troops of the arbitrary
    Crown.
To the houses and the barns, right and left the torch
    was plied.
Roaring conflagration burst from the roofs on every
    side.
Pillage, got of robber blood, did its petty, coward
    shames.
Villagers in flight looked back and beheld their homes
    in flames.
All great things, ere they are won, toil and sacrifice
    require,
And this, in the New World, was Liberty's first altar-
    fire!

But a gentler flame upflares here beside the flame of
    war.
To the fair Van Steenbergh's home it was more than
    bolt and bar.
" Yonder stands," said General Vaughan, "an abode of
    wit and grace.
Colonel! it is my command: let no harm befall the
    place!"

So that house alone was spared; even to this hour it
    stands,
A remembrancer in stone of Colonial days and hands.
It is said, our Kingston belle with her lover had no
    part;
Cupid's Tory arrow glanced from her Continental
    heart.
    January, 1893.

A SEA–FIGHT.

WE sailed the trim brig Enterprise, and scoured
The seas and bays and inlets, swooping down
On British navigation, beak and claws,
Till Terror snatched the trumpet of our fame
And blew it loud. A hundred strong we were;
We liked our canvas plumage, wooden walls,
And brave commander Burrows. He so well
Had trained us to our service on the brig,
That by one will, which seemed to be her own,
The vessel was inspired; and gracefully
She moved or stayed, like some strong-pinioned fowl
Whose life is air and billow.

                    On our track
Was sent, to sink or capture us, a brig,
The Boxer, in command of captain Blythe.
Above a hundred manned her, chosen men
Well versed in sea-fights and not dreading death.

In any part her outfit nothing lacked
That forethought joined to long experience
Could with free hand bestow. She crossed the deep
Hope-winged and steered by warlike confidence.

Ere new September's sun had quite forgot
His August anger, and when that ardent god
Had sent his gray forerunners up the east,
In shore, scarce three leagues south of Pemaquid,
The Boxer lay at anchor. We could see
Her upper half of rigging, yards and spars
Against the starry sky above the shore.
The wind was south by west, a freshening breath
That filled with steady progress all our sails.

Things dangerous give warning ere they strike :
The baned snake rattles and the lightning's ship
Darkens the verge. But we, to warn the brig
And rouse her from her slumber, as she lay
Rocked on the breathing bosom of the sea,
Sent her an iron message round and swift,
That chipped a mast and cut a stay in twain.
The sending woke the echoes of the coast,
Ran up the flag of England to the peak
And strained upon the digging anchor-fluke.
We heard the alien orders trumpeted,
The roll of drums, the hoisting of the sails,
Then swung our helm to larboard, stood to sea,
And showed the British mariners our heels.
With all sails set we stood away to sea ;
And knew that, having sent so sweet a kiss,
We should be followed by our charmer soon.

Out of the wide Atlantic rose the sun,
As red as Mars and girt with pageantry.
Dismissing satiate Sleep, he scattered far
.The insubstantial navies of the dark.
He cast a splendid presage on our sails

And showed us, far astern, the English brig
Crowding her canvas in excited chase.
Her sails were puffed out like the blowing cheeks
That the old painters, picturing the sky,
Gave the personified, loud-rushing winds.
Tho' thus she strained, until we clewed and reefed,
She fell behind and faded from our sight;
But at his post the lookout ever kept
His glass set on her, if she waxed or waned.
And now, with zest expectant, each man broke
His sleepy fast; and, at the fragrant board,
The frolic spume of quip and badinage,
Cast up by surging thoughts too deep for words,
Ran on and sparkled with misleading light.

But leaning forward under press of sail,
Hull down and far to leeward, gained on us
The Boxer, plunging, tearing through the waves.
We lay to for a while, then luffed and tacked
Until an eighteen pounder at her bow
Sent us a bare-back rider on the wind.
We heard him cry and saw him as he leaped
Lightly at our curved mainsail, piercing it
As if indeed it were a paper'd hoop
Held up to jump through in a circus-ring.
And we, ready and waiting for the fight,
With bulwarks down, screens up, the shot on deck,
Guns loaded, tackles rove, yards slung, fires out,
And powder filled, stood silent at our posts
And meant the battle should be sharp and brief.

But on the Boxer they had yet no will
To close with us so soon; for, coming up,
They at respectful distance ministered
Their broadside thunder, damaging in chief
Our topsails, flying-jib, top-gallant mast.
But we took lower, readier aim, and when,
On the white summit of a hill-like wave,
The lifted Boxer rose and showed the green

Below her water-line, we paid her back
With the fierce best that our loud guns could do.

No fabled dragons ours that, roaring rage,
Belched flame and smoke and dealt destruction dire,
With instant iteration, peal on peal —
No fables these the Boxer surely found.
We paused to let the smoke lift, and beheld
A hurrying to and fro upon her deck,
And saw her veering to the starboard tack.
We followed gleefully, and twice with grape
We raked her, fore and aft, as to the wind
She came up shivering. But St. George's cross
Yet at her gaff-peak flaunted enmity.

Her captain, seeing his unhappy case,
The dead and wounded thick about the guns,
The leaky damage to the hull, the masts
Half cut in twain, stood on the quarter-deck
And propped the failing courage of his men:
"Tho' sorely pressed, we shall not lose the fight
If yet your hearts are equal to your hands;
For victory of valor and of strength
Is evermore begot. And will you strike
To Yankees her great flag that rules the seas —
To rebels that, with open aid of France,
Wrested the fairest jewel from our crown?
They fought, they said, for precious liberty —
For liberty! and have not freed their slaves!
Nay, nay, you shall not haul the ensign down;
Go nail it to the mast: we will not strike
The flag of England on our brig to-day!"
The leak was stopped, the masts were stayed, decks
    cleared,
And, ready again for action, down on us
The Boxer bore to scatter us to the winds.

Far west, upon our inland prairie sea,
Two buffaloes with deadly hatred meet,

And one is gored and suddenly slinks away
To lick his wounds and gather his spent strength.
His pain excites his fury, and he turns
Undaunted on his stronger enemy
With tenfold greater violence than at first.
So on us now the Boxer, bellowing war,
Her oak flanks smoking and her head bent down,
Turned furiously. The sea, struck into foam,
Dashed over her like pawed-up prairie dust.
But ever, as she rose upon the wave,
We welcomed her with carnage and a roar,
And riddled her in rigging, sails and hull.

Thus, when the eastward shadows for three hours
Had flatly rigged the rounded, seamy decks,
Did the two brigs approach, discharging death,
And, scarcely half a pistol-shot apart,
Stand wrapped in battle. Loud and fiercely hot,
The grim ingredients of floating war
Mixed in that witches' caldron. Blythe was dead.
Burrows lay dying; carried from the deck,
He saw our colors through a rift of smoke,
And pointing toward them, said, "Strike not the flag!
The stars of dawn are in its azure field
And in its stripes the sunrise; it denotes
A strife with dark oppression, old-world wrongs —
A progress toward the goal of liberty.
What Hampden, Cromwell, fought for, we to-day
Are fighting for; we carry on their war.
Our guns wake echoes of great Milton's songs,
Of Burke's appeals. Lower not fair Freedom's flag!
For England's noblest dead look down on us,
And Washington and our slain patriots
Look down on us, approving our just cause."

We cheered and fired, and cheered and fired again,
Unmindful of the faltering replies
The Boxer sent from her remaining guns.
But they who manned them soon for quarter cried:

"Our colors nailed, we cannot haul them down."
Then Burrows heard that victory was ours,
And clasped his hands and said: "I die content."

At Portland, to which haven we had borne
The mass of shreds and splinters called the prize,
We buried the brave commanders, side by side.
The sympathetic music of the bands,
The solemn throbbing of the muffled drums,
The slow procession, stepping rhythmically,
The somber drapery of the crowded streets,
The farewell musket volleys — all of these
Were salient, undivided honors paid
The victor and the vanquished, now at peace.

Dust in their graves upon our northern coast,
They sleep away the ever-passing years,
Burrows and Blythe, true heroes, worthy types
Of valor, English and American —
Brave hearts, firm wills, that shall not be forgot
While glory waits on patriotic deeds.
   1887.

GETTYSBURG.

THE RECORD OF A NORTHERN REGIMENT.

THE FIRST DAY.

HIGH-HEARTED with many successes, and never so
     strong as then,
Lee marched into Pennsylvania with a hundred thou-
     sand men.
But the Army of the Potomac caught up betimes with
     his van,
And at Gettysburg fronted invasion valiantly, man for
     man.

Then the splendid Eightieth Regiment of New York
    Volunteers,
Named "The Ulster Guard" for their county — may
    it never lack their peers!
Tho' last of the Federal army to strike their Virginia tents,
Were first to arrive at Gettysburg and first to wage
    its defense.

Save that Buford's cavalry only, had come on the day
    before;
And the Ulster Guard, as they double-quicked, could
    hear the far-off roar
Of the horsemen's guns, as they thundered to hold the
    coveted ground;
For eagle-eyed General Pleasanton the vantage place
    had found.

He had given the duty to Buford hereon to make a
    stand,
And Buford repeated to Devin, a colonel in his com-
    mand,
That here must be fought the battle, and he feared
    that it would begin
Ere the infantry could assist him, for the scouts were
    driven in.

But Devin, who doubted the foemen in positive strength
    were near,
Said that he would "take care of any who might at
    his front appear."
"You will not!" said Buford, "for early to-morrow
    they will attack,
And we shall do well, Tom Devin, if we are not soon
    driven back.

"For the enemy then will come booming — his skir-
    mishers three deep."
So boded the chevalier Buford, and turned him to
    warless sleep;

But he spoke to his signal-captain, reminding him of
      his trust,
Saying, " Look out to-night for camp-fires, and in the
      morning for dust."

There was dust enough in the morning, and lines of
      camp-fires that night ;
And Buford and Devin, a-saddle, were early forth for
      the fight.
The enemy's van was at them.   And where was our
      army delayed ?
In a belfry stood gallant Buford, and watched for the
      northern aid.

The dust of the First Corps' coming was a trailing,
      glorious cloud.
The full, red disk on the banners was a sun-like sym-
      bol and proud.
The blue-coated succor and rescue marched up the
      Emmitsburg road
And across the swale where, like silver, Stevens Run
      peacefully flowed.

Welcome, magnificent, thrilling was the spectacle to behold,
As the ranks, at double-quick moving through the har-
      vest's swaying gold,
Swept up Oak Ridge and deployed there, on the crest,
      in battle array,
Their arms and accouterments gleaming in the July
      light of day.

When Rowley's brigade reached the ridge that is west
      of Willoughby Run,
In a sheltering wood they halted ; their wearisome
      march was done.
But in Hagerstown road, which rudely of quietude was
      bereft,
They at once formed line of battle, with the Ulster
      Guard on the left.

Then the prompt brigade, by the right flank, in solid
    column advanced
Through the wood and the fields beyond it, where
    yellow butterflies danced,
Toward Gettysburg, to the ridge-slope that is east of
    Willoughby Run,
Where they formed new line of battle, with their backs
    to the mounting sun.

But ordered over the ridge-top and into the valley below,
There the rifle missives were pinging, and there were
    who got their woe;
Beyond, in a grain field, swarmed hornets, sharp-
    shooters plying their trade.
So, back to their place on the ridge-slope, discretion
    sent the brigade.

They had been to the spot where Reynolds, their great
    corps commander, fell,
And Doubleday, of their division, now served in his
    stead right well.
They had Biddle in place of Rowley, for the hour its
    needs creates;
And the Federal left wing, this day, fought under our
    colonel Gates.

Across from that left, nearly westward, stood a dwell-
    ing-house of brick
And farm buildings other, not distant from where the
    foemen were thick.
From the buildings our captain, Baldwin, after a spir-
    ited fight,
Drove the enemy, took possession and checked and
    harried their right.

Then Cunningham daringly followed, to give brave
    Baldwin his aid,
And, for two hours, they and their soldiers the left
    flank covered and stayed.

This deed of a handful excited the growing enemy's
      ire;
He partly surrounded the buildings, the smaller of
      which took fire.

The companies lost their defenses, and soon thereafter
      were seen
Retreating under the cover of cavalry and a ra-
      vine. . . .
The fear that is felt by the soldier ere the first few
      shots are fired,
By the Ulster Guard was forgotten; for they fought
      as if inspired.

The enemy's musketry rattle and dread artillery roar
Made ever a louder minute than the one that thun-
      dered before,
As fresh, impetuous foemen arrived on the furious
      field,
And their batteries quickly unlimbered and into action
      wheeled.

Their division of Rodes arriving on Oak Hill's summit,
      was seen
Overlooking the uplands southward and the basking
      meads between.
On the crest they planted their cannons, and with shot
      and shell they cleft
The ranks of Federal soldiers, from the right to the
      utmost left.

As the sickle of pest, for ravage, was this reaping en-
      filade;
To get from the sweep of its anger, the Federal
      troops essayed.
By the left flank, Biddle retreated, the Hagerstown
      road to try,
Supporting the cannons of Cooper, which to Oak Hill
      made reply.

The Federal line was bow-shaped, the apex on Cham-
        bersburg road,
The left on Hagerstown highway, and where Rock
        Creek trippingly flowed,
On the north of Gettysburg, rested the dexter end of the bow;
For the bow was bent backward strongly, as if to
        shoot at the foe.

But where was the arrow, the army, that should
        straightway pierce his heart?
The bow was soon palpably broken, or broken, at best,
        in part.
Too great was the strain for endurance, and the strain
        each moment grew;
For what could four Union divisions, with half of
        Lee's veterans do?

When Ewell's Corps, formerly Jackson's, had entered
        the clashing field,
They meant that the Federal forces should presently
        die, or yield.
There were thirty and five armed thousands with this
        savage, warlike will,
Slave-holders and proud work-scorners, and for being
        that, fiercer still.

But, fewer than half their number were the blue in
        battle array
Round Gettysburg, northward and westward, on that
        first unequal day.
They were cool, effective fighters, and the enemy
        sadly found
That the price was his heart's red current, for each
        rival inch of ground.

But the westering sun drooped hapless when long
        Confederate lines
Of closely-formed infantry, moving as pawns in their
        player's designs,

Began the advance; and behind them came strong re-
    serves, and the fight
Blazed loud. But the Union's defenders broke at the
    center and right.

Then Gettysburg groaned and was crowded and chok'd
    with the men who fled.
The rebels, hotly pursuing, fed havoc on murderous bread.
The town was streeted with slaughter, and even in
    alley and lane
Was the thud of the leaden summons and the cry of
    deadly pain.

But the First Corps had not waver'd, and strove to
    recover the day,
Tho' a half of the Union forces was scattered, as
    leaves, away.
Yet the left of the line was holden by Biddle's superb
    brigade,
And Cooper's four deep-throated war-dogs were loud
    with their iron aid.

On the left of these baying creatures, the Ulster
    Guard, true and tried,
Stood under the Federal standard — their starry, bullet-
    torn pride.
They held their strong morning position, eastward of
    Willoughby Run,
On the ridge; but a darkling onset in the distance
    had begun.

For a cloud of troops, a division, from the tempest's
    bounds afar
In the west and south, hasted forward in powerful
    lines of war.
Awaiting the grim adventure with calmness not void
    of delight,
Stood the Ulster Guard in their prowess, undauntable
    in the fight.

As the enemy came from the cover of woods, where
    he had formed,
With a torrent of screaming death-shots his solid ad-
    vance was stormed.
Our infantry fire lightened sharply, our guns were
    cleverly served;
But the living took slain men's places, and the ranks
    came on unswerved.

They came in their might, and outflanking Gates's
    intrepid command,
Fired oblique, destructive volleys, which madness might
    scarcely withstand;
But our soldiers knew they were fighting, on their own
    free northern ground,
For their homes, their country, and all things that in
    these birthrights abound.

And their zeal and enthusiasm were their very light
    and breath;
Each soldier did valorous actions and smiled on wounds
    and on death.
Tho' the dead there fell till the living fought from
    behind them at last,
To the ground our Guard seemed rooted, for they
    stood unshaken and fast.

Above them the smoke of the conflict heavily lifted
    and curled,
And the hot sun floated behind it like some fulvid
    phantom world,
Toward which foregone souls were ascending, in sacred
    columns and slow
From the pitiless field of slaughter in the real world below.

The mingled thunders of battle shook widely the val-
    orous ground;
Not since the hills were heaved upward had they
    throbbed with such mighty sound.

The sooty air, split with concussions, bore bruit of the
    fight afar,
And hurried the long, forced marches to this suck and
    whirlpool of war.

The Ulster Guard, fearless and hardy, outflanked by a
    whole brigade,
Stayed the whelming wave of onset and retreated no
    whit dismayed.
They were last to leave the position, and as they slowly retired
(Often loading, halting and turning) they on their
    pursuers fired.

On his horse Gates shouldered the colors (lest, haply,
    it should be lost)
Till he knew the chance for its capture was safely
    weathered and crossed;
For not far from the Seminary, where a stone and
    rail fence stood,
He again formed line with Biddle, at the edge of a
    narrow wood.

Here, with five brave batteries near them, and Meredith
    on their right,
Assailed by a Southern division, they made a despe-
    rate fight,
Till the enemy fled the carnage, and retreated toward
    the sun,
To the dank and sorrowful valley of sluggish Wil-
    loughby Run.

Our forlorn hope saved from destruction the greater
    part of their corps,
Whose confused retreat they defended, and they could
    not, that day, more.
For the bulk of the Union army they had helped,
    with courage grand,
To hold the great natural bulwarks, which back of
    Gettysburg stand.

Thus the Ulster Guard nobly combated, in open field,
    eight hours,
'Gainst double and triple their number, secession's
    violent powers.
Then the Guard retired to the bulwarks where, on a
    commanding height,
By the verdant graves of the townsfolk, they bivou-
    acked for the night.

At midnight the sleeplessly anxious took heart and
    rest at a sound —
The advent of Meade and his army on the rugged,
    rising ground.
The orderly footsteps of thousands, the iron trample of
    steeds,
And the rumble of guns and caissons, made music for
    Union needs.

THE SECOND DAY.

On the second day of the battle the Ulster Guard was
    arrayed
With a Pennsylvania regiment — a special demi-
    brigade,
Whom Colonel Gates took the command of — and if
    one regiment durst,
The other durst more; none braver than that Hundred
    and Fifty-first.

Not till afternoon did the foemen begin their flanking
    attack,
And the demi-brigade went forward when Sickles was
    driven back.
So they helped to check the invader, and when the
    darkness divine
Closed the terrible strife, they were posted centrally in
    the line.

In the whistling forefront of conflict stood firm the
     demi-brigade,
And a fence of rails, which was near them, they
     changed to a barricade.
What the shield was to the crusader, this was to
     them in the fight,
And behind it they lay on their muskets throughout
     that sullen night.

O Night! on the battle-field tarry; thou truce, two
     armed days between.
The troops asleep in their blankets and sentinels dimly
     are seen.
The hands of Darkness and Silence are over the
     mouths of the guns,
And, in dreamland, dove-like are homing our country's
     bivouacked sons.

Yonder, stretcher-bearers go laden; here runs a trench
     for the dead;
Hark! moans of wounded and dying, and the caw of
     hunger o'erhead.
Oh! what shall eventful to-morrow bring forth for the
     dreaming brave?
Shall he be the hero and idol, or rest in a nameless
     grave?

THE THIRD DAY.

At noon, on the third day, the prelude to Pickett's
     wild charge began —
A dirge, by the guns of rebellion, for the Lost Cause
     and its ban;
And the Ulster Guard's covert station, it fatefully so
     befell,
Was swept by a hideous tempest of shot and explod-
     ing shell.

Unknown in their sharpest warfare was the like to
     these men of ours;
Full a hundred bellowing cannon played on them for
     nigh two hours.
The sky was a burst of black missiles, the ground was
     harrowed amain;
But, by their barricade shielded, a few men only were slain.

When the cannonade had subsided, Pickett's division
     began
To debouch from the woods and orchard, where their
     strong right center ran.
With shouldered arms, with their battle-yell, and at
     double-quick, they came,
Devoted, that brave eighteen thousand, to death and
     immortal fame.

The charge moved apace through the open; the mili-
     tant ocean of men
Surged inland in three awful billows, submerging
     meadow and glen.
The steel was as water that sparkled, the standards as
     flying spume,
And the roar of guns was the breaking on irrevocable
     doom.

When Pickett's men entered the valley in front of the
     Ulster Guard,
That Guard opened fire on them briskly. Did this
     their approach retard?
Into one their three waves melted as they marched by
     the left oblique;
Then the whole to the right surged quickly, to dash
     where our line seemed weak.

Through their lines of advancing battle, great, horrible
     rents were plowed;
Yet the ranks closed up in a moment, and came on,
     fearless and proud.

But angrily toward them converging, the daring demi-
    brigade
Moved down like a storm-cloud, and met them with
    a deadly fusilade.

There rested the left wing of Hancock back in the
    Ulster Guard's rear,
Behind the guns on the bluff-top, and the right of
    Pickett was near.
What was it that led Gates forward, from his barri-
    cade and shield,
To fulfill, at the one great moment, this gap in the
    foremost field?

Till beneath the height at our center, Pickett had
    charged with a will;
But he paused at a fence for shelter, just at the foot
    of the hill.
There, over the fence, was a slashing, a grove that lay
    felled and dense —
Felled to clear the range for our cannons — and this
    he made a defense.

His hardihood showed his purpose in striking our right-
    center line.
The demi-brigade battled fiercely, set teeth to foil his
    design
To reach, on the bluff-top, our cannons and silence
    them then and there;
But, for guerdon, the enemy's effort had flagrant loss
    and despair.

For fate stood over against it, espoused to the worthier side.
Tho' the oppressor a while may prosper, fate ruins him
    in his pride.
Bringing vict'ry the Proclamation had bid that the
    slaves be free,
And the side of the wronged will triumph, whatever
    the odds may be.

The desperate onset of Pickett, this far, was fruitless
    and bare,
As yet, for the battery'd summit, he had to do and to dare.
The Union troops that opposed him, he outnumbered
    as six to one;
But the fewer had cooler courage, and willed to be not
    outdone.

So the strife for the fence and hillside was stubborn
    and most severe;
Both sides knew well that the title to the guns was
    the question here.
At quarter the range of a pistol the enemy swarmed
    like bees;
But he was screened and protected by the fence and
    the fallen trees.

Then the demi-brigade, through the slashing, charged
    with a right good will,
And they sent up a cheer that gladdened the cannon-
    eers on the hill.
In the fierce, hand-to-hand rencounter, where the thick
    in the brunt contend,
The enemy's guns played among them, alike on foe
    and on friend.

But Pickett's men turned in confusion, all hindered of
    their desire,
And into them, whipped and retreating, Gates volleyed
    a scathing fire.
The hundreds of prisoners taken now seemed the best
    of the gain;
But the place of the strife was covered with rebel
    wounded and slain.

Give pause for a tear for Baldwin and weep for them
    all who died,
In the three days' fight on the ridges, that the Union
    might abide;

For when the gray billow of Pickett fell wasted back
      from its strand,
Gates found his own loss in the battle was more than
      half his command.

At Gettysburg this charge ended the Ulster Guard's
      part in the fight.
The broken Confederate army fled, with their wounded,
      at night.
On our troops and those rock-ribbed bulwarks, which
      seemed for the hour to wait,
Dashed in vain the flood of rebellion ; and the fiat of
      God is fate.

ELEUSINIA.

THE sun-bronzed Arabs, living at the base
Of Karnak's mighty ruin, see in it
The work of no man's hand. They cannot think
Its lofty beauty and majestic form,
So awe-begetting, even in decay,
Are the unaided deed of their own kind.
But, as most men are wont, when sharply faced
By problems that they do not understand,
The squalid Arabs, quite too ignorant
To seek in natural causes for a key,
Exalt their case to the miraculous
And supernatural, and so believe
That monstrous genii, in antiquity,
To please the holder of some magic ring,
Built Karnak in a night!

                    All governments,
Books, customs, buildings, railways, ships, and all
The stark realities that men have made,
Are but imagination's utterances.
The invisible speaks in the visible,

And over all, the high, far-reaching thoughts
Of great imaginations domineer.
First of the Magi, Zoroaster yet
Colors the Western theosophic mind,
Besides the minds of Asian myriads.
Nor have his genii lost hold on men;
But are an explanation, in the East,
Of architectural victories, which appear
Beyond the power of human hands to win.

But we, of higher credence, think not so.
Of larger literature and ampler range,
We know the same full-browed intelligence,
The same Masonic wisdom, that upreared
High-girdled Babylon and purple Tyre
And built the Temple of King Solomon,
Built also the sepulchral Pyramids,
Built Philæ, hundred-gated Thebes, and all
Those works stupendous, whose calm grandeur yet
Shows the departed glory of the Nile.

It scarce seems longer past than yesterday
That men undid the brazen clamps which held
Upon its pedestal the Obelisk —
That ray-like shaft, which Thutmes raised at On
To grace the Temple of the Setting Sun —
And found Masonic emblems there bestowed.
Such useful emblems have been found withal
In prehistoric ruins Mexican.
If other clue were needed to connect
Our modern Craft with builders of the past,
We have the evidence of what we know, —
That nothing can be operative long
And not be speculative too; for Use
Is more than manual. High intelligence
Must see the ideal in the real, and clothe
Upon the impalpable and naked truth
The palpable resemblance; it must needs

Behold in all that is material,
External, the express embodiment,
Or signature, of far more lasting things,
Which are internal, spiritual.

        Swedenborg,
Upon the other worlds of heaven and hell,
His ideality imposed, and strove
Them to describe, the universe and God,
Using the splendid words of holy writ
As signs and tokens of the mysteries
That, in imagination, he beheld.
But not so far the wise Freemason dares.
In square and compasses, in setting-maul,
And in the other stated working-tools
Used by the Craft, he sees an ideal use.
To him they are the emblems of such things
As have been found alike in every soul
And make the world fraternal.

        Symbolism
Is the rich blood and life of Masonry.
A symbol is the solid link between
The real and the ideal. It must be
That man himself, the crown of earthly things,
Made in his Maker's image, is the true,
The only symbol of the Power Divine.
It follows that sublime Freemasonry
And heaven-born, strong-pinioned Poetry
Are one at heart; for, whatsoever be
Sincere, commensurate, symbolical,
Is native of the Muse — her work. To think
In symbols is imagination's house.
So the fast hold which Masonry has kept
Upon the minds of men for centuries —
For long millenniums — is, in truth, the same
As that of Poetry. For Poetry
Drank from the fountain of immortal youth,

Then rose in beauty, like the Morning Star,
And lit the holy, intellectual fire,
Guide of our faith and practice, that is laid
Upon Masonic altars.

                        When expressed
In buildings she is seen, as in the tree
The hamadryad, we but change her name,
And Architecture nominate the Muse.
But the broad tenets, on whose soil is based
Our Ancient Order, are a fertile land,
And all the arts and sciences alike
Find in it healthful sustenance, and, nursed
In genial sunshine and condensate dew,
Burst into bloom and yield abundant fruits.

EMANUEL.

In the New World, the hemisphere unknown
When, Hebrew-wise, Moriah uttered praise —
In a new land of liberty and hope,
Of golden harvests and of broad, fresh fields —
In the new Promised Land — we dedicate,
We consecrate this House of Righteousness.
     Be in our hearts, Shekinah!

In all this land there is no king but God.
He is our God, and we have built to Him.
To men of every creed, who serve his law,
We make the doors of this that we have built,
As wide with welcome as are freedom's doors,
As open and as tolerant as they.
     Be in our hearts, Shekinah!

Of us the Branch to whom the nations bow.
In us is testimony and the root
Whence sprang the palmy, Messianic New.

The New is of the Old to which we cling.
Not to destroy the New we plant the Old,
But that the Old may flourish with the New.
    Be in our hearts, Shekinah!

The end we know not; but we wander on,
Down the regretful wilderness of time.
Nations have risen and dissolved away;
But we remain, and are together bound
As are the glad, innumerable suns,
The blazing jewels in the Almighty's crown.
    Be in our hearts, Shekinah!

Here may we ever worship as we will,
With strong simplicity and manly trust.
Here may the wistful aspiration, prayer,
Fire the neglected voices of the soul.
And may Jehovah this, his temple, give
The rapture of cherubic wheels and wings.
    Be in our hearts, Shekinah!

1892.

THE LONG REGRET.

Two angels stood without The City's gate
And down beside the wall where ran a stream,
And palms hung over, and the day was mild.

These angels' chosen duty was to aid
Weak comers to The City from our world.
For when they saw a spirit down the void
Mounting on weary, nigh exhausted wings,
They flew to it and helped it to The Gate.
So, often in communion with the souls
That from this life depart, these angels learned
Much of our world, which, to their sight, was like
A glowing topaz far below in space.

Beside the jasper wall where fell a stream,
And palms waved over and the light was soft,
I marveled much to hear the angels speak.
For both were weary of the long regret
That, tho' the Christ is worshiped in the world,
And tho' his name is great and spread abroad,
There are so few obedient to his will.
Old, savage error in the blood survives,
Ignores the truth and sullies its domain.
Of those who hopefully avow the faith,
Few for their enemies pray, or aught forgive,
Or with fair favors unkind acts return.
And fewer still judge not lest they be judged;
For most fling wide uncharities of speech,
Warped prejudice all false, or calumny.
Many evil with evil resist, nor fear
To punish those who wrong them, as if God
Were not a jealous God, and had forgot
That vengeance is his fixed, essential right
And his alone.

    Both voices swelled and chimed
All variously and like cathedral chimes.
Then the swift angels, with white wings outspread,
Plunged down the abrupt, interminable gulf.
They disappeared, but soon to sight returned,
And I beheld a ray of love divine
Illumine their calm faces, as each bore
A rescued spirit Godward to The Gate.

www.ingramcontent.com/pod-product-compliance
Lightning Source LLC
Chambersburg PA
CBHW020945120726
47905CB00008B/2680